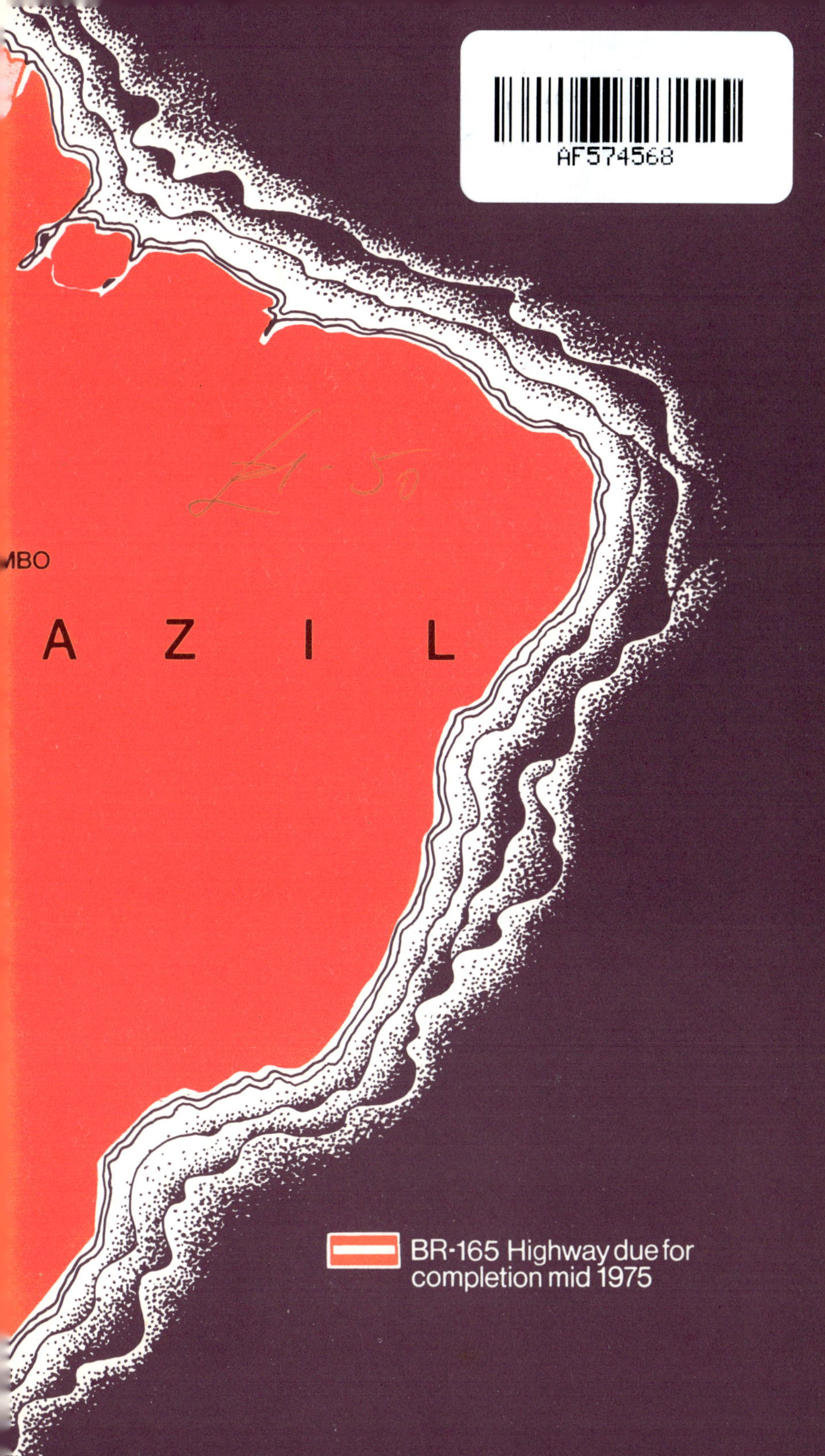
AF574568
MBO
A Z I L
BR-165 Highway due for
completion mid 1975

Bart's Mornings and Other Tales of Modern Brazil

By the same author:

THE GAME

TUSSY IS ME

THE NIGHTCOMERS

Bart's Mornings and Other Tales of Modern Brazil

by

MICHAEL HASTINGS

HODDER AND STOUGHTON
LONDON SYDNEY AUCKLAND TORONTO

The author wishes to thank Tracy Ullveit-Möe and Victoria Hardie for their research and investigation into the story of Padre François Jentel.

 ISBN 0 340 19692 0. *Printed in Great Britain for Hodder and Stoughton Limited, St. Paul's House, Warwick Lane, London EC4P 4AH by Northumberland Press Limited, Gateshead.*

CONTENTS

BART'S MORNINGS

Now I know who to blame. It was Bart. It was his fault all along. If I hadn't have bumped into him I would have really enjoyed Campo Grande.

You see I had fallen in love with the Brazilian rail service. Been up to Porto Velho to see the remains of the Marmoré-Madeira line, even followed it by car right through to Guajará-Mirim on the western border; this was the famous rail that killed a man for every sleeper they laid in the last quarter of the nineteenth century. I believe they were forced to import Scots engineers and other labourers from Peru to complete it; disease and plague were so rampant and the Brazils themselves got so frightened of the death toll.

At Her Majesty's expense I had just completed a two-year course in sack darning in one of Her better institutes for penal reform; my wife – who I had almost killed in a driving accident when I was discovered to have, according to the Court, an excess of alcohol in my bloodstream hitherto almost unknown in medical history – had already divorced me by the time I was released. I was alone again and I wanted to travel. I wanted to get out of this pale land. I chose a country which, if it did not possess drinkers of the same calibre as myself it, sure as port goes with brandy, possessed the mesmo drivers as eu. I chose Brazil.

I had driven up from Araçatuba, Estado do São Paulo, and I had followed the Bauru rail link as far as Campo Grande. And, if I had not met Bart, I would have gone on west to Corumbá where the rail crosses into Bolivia towards Santa Cruz

In the last century Bolivia, being landlocked, needed that Marmoré-Madeira line to send goods up to the Amazon and on saída ão Atlantico. Now, once again, with no viable sea port, Bolivia needs an out, and Brazil has invested enough cruzeiros in her to warrant a great rail line across the entire continent.

So . . . after all this driving, I was tired of seeing tiny rail halts and shaking that dust out of my ears, eyes, nose and throat. And this Avis hired Impala was costing me too much money per week. I made up my mind to dump it in Campo Grande near the station and cable desculpes to the Avis office in São Paulo.

I locked the car and carefully placed the keys behind the off-side tyre hubcap and wrote out my apologetic telegram. I put all my belongings into the army shoulder sack I always carry and I stood in the dusty Avenida São João inhaling Campo Grande's fumes of convites.

The Hotel Colombo is the oldest place in town. But, alas, it was not going to serve my purpose. When I reached it, I saw the scaffolding on the outside and I could hear the bone cracking rip-off sound of construction drills from inside. Either it had changed hands and was undergoing new ownership or, and much more likely at that, certain conto hungry Brazils had discovered it was indeed the oldest two-storey mansion in Campo Grande and what better excuse (for pulling it down) could there be than that?

Before I moved on, I took a peek through the thick red dust in the main hallway. Conveniently for me the builders had removed the entire first-floor landing, and I could see the gentle curve of the oak staircase as it snaked up to the lattice skylight oval-shaped against the attic ceiling. I must admit that I felt a little sentimental about it. After all, here was the only genuine eighteenth-century oak staircase in all Campo Grande and underneath it were three construction trabalhadores attacking the thick end of the balustrade with an electrically operated adze.

Then things began to look up. I knew an English agronomist who worked out here on an exchange contract between the governments; all that really signifies is – we send out one humble itinerant loyal subject of Her Majesty the Queen in order for the Brazils to eat his pick his brains clean and then discard him with a 'now we learn how we don't want you anymore, mister', and the Brazilian government posts us by exchange a youthful but eager brasileiro who, to his abandoned delight, discovers little England has long done away with the Catholic Church solely in order that he may while away his hours stuffing his hands up pretty English maids' skirts.

The agronomist, it just so happened, was leaving town for

a month, and if I liked, I could borrow his house and take advantage of his daily empregada. I grabbed the gift and moved in. My friend introduced me to the sole card playing mates he knew – an ex-CIA US Army Colonel and his wife, with the instructions that they were the only civilised decent people in the town; and he left me master of his pretty pink cottage up in the hills back of Campo Grande wallowing like a mato seco jacaré under my first hot shower for two months.

The Colonel slapped me on my back, insisted on calling me *Hal* (I have been Harold all my life), and had me in that night to his place for a couple of Bridge rubbers. He and his golden-haired pagoda quoiffed wife were a nightmare. They had twangy voices rough as the face of the moon and the Colonel had the most irritating habit of keeping a plastic ready-reckoner in his top shirt pocket while we played. Every so now and again he'd glance at it, just to be sure he got the best aggregate from all the calls.

As the evening wore on I became incoherent with a sudden tiredness. The driving had made me bone weary. I had done some three thousand kilometres down those red dust roads and I was dying from it. And the Colonel and his hideous wife, God bless 'em, were rich at least in native yankee hospitality. Result being – I got so drunk I couldn't remember the following day who in hell my partner had been in the game, even his, or her, face. I could not recall.

All I remembered was a phrase of the Colonel's—

"Tell ya one thing, boy, I learned in all my experience overseas," he hammered his rockdrill adenoids at me, curling and twisting his readyreckoner card in his fingers, "you must never tell the truth. Never do it, son! It makes ya *vulnerable*!"

His wife kept the gin fizzes in the freezer. All I ever heard that night was the delicious sound of the air-tight clap of the freezer door, as it opened and closed, that it might bring me the fizzy oblivion my bones yearned for; so ... good on yer Colonel more power to yer arm may yer shit gold bricks and play rubbers until your eyes turn the shape of Game Spades with Full Honours but keep pushing across those gin fizzes.

I recover slowly. All the following day I slept.

When I woke I felt really guilty for what was undoubtedly a disgraceful exhibition the previous evening. I knew I had spilt one whole bottle of pimento sauce with the home-made kibés over the wife's new baize Bridge cloth, and I had insulted the partner though I could not recall exactly what it was I said, or indeed what I didn't say.

There'd be no more Bridge for me in Campo Grande. That Colonel's last words to me were along the line of—

"Now ya be sure, Hal, any evenin' ya wanna cut the cards with us, just ya feel like you was one of the family!"

In other words—

"You put your gin sodden limey chin across my front door shoe mat I'm gonna poke you as Rocky Marciano far as the front gate, son, never heard of no one before do that, come in to civil folks' home drink whole month's supply of gin fizzes and crown everything walk out of the house and piss ruin all over my favourite Queen of the Night orquidea blooms, Jesus in Heaven, boy!"

In the late afternoon I drank down all of a miniature of Fernet Branca and took a bottle of beer from the agronomist's freezer and washed my hair in it. Not even the black café sem sucre could make me vomit anything up, so I cleaned my teeth and sucked lime-lemons to ease the throat.

The early night suddenly cooled and I felt a lot better. Up top of the tall buriti palm, end of the garden, a breeze fingered the immense raffia leaves. The last of the sun slipped away it left a mamão rind of sugar pink dreamland like a nursery idea of sangue da boneca. A white silent garça flew low over the house, wide wing span milking the air, gracious garça heron happier in the pantanal where it was headed for due west of here. Now I was fine.

The University of Campo Grande boasts the best swimming pool whole damn Estado do Mato Grosso. It was olympic-sized, with twenty-metre diving boards and Podium of Marathon tier benches. Trouble was – no one ever used it. First you had to obtain a medical certificate for about fifteen US dollars to prove you were fit enough and rich enough to swim in it. Then you had to be lucky, withal, because it wasn't every day of the year that the authorities allowed the pool to be filled with water.

There was a nice bar behind the piscina, in front of the boating lake at the University complex. All pillars of sheer concrete in vague architectural artistry. Distant matogrossense echo of the great Oscar Niemeyer. But everywhere, all around at your feet, detritus of cans and unvanquished garbage.

Each day this week, apparently, there had been parties in

the evening beside the boating lake. And on my second night in Campo Grande I ventured out that way. And it was there I bumped into Bart.

He was sitting with a bespectacled Brazil sharing a Brahma Chopp grande beer. There was a crowd out here. And I asked Bart if the chair at his table was free. He immediately jumped up and said he knew I was a britisher moment I walked by. We introduced ourselves. He was from Holland. An engineer. He had worked out at Três Lagoas on their huge twin hydro-electric dams.

"But now..." and he shrugged, "the Brazilians decided they didn't need my know how anymore and they terminated the contract. Stupid of them. Most uneconomic. They had to pay me off with a full two year salary. So I'm staying here. Spending the money. When it's gone – I'll go some place else. Maybe America."

His Brazil friend was called Aragão. I knew I didn't like him the moment I said 'prazer'. I just could not make it sound convincing. And he knew all right. We were just not made to hit it off. So he got very nervous. He started to order all sorts of caiperinhas and batidas caju with mock generosity. And he began to talk money.

He began to talk so much nonsense off the top of his head even Bart had to raise his eyebrows. He obviously knew this Aragão. The man didn't usually blow lies this strong.

On the other hand, it could easily have been all my fault. I didn't like Aragão's language. He'd say to me—

"You want to come up and see the office I work in? The Diário de Serra. I write whole paper, gringo. It got air conditioning in every bathroom maybe even!"

And—

"I tell you I want you to come out see these two fazendas I bought, gringo."

More—

"I got this piece of land. It 25,000 hectares. That almost big as whole Inglaterra, no é, gringo?"

I have lived at various times in a number of places on this continent. In Bolivia, Columbia, Peru and Dominica. And now I have spent almost a year and a half in Brazil. Nunca nada nobody, ninguém not even once, has anybody addressed me to my face as a 'gringo' before.

What I need for to sit there listening to this drivel from one

Aragão who I don't like anyway? And Bart drank quietly, he moved his chair as far away from us as the space would allow, and he just poured caips down his throat as if he was seeking to float away.

Maybe the alcohol was too speedy for me. I felt a flush across my face. My fingers scraped my palms. Distinct irritation all over my skin. Prickles of hate.

"How much land you got, gringo?"

"About half a hectare," I answered.

"That what you are, gringo, a pobre gringo, hah?"

"You haven't asked me where I keep my half a hectare."

"Oh gringo – where you keep it then?"

"Right slap centro Piccadilly Circus, Londres, you mother fucking bullshit artist Brazil nut!" Not to put too fine a point on it. And I made it in quite passable Portuguese.

Well . . . that did it. Aragão, he jumped off his chair and threw back his head in a lion's roar. Jumped and jiggled up and down on his pointy toes and waved his arms in girations to attract as many people as he could in order that they may listen to his side of the story first (with the speed he was talking there was precious little chance for me to interbutt) at the top of his voice as if his lungs would burst. Because out here this is how a Brazilian likes to tell you – it is war, senhor, between us – and usually after a few more tanking-up moments like this you simply set to with knives, fists, toe-caps and your dead mother-in-law's false teeth.

Only . . . Aragão really was serious.

And I knew there was no point in hesitating. I stepped forward. Raised my right arm theatrically high in the air, for a split second Aragão studied with curiosity what appeared like I was trying to impersonate a set of railway signals, and I hit him once plum centre of his throat with the left. Aragão stopped talking instantly. Bart pulled me away by the arm. And before I heard the impact of Aragão's skull on the novo concrete Bart dragged me running across the swimming pool compound to vault a low iron railing, towards his car.

We fell inside his Volks which, mercifully, he hadn't bothered to lock. And I heard them running up behind us, and their shouts. But he was too quick for them and the ignition bolted the first gear like a tin hare.

"You been drinking . . . ?"

"Sure. What's that do with—"

"Mothering pinga fed whore you can't do that sort of thing out here..."

"Late in the day to tell me—"

"Man like Aragão – make him look silly like that in front of all those people he knows – he'll come after you with a gun. I would in his place."

I laughed nervously. Bart frowned. He reached down to the foam fire fighter bomba holster and pulled out a small calibre pistol.

"Sure I would," he added, "and I'm not even a Brazil nut."

"I've had bragging loud-mouthed Brazils up to here!" I said crossing my throat.

"So have we all – but this is their country not yours, never forget that."

"Right."

"They may be pig stupid nationals and all that – you offend one he never forgets."

"...All right...you never offended a Brazilian?"

"I have...do it all the time," he replied, "but there are ways of doing it – com jeito, how you say – with finesse."

We found a quiet bar and sat together at the back against the white and blue ceramic wall, just in case a guarana crazed Aragão with pistols in his ears came running down the street for me.

I hadn't realised how much I was shaking until I sat down. We ordered beers and more caiperinhas, and I insisted on the caips being se pode espremer o limão direto down the bottom of the glasses because they never ever tasted quite right any other way like when they just throw the stuff in the glasses, or keep it pre-made in the freezer all night.

He was watching me carefully. Weary smile on him—

"When I first came out here...I was like you. Real piss artist. Never sober. Nothing but sneers for the Brazils. You learn – it fade away."

Bart must have been an object of fascination to the Brazilian girls out here when he first arrived. White blond hair and very loiro features like a German movie star of the thirties more yer actual Fourth Reich stud hun appearance, strongly built with pale blue effortless eyes which never seemed to linger há pouco on the mere surface of objects, but lazily bored right through them. And then I remembered why I thought of the movies. There was a well-known American action star – George Peppard;

now Bart and he looked identical twins (seeing as in fact I haven't taken in a George Peppard oater for many a year I might not be the best judge right this moment).

For all the moral code Bart was trying to instil in me, I noticed how he drank just as damn much as I did. And so ... in the course of these delicious blind hours, when you sit in the soft night at a bar surrounded by those totally familiar strangers, real and shadowy, alive or in your boozing eye, giving yourself up to that twilight god who beckons pinga oblivion, bearing you on chariots of incoherence lifting you up from the dust on the street like you were a babe in arms, I learnt of myself that perhaps I have indeed, all along, been a trifle over-confident and true brit patronising bullshitter; and I had to admit, under Bart's pale stare, that a nut (and he was a Brazil nut) like Aragão had every right to come gunning down the Rua Marechal Rondon in Campo Grande for me.

Bart stood up abruptly. The table caught his knee and he kicked it until it rolled to the front step of the bar. Maybe he had only wanted to drink to keep me company. I think he felt angry with himself. Angry for his lack of control.

"Now..." he murmured, flecks of teutonic thoroughness in his blurred speech, "We go find the whores."

"Ah yes ..." I replied soulfully. That made a lot of sense. Feeling the way I did I needed a putaria like I needed Aragão's pistol in between my teeth.

"As of last month – I know every puta in this whole place. You see my girl's been in hospital – for something nothing – and I went back to my old ways. Like I was saying – when I was once like you a real piss artist gringo!" and he grinned at me mischievously.

It was a tiny grey casa up a red dirt strip. Four cars jammed together outside including Bart's Volks in unlikely intimacy. I don't know quite why we did take caution. A last gasp of a sixth sense breathed a warning. Bart pocketed his pistol he kept in the bomba holster. And I thrust the car tyre wrench into my baggy trousers.

"I thought you said you knew every whore house?" I asked him.

"Well ... this is a new one, I never heard of it until this morning." Now he grinned at me again, "It was Aragão who told me. He says he often comes here..." I fingered the Volks flat iron against my hip.

"How much money you got on you?"

"Hundred and fifty crucs," I told him.

"About all you will need."

A dance floor the size of a double bed. Fat dona on the stoop. Thin nothing nut behind the corner bar. One yellow light glowing. Old tape blatting out old Neil Diamond. And at the back a curtain which swung to and fro when we let the dust in from outside.

Bart's was called Alice. Mine was Edna. She pronounced it Eednii. I didn't have the energy to summon up a smile. It was ironic a puta from Campo Grande should invent a name so plebian typico like Edna, with the belief it had some western movie house estrela magic. Alice, from Hot Springs, Nevada, yearh! But Edna, from Avenida nada Boondocks, putaria favela suburb, Campo Grande! No, senhor!

All girls sound nice in the dark. And the dona put the yellow bulb on the wink for us. I do remember we ordered a couple of beers which never arrived. Bart was untying the lace of Alice's blouse. I caught a glimpse of Edna's long legs and knew she stood a good inch taller than I.

Edna put her arms around my neck and started to explain her family problems. Ran away from home. Parents died young. Had to take care of the kids. Now she has a son of her own, three years old, and did I want to see a photograph of him?

Bart had untied the little silver laces and Alice's blouse crumpled away silkily from her breasts. He put his hand in and with a certain teutonic clinical precision pulled out a perfectly moulded right breast which he proceeded to squeeze at the nipple. The nipple was a slight oddity. Very long and peaky, as if an ungrateful client had distended it with a pair of callipers. He invited me to take out the other breast but Edna would have none of it. She slapped my hand down and asked me to buy her a whisky. No, I wouldn't.

"You want have fetch bring negociate an orgasm with me?" Edna asked. I told her to speak to me in Portuguese. Then I could explain just exactly what it was want have fetch bring negociate I had in mind.

"How much?"

"Three hundred meu minha, I give pussy away."

"Hundred twenty top, lover, what does the dona want for the room?"

There followed a certain disgracefully seedy dialogue to the effect that I wouldn't want have fetch bring negociate Miss Universe for more than a hundred and twenty crucs, in addition that fat old bag dona was going to take another twenty off me. Edna came round to my way of thinking. She said she had to make sacrifices from time to time, giving me a kind of – *maybe you not got any testicles waste my time anyway, gringo* – look.

Bart had already disappeared behind the curtain.

"What you like, handsome? You know you are handsome you look like an Argentino that what you are?"

"No..."

"How you like Edna?"

"Fine fine..."

"No, I mean how you like it?"

"Well, let's see ..."

"Like it like a dog?"

"Could be..."

"Like me on a prong like churrasco?"

"Maybe that too..."

"Like fucky right up back passage?"

"It's a thought..."

"Want me to beat you up make you spill it on the floor?"

"I don't think so ..."

"Like me take it in mouth chew it right off?"

And I told her that I didn't believe such a strenuous act of human demolition would do either of our digestive futures much good.

In the corridor behind the curtain the little rooms were screened from one another by a wood partition. Somehow, I managed to contrive an alternative want have fetch bring negociation with Edna than those first options she had offered up.

Bart was making one hell of a noise next door. The fucking wood screen was bending and bowing. Edna hammered with her heel to quieten them down. Then I heard the dona's voice. Then Bart was shouting out loud and when I peeped round my door I found him jammed up against the washbasin end of corridor with the dona and Alice making a wingding din of a Portuguese racket. It transpired that Bart's appetite was by no means sated and he wanted a second go at Alice all inclusive of the fixed price. Alice, no mean economist, said go screw yourself. And the dona demanded a further hundred and twenty crucs. Bart was in flames. All pinga shot in the eye and pink cheeked and white blond hair standing on end.

I hastily pulled on my trousers and laid Edna's money under the water flask. Three men were suddenly leaning against Bart out in the corridor and Alice was screaming she had seen a revolver on him some place. I took out the Volks' flat wrench and belted one Brazil nut across the neck. The dark skin blanched white. He stumbled forward. Bart produced his gun but in the mêlée he had no chance, what with the dona on her knees for some curious reason attempting to take a huge bite out of his toe-cap. A fist just blew out from nowhere, like a magician's dismembered limb, and caught Bart so hard the side of his face he twisted and rammed his temple into a chin-level wall tap. He sank without trace somewhere in the vicinity of the floor where the fat dona still lay contentedly chewing off strips from his toe-cap.

I remember being swung around, and a very wiry Brazil with a stone hard tiny fist balanced me on my pinga feet for an instant and landed his knuckles slap centro my forehead and that was it. Feet skidded from under me. Edna screamed. And the back of my head vaulted hard down on to the tile floor. Good-night, senhor.

It was less than an hour afterwards. Bart and I regained consciousness bottom of a red dustbowl erosion pit filled with canned detritus and the stench of one very dead animal. We climbed up to the road and took stock. Both our wristwatches were gone. Bart's Volks' keys had vanished. So too had his permanent work carteira and his driving licence.

We didn't speak for a long time. Just walked a bit. Stopped and took a breather. Then tried to make out just which side of favela Campo Grande we had been dumped.

We made it to my little house with its neat and tidy agronomist garden out front. We both showered and inspected the bruises, I got two Brahma Chopps from the freezer and we lounged about draped in toga towels. Very little was said, until the beer began to flow again, blood tingled just enough to—

"You know..." Bart mouthed through fat punchy lips, "you just have got to be kiddin'!"

"What...?"

"What in hell I ever done," Bart's European inflexion quickly gave way to this curious pidgin yankee English we all end up with out here, "to deserve meeting a piss artist sodden mothering son and heir to two whisky bottles like you!"

"Hmm...?"

"I was a happy man until I met you!"

"Ah..."

"I had a friend called Aragão who no friend any longer, he was my jererê traficante you bum, I relied on the dreaded weed from time to time in this town to make it appear more hospitable, now he's gone."

"I'm sorry, Bart..."

"Now I got a girlfriend, who I live with, now she knows sure as night turns into day I been whoring up putarias, and she may not even be home waiting for me after this – she is so jealous all the time."

"I apologise... I do..."

"I lost my watch my mother gave me twenty-first birthday. I lost my work carteira, my revolver, my driver's licence, and now my liver hurts, and you got nothing better to do than sit there looking like an empty bottle of pinga desculping bullshit at me!"

"I grovel... I mean it..."

Bart paused.

"... I was once a piss artist like you true piss artist drunk."

"Yes..."

"I truly was."

"You said..."

"I don't know why, no senhor I don't, but when I consider it, I think I still like you."

"Thanks..."

"I must be louco crazed out of my mind, gringo, but I like you."

One of us just had to laugh.

Quite understandably, for a few days after, I saw very little of Bart. I imagined he was doing his best to make amends with his girl Apareçida for that shameful night on the tiles.

I was gloomily contemplating my agronomist's near empty freezer counting up three cases of opened Brahma Chopp beers when Bart returned to ring my doorbell. He was all smiles and chock full of the casual you old dog you what you been whoring at since I last... and I shrugged it off.

"My girl wants to meet you," he said.

"Very nice too."

"No no... really, she thinks she has forgiven us now. In any case you are forgiven."

"What about you?" I asked. Bart pulled up his trouser leg

and showed me the yellow and brown bruises.

"She's still kicking me. Every time I open my mouth she kicks me."

"Those things you lost, Bart... ?"

"Not a chance. I've renewed one, and told the authorities that I had an accident. Fell out of my pocket. And I have new car keys."

"The revolver?"

"Who cares. I had no licence for it anyway."

We drove to collect Apareçida from her doctor's. She was there for a final check-up. On the door I noticed the man's name. And his professional speciality. He was a gynaecologist. From there the three of us found a clean Lebanese restaurant. Little red table cloths and fat lacquered statuary of girls and boys of no specific genitalia, glazed hermaphrodites poised with an arm extended offering up a fruit bowl, dripping marble grapes.

"I heard all about you," Apareçida began, as we sat down, "and I thought oh but does he sound like a heel. But now we meet – maybe I think differently."

I had the grace to blush.

I didn't talk much that evening. But I could tell that she wanted to. There was a strange buoyancy about her. Though she kept her spirits high I could feel a sadness and an unhealing wound of desperation in her.

Lovely, all right ... very: Apareçida had a small face of tiny features in repose, but when she talked those black Brazil eyes bloomed and her broad thin lips laughed a lot and she revealed very carefully capped white teeth. I would not as a rule use the word 'carefully'. But in her case, it applied. She was not a girl any longer, about thirty-five or so, but beneath the restrained cosmetics and neatly tied dark hair there were worry lines and tiny time-laden furrows which crinkled at the corners of her mouth and her eyes; it would take more than a passing glance to register the dye in her hair and how the tinted white strands were hidden away with care.

Apareçida had perfect English. As good as Bart's. She had French, too. And still she could surprise you. Two years ago she qualified as a lawyer out of night school. In Campo Grande it was unheard of. There could not have been two other women in the whole town who practised law.

Bart and she had a way of sitting together. Never too close.

None of that awful enamorado rubbish. But there was another kind of tension between them. A nicer kind, you sensed that in all their loving they had never been so fulfilled as with one another. And though their bodies were apart, they shared an equal grace, an intimate understanding, an acute awareness of touch. You felt that – as animals they were totally and evenly matched.

How so often their nights together, whatever their skills to obtain those crises of pleasure, cry against cry, flesh seeking a death of the senses, Bart and Apareçida were one.

She had never married; and, in a place like Campo Grande it doesn't take a priest to tell you that if you are unwed by the age of twenty-two you heard whispers all along the streets. In some cases they'd be tender sighs of regret, in others sheer bitch words. A primitive papist yoke in the name of innocence and salvation.

"But it's insane," I broke in, "you could be practising law in São Paulo making a fortune from American clients."

Bart put his thick arm around her and grinned sheepishly—

"My Apareçida hasn't got the courage to. She's frightened. She has come so far – you see, so far, and she can go no further."

Naturally, I asked why.

Her father ran off leaving the mother with three kids. He never came back. The mother committed suicide in front of Apareçida. She gulped at a mouthful of sulphuric acid and sat on a chair convulsing. After moments something heaved with wicked pain in her belly and she threw back her head and died. Apareçida was eleven.

There was nobody else to turn to. She brought her two brothers to Campo Grande and they squatted in a favela shack hidden behind tall colonião grasses by the river. Apareçida sold newspapers in hotel rooms and walked all the bars unloading lottery tickets. She fed her young family and the authorities never found out. She took night school and became a tall skinny wide-eyed creature tripping about town in slop sandals and near no nothing skimpy dresses which she stole. All her available money went on textbooks and food for the boys.

Bart egged her on. Perhaps he had heard the story a thousand times before, but clearly he was not tired of it. The pride in his voice when—

"You tell him . . . he's a britisher . . . they all good listeners."

"Well..." she hesitated.

"No. Go on."

"There was this hotel here – maybe their business wasn't so good, anyway – they would send me up to the rooms with the papers and I'd knock on the door and try to sell two contos of rubbish to a man. But ... I kept getting these offers. The man would look at me and say – the portaria send you up? Yes, I said. You a virgin? He asked. Oh, yes, I said. One day..."

She stopped. It was a crick in her mouth. She wiped her eyes but I could find no tears there.

"Go on go on," said Bart, "does you good. Hang it all out as the Americans say."

Then came the tears. Large, and blobbing and real, window paning down her sweet up-tilted nose. She drew breath.

"Am I boring you?"

"!"

"Another time it happened – and some man in a room offered me fifty cruzeiros. I was so young at the time – what? Fourteen. Yes, about that. And I went into his room. I let the man do what he wanted. I remember I couldn't take my eyes off his boots. He wore enormous yellow boots, and, well of course he took his pants down, but he never took those huge boots off."

"Were you afraid?"

"I felt nothing. I hurt a little. Naturally. But I let him do just what he wanted and I said nothing."

"He paid you..."

"No. He threw me out of the room. I could do nothing."

"You should have put a knife through his throat."

"But I learned quick. I had nothing to lose then. It was all over for me. And I became hard. Very hard. Every new man I met in those hotel rooms – oh, I gave it to them, I did, good and strong, I had their money out on the table and inside my shoe before they could touch a button on my dress."

She was crying so much now, I couldn't make out all the details. She lived with an American, and that was how she learnt the language. Then there was a Frenchman. And that was the way it went.

"Then...I met Bart," she said simply.

They took me back to their house. It was a nice blue wash fronted low casa, with a garage, up in the dirt road hills west of the town. The large untidy room was filled with air-condition cool, and Bart kept two freezers behind the dining table. Apareçida said she had stopped crying, and had pulled herself together, and though she still did not trust me she liked me a little now. I watched her take a musical longplay of the famous drama 'Morte e Vida Severina' (Cabral de Melo Neto) and place it on the gramophone deck. She apologised again and said she had to tidy herself up.

"Freezer full of gin tonic, you want?"

"I should say..."

"You know, you are just like Bart when I first met him. You keep your nose down every glass you can find."

"Safest place to put it, a nose like mine."

She didn't smile.

Bart placed the drinks on the side table and cracked a tonic bottle. I cut up the lime-lemons and snookered the cubes from the ice tray.

"A warning..."

I looked up.

"We must take things steady tonight. She's a little bit afraid."

"Bart, that's the second time this evening you've said she's afraid. What are you driving at, man?"

"Look at it her way – I'm seven years younger than she is, did you know that?"

I didn't.

"And things don't always run smooth here. Now that she has just come out of hospital I have to go careful with her. She knows – one day I'm going to leave her. When the money runs out. Go to the States. Or France. And when I leave, oh boy... there won't be anyone around to pick up her pieces."

"Take her with you."

"No..." he whispered, as if he was ashamed of the finality in his mind.

"Girl like that, Bart, she's a million – you can take her anywhere you like. Christ sake – there's not one fucking girl with one thousandth of what she got all Campo Grande!"

"I know..."

"If I found a girl who'd done all that and come through like she has I'd be down on my knees sober thanking Somebody up there whose existence I'm not too convinced about anyway!"

"True..."

"I don't understand."

"When I came here, I had this house, the car, free petrol, and a thousand US dollars a month. I was king. And I piss artisted it all away most every night. Just like you. Then I met her. She picked me up in a bar and floated me back home. Soon enough I discovered I was leaning on her like a baby. She was so wise. She knows things has seen things people like you and me don't have the time or the sensitivity to recognise let alone understand. Don't get me wrong. I worshipped her."

"Don't stop. Good medicine."

"But... and here's the irony... it has been a long affair. I haven't always kept true. No, senhor, I haven't. Now, I feel it deep inside me. That I'm now at the close of the affair. It cannot get better it cannot get worse. A marriage would do nothing. It would simply prolong an affair that was inevitably bound to finish. Is that so disgusting?"

"You never wanted children?"

"Look at me, I'm single, I'm alone, a thousand US dollars a month out here, can earn twice that anywhere in the world," and he paused. He laid his fingers over his eyes for a moment, his head lowered. "Oh, shit it! ... I want children. I'd have hers. I'd stay with her, then."

"Have you discussed it with her?"

"She just cries bursts out crying at the mention."

"Have you discussed leaving – with her?"

"No. But she knows. She's so wise she knows all the secrets in my mind. Don't doubt."

"You leave her, Bart, she's finished in a place like Campo Grande."

"My answer is – I cannot stay. I cannot." And I recognised that stolid teutonic reasoning behind his eyes. Nothing I could say would alter that.

Apareçida breezed into the room wearing a transparent thin dress and I appreciated how her legs climbed up to her hips as if they were never going to end.

"How're you two piss artists doing?" she called out. And it was a charming thing to see the way she blushed. She caught my surprised glance at her use of the words pejorative.

"Excuse me, please," she murmured, "I pick up all this bad language from Bart. I never used to talk like this."

In the course of things, I learnt that it suited Bart to have me around, albeit only for a few weeks. He was pleased enough that, though she distrusted me, Apareçida had not lost all respect for her servant Harold. All right, I was an echo of the kind of bum she first discovered in Bart and rescued him from; but I constituted no threat, she knew he wouldn't lower himself to my way of life now that he had leant on her so much.

At first, he came round only in the early evenings for a drink. He'd excuse himself come supper time, saying—

"Well, it's time for my slippers. Old pinga rake like you got plenty to find in the town on your own. Goodnight."

But, there were visible cracks in his surface. There was a new tension, a longing for things greener the other side of the hill and you name it cliché etcetera. More and more he talked about America. Did I know Wisconsin? No, I didn't. He'd been offered a good job there. Did I think Wisconsin women were liberated? I talked a lot of nonsense about hearsay to the effect that American women are sexually combative and that their physical liberation is an assertion of power (God forgive me my glibness in Campo Grande).

Then a curious thing happened. He appeared one night. He said Apareçida had to meet some people (a palpable lie – a guess, but I was right) and we should do a round of the bars.

"Now you know what that means," I warned him.

"Just this one time."

"Who takes the blame if—" I tried to admonish.

"Go to hell! I do. Don't ask me again!"

We got back around two in the morning. As I pushed my agronomist's front door, I could hear the telephone ringing on the wall in the kitchen. I was going to run for it, but Bart put his hand on my arm. In the pause the phone stopped. He shrugged. I thought those light eyes of his looked oddly cowed.

He tried to put a cassette tape on the machine. It wouldn't play. He jerked it loose and the brown filmy strands were twisted around the loop. He pulled at it angrily. The tape snapped.

"Oh shit! ... shit it!" he cried out loud.

"I can replace."

He stumbled by the door. He had to grip tight by the jamb to stand up straight. He was swimming.

"Gringo goodnight ... !"

He was out the door, and from the strange noises of the car's manual, I received the clear impression he was trying by force of will power to reverse the Volks in first gear.

Now I had slept let's say an hour and a bit. When all the lights flooded my frost-glass bedroom door from the room out front. I didn't think I was being burgled. I just thought of Aragão. Could this be the end? I looked out at the night through the window above my head. Stars were fading. There was a smear of lemon on the horizon below the window ledge.

Bart was standing in the kitchen boiling black coffee when I got up the courage to find out who.

"Hi..." he said without looking round.

"What time?"

"Four..."

He was wearing cotton riding breeches and a white t-shirt. He had on a pair of tall black boots, wide at the ankles, with silver spurs. I couldn't believe my eyes.

"You out of your mind?" I enquired.

"No, senhor."

"You in fancy dress?"

"Nope neither..."

"I thought I'd got rid of you an hour ago – you went back home?"

"Yes, I couldn't sleep."

"You saw your girl?"

"Yep."

"I'll have some of that café," I sighed. I could feel the night's intake of alcohol beginning to stir. It had thought it had got away with at least one good night's sleep. Now I was kicking it around. Oxygen getting at it. Firing it. I could feel it waking. Asking for more help. Keep to the café, you bum.

"I'm going riding. You want come?"

"Now!"

"You can ride?"

"When I'm sober I can, yes."

"Best thing in the world to sober up with. I always used to do it."

"Where? How?" I asked, all além da imaginação.

It appeared that one of the few friends he had ever made in Campo Grande was the coronel at the 6th Battalion Cavalry Division. He had permission to take out any horse he wanted and ride it round the gallops inside the quartel. They had jumps there, too, and a white sixteen-hand high animal no one but the coronel was allowed to ride.

This was Bart's one concession – in his early piss artist days in Campo Grande – to the respectable life. For all the doctors and lawyers and dentists who were anybody in town had this same permission to ride the coronel's horses in the early morning hours.

"We go now?" he said almost menacingly.

As we drove down to the militar section I was aware how quickly the light comes at this hour. The dark of the cool clouds pulls back and a most beautiful lemon meringue texture lifts across the sky, more than an hour to first sun, and mist still on the trees like spume from a cachoeira valley. You could hear the winsome sabiá call from the bushes and the red dust on the road doesn't powder so finely in the wake of the Volks' wheels.

"I used to think," he said as we stopped the car inside the quartel gates, "when I saw these mornings like this, well I thought, there must be a pattern to life. God is in it somewhere. At least, He is until nine o'clock in the morning when the heat rises from the pavement."

"I've never seen it before like this."

"Every morning," he told me, "I used to do this. Sometimes I kidded myself I liked it even better than drinking."

"Why did you stop?"

"When Apareçida moved in with me she got a grudge against it."

"Why?"

"Everybody knows who she is. She can't get permission from the coronel to ride the militar horses. For that matter – she'd never lower herself to ask. But she spits on them for that."

It transpired that the lawyers and the doctors and the dentists didn't want their virgin daughters attending the privileged riding quartel of the 6th Cavalry with a creature like Apareçida. That was too much for their propriety.

"So she invented things about my riding," Bart continued, "she said I was having an affair with an American girl who rode in the mornings. She hated me going there. Always the same grudge."

"Was it true?"

"There . . . was an American girl who used to ride out here."

"Were you screwing her?"

"I . . . all right, yes I was."

"What happened to her?"

"Nothing. She's still here. But I don't see her any more. That was my promise to Apareçida. And then . . . well, I stopped going to the quartel."

"Until today."

He sidestepped. He asked me how well I could jump. I told him I'd made some gymkhana leaps over a metre and a half.

You can say what you like about those DOPS thugs and those SNI Brazil nut CIA type groups, but it was a revelation to see how this Cavalry quartel was run. The young squaddies were the nicest bunch you could ever hope to meet. They'd do anything for you. Nothing was too much trouble. They chose for me the least tired animal, a calm girl, but tall and springy. They brushed her down until she shone and they insisted I wear one of their special t-shirts with the Cavalry Insignia. They griddled the calm girl's shoes with an iron to clean out for stones and I picked a double-barred bit in case I couldn't control her properly first time out.

And Bart was right. The sobering effect was incredible. I declined any of the jumps, but I trotted her in figures-of-eight around the poles and took her for a gallop up a red dust and sertão ridge while Bart concentrated on a series of tight sand bank jumps where his horse had to gauge without knowing how deep lay the fall on the other side.

And high above us the lemon light began to cream. It became a thicker texture. Plops of green-tinged yellow and lemon sky climbed across the receding stars. Only clouds muddied the picture. I don't believe I ever had seen a morning in Brazil so breathtaking. You could add, I suppose, as a rider, that I'd never ever seen one morning in Brazil this early before. The air smelt of cinnamon and vanilla and sweet horse breath. So cool was it, not a drop of moisture, humid morning tears, lay in my palms.

These riding mornings became a habit with us. No matter how late Bart made it back to his house, he always came round to me at four in the early light. I had no idea how he explained it away to his girl. As for me, I knew that I was true persona non grata in Apareçida's eyes now, but sad as it was, I did not think I was doing anything very wrong.

These were Bart's mornings. Tactile and attainable, yet filled with his infinite yearning, his heart married to excess, a love vessel all shot up but bearing no exit wounds. Obvious enough – it was his way of saying that one day, Apareçida, I will leave you. And from his expression, the sense of sheer happiness which radiated from him, I knew these mornings meant more to him than this girl, than all the pinga he could take, than any companionship I could offer him. To Bart they had a pattern, out of holy nowhere a grid had been shaped, they were his grip on a sliding world.

Each day we boozed away the early evenings. Sometimes we made it to a putaria to haggle over prices with the girls. But my few weeks in Campo Grande were coming to a close and I would have to make that trip I had promised myself up into Acre where, it was said, this novo movimento in Brazil had not yet penetrated. In a matter of a couple of days I'd say goodbye to Bart, and I'd ask him to send my best to Apareçida for, though he never as much as admitted it to my face, I was certain she would not want to meet me again.

I galloped hard up the sertão ridge. My good friend beneath me had become accustomed to my ways, and I no longer needed to use that hard bit on her. Just as we turned, on a particularly gritty level of ground, I heard the clink of a front shoe. She stamped her hoof, and cocked her ears at me. When I peered over I could see the iron rim jutting out to the side. I jumped down and tried to lift her hoof. But I couldn't get a good look at it. The nails had come out. Or there was a softening in her tissue. I wasn't sure.

I walked her back past the jumps where Bart trotted. He waved at me, and I grimaced. He wasn't going to stop for me. The Cavalry boys in the smithy room took her in from me and I hung up the girths.

There is a wide road outside the quartel. It is on a rise. High enough for someone passing in a car to watch the riders jump beyond the wall. I guessed Bart would be another hour or so, and I walked out of the main gate and stood on the unusually cool quiet pavement. At first I did not notice the car. Something made me look twice. There, about forty metres away sat Apareçida in a Volks car I did not recognise. It certainly didn't belong to Bart.

She was oblivious of me. She stared out across the quartel wall to where the jumps were. She watched as Bart trotted back and forth trying to decide on a further sand bank leap. She had an impassive stillness. You couldn't see her head move.

Apareçida didn't hear me approach until I reached down to open the near-side passenger door. I leant my head in.

"Are we on speaking terms?" I asked facetiously.

She startled. Then she took a deep breath and flushed violently.

She looked years younger, like a child caught out on a silly prank.

"Why ... yes!"

"May I come in?"

"If you want."

"You not going to start kicking me or—"

"Please please – don't be so silly."

I opened the window and lounged in the seat beside her; if I'd been a real no thinking bastard I would have decided I at least had the advantage, I had the drop on her. I wasn't that bad. And if she didn't want Bart to know she came down here to watch him ride the jumps, I wasn't going to tell on her.

"This isn't your car ..." I began.

"That's my business."

"Sure it is ..."

"I borrowed it from a friend."

"I was only asking."

"When are you leaving Campo Grande?"

I told her.

"I suppose ... you want to know why I'm sitting here, snooping you call it, no?" she asked, in a slightly tremulous voice.

"I think I already know ..."

"How?"

"You wanted to see if that American girl was down here."

"Go to hell!"

"I don't mind, I don't mind! Don't kill me!"

"Bart told you about her—?"

"He did."

"He would ..."

"But it isn't true, Apareçida. You can see with your own eyes. How often you come down here since we been riding?"

"This is the first time."

"There never has been an American girl while I've been riding these mornings."

"So you say. I'm not going to believe you."

"I swear to you, girl! All in your mind!"

"No ..."

"Sim sim, senhorita."

"Sometimes ..." she paused, rolling her fingers around the steering wheel, "I wish to myself I wish to God that there was."

"Masochist."

"I mean it. God it would be so much easier if there was

an American girl! You understand that don't you?"

"I think so."

"Course you do. I could grip on to something. I could have a hold on to something. I'd know what was coming. I'd be armed!" she said.

"You could leave him first ..." I murmured, glancing around at the car we sat in which I did not recognise. But I felt treacherous and dirty in saying so.

"I have nowhere to go. This is my place. Little Campo Grande," and with bitterness, like salt and lemon and cocaine snorted at one into the nostrils.

"I'm sorry ... I take that back."

"Don't think my brothers will help me. They don't live here now. Even so – they won't talk to me. Their wives won't allow it."

"Please ... babe, I apologise."

"Bart will leave me ... He will. It is just that, I cannot stand the waiting. Not knowing how or when. Not having a clue. I'm walking blind in the dark knowing that somewhere there's a big fall ahead of me and there is no one to warn me!"

You can't call that self-pity. It didn't come out of Apareçida like that. It came like a voice distended on eyes which have watched sulphuric acid pour down a grown woman's throat, and skin which has grubbed childish unknowing pleasures for fat stomachs and tall yellow boots in hotel bedrooms promising cruc notes.

"It may not end like that. You could hold on. Bart needs you. He leans on you. He could take you to America."

"I had my chance to hold on."

"—?—"

"Sure I did," she continued, "why do you think I was in the hospital for a month?"

"I never asked."

"Just before you got here."

"Yes, I remember. You had a cyst on your pussy or a feminine problem like that, huh?"

"I was carrying his child. I went into the hospital and had an abortion. That's right. That's why I cried so much that night we ate together, remember?"

"An abortion! In Holy Brazil! You kidding me!"

"No kid."

"Why? Why when you could have held on? That was the

very thing Bart would stay for. You would have kept him for ever. What's the matter with you, Apareçida?"

"I asked myself that ..."

"Bart never knew?"

"And you will never tell him, gringo, or I cut your throat!"

"Cert ..."

"All I ask of you."

"You threw everything away?"

"Yes."

"You did it for him?"

"In the end, he will leave me."

"You make me think I'm the worst heel in the world."

"Oh well ... that's nice," and she threw back her head and laughed. It was a distant laughter, without any pity or gaiety. "Because that's just what you are!"

"I'm a heel."

"And a piss artist."

"Don't stop at that!"

"I won't! ..." a sudden flaring anger in her face, her neck grew taut with laced fibres beneath her skin, and she snake snapped round on me, "People like you come into this town by the dozen. Think they can tell us what to do how to do—"

"Now wait a minute—"

"You tell me I ought to leave Bart! Who the hell do you think you are gringo telling me what I should do! What do you know about living in this place out here! Know fat nothing!"

"Slow down."

"You raise your eyebrows and say to me you don't believe it is possible to have an abortion in a country like this. Let me tell you this is no backward country, and when people need help even people like me they can get it!"

"OK OK."

Behind her head, I could see Bart's ash-white hair bobbing in slicks over his pink face as he cantered for a jump. His horse rose beautifully, back legs just scraping the rail, and both rider and beast disappeared below the quartel wall from this side of the street.

"This damn country not the ass-hole place you seem to think it is!"

"I never said—"

"It's not a banana republic gringos like you can walk in and tell us what to do where to do it and how to! This is Brazil!"

"You getting through."

"This is the greatest country in the world. With the greatest future. No matter what you think of me or what future I got. In the first place I am here and this is me, and I can take it. Whatever comes. Because I love this country. It is mine, not Bart's, not yours. Lovers pará la lovers pará ca – but I stay! I'm a Brazilian!"

"You finished screaming?"

"Now get the fuck out of this car, gringo, and don't expect me to say goodbye to you! Because I won't, ever! Tá?"

When I returned to England, friends offered me a little cottage near Glastonbury to dry out in. Oh . . . it is so far away from any pub or off-licence you won't have the energy to walk there. We'll come and collect you when you are better.

At first, I found it a pretty appalling plight to be in. If you loathed the English countryside as much as I do you'd understand. Night sounds make me paranoiac. The least feather of pollen makes my nose drip like grannie's old faucet, and my eyes run red. And I also have a manure allergy. One look at a pile of it and spots come out in a crowd.

And it was lonely. For I too had my memories. The wife I had almost killed in that car crash. The sentence at the trial for driving so much under the influence of etcetera. How she swore she'd never ever speak to me again. The divorce proceedings speeded up by uncontrollable bouts of drinking. Wife whom I had loved but wife who could not understand I needed the wet veil to reach out to her this love. Hard though she tried to understand, it never quite got through, no matter how often I explained it to her, that the drinking made me sober. It had always been my clarity. Without it whole world was on the blink, with it blood was ecstatic.

Some can read in certain romantic fiction that drying out is just a matter of waking in the morning and testing your control by the amount of shake there is in your fingers. It is my experience to dry out properly, you have to hypnotise yourself to hate the alcohol. It has to become the real devil instead of the devil disguised as an angel of mercy you have always believed it to be, and even then you see shadows that aren't dreams and ghosts climb up your spine tricking you into thinking you are safe from the rot when all the time it is just another lie you have to uncover. And what they call the shakes doesn't start at the end of popular fiction fingers, it is a rattling, it is a palpable unsticking of the flesh from the bone, until like a burnt-out cob juggling in its husk, the rind of you has come apart from the core.

The months had gone by. With care I had dried out. I was allowed piss like cider and the occasional sherry before dinner. My mornings were never quite those same incomparable mornings of that lemon light and the way it bathed me in a stilly coolness of cinnamon and vanilla and sweet horse breath when, so cool was it, not a drop of moisture, humid morning tears, lay in my palms, and mist still hung in the trees like spume from a cachoeira valley.

To my delight I received a card from Bart. Then I saw the stamp. It was franked Wisconsin. All it said – 'Sixty-nine women, you damn gringo, and I'm still counting! Yours, Bart.'

Quite alone, as I most frequently am, nowadays, I sat down and wrote a letter—

Cara Apareçida,

I do not know what I can say to you which will make any difference. I think of you often, and I burn with shame. I want you to know I hope you can hang in there as the Americans say hang in there with the whispers in the street. And there might come a day when you'll forgive us – by us I mean all those tired souls who travel to you from this antique kingdom of Europe in your east bringing gifts which only turn to debts – and even forgive me my arrogance. You said to me you are a Brazilian and your fight's there. I'm humbled. The pie is under my nose. Some mornings, dull and grey and wet, I think I can still hear your voice crying out, and I ache with saudade. For as much as I'd like to help you I cannot even help myself. More power to your arm babe, and luck too,

Felicidades,

Though I sealed the envelope and stamped it and kept it neatly placed in my wallet pocket for days what, in all her heavens and hells, would she want with a letter from a piss artist gringo like me? . . . I never posted it.

'I HEARD THE CRY OF MY PEOPLE'*

"Is this your doll?"

"Yes ..."

"You love her?"

"She's my dolly."

"What is your name?"

"Adelia."

"And dolly's—?"

"Adelia – after me. You see – I'm her."

"I tell you what we're going to do. I want to keep your dolly for a while."

"Why?"

"We are going to ask you a lot of questions. If you give us the proper answers I will give you back the doll."

"Why did Daddy and Mummy leave like that?"

"Adelia – if you don't give us the answers we must have I will break the dolly and burn her."

"You won't! ... Why!"

"Yes, I'm afraid so."

"You can't ... !"

"You do want to have the dolly back?"

"Yes ... !"

"Then you must stand over here – and listen carefully to what we say. And you must answer truthfully."

"I want dolly back ..."

Adelia was seven. She lived with her mother, Darci, and her father, Dermi, in a single-storey house on the Santos road to the coast out of São Paulo. The Flores family rented the yellow stucco cottage. It stood so close to the road – although it was

* 'Eu ouvi o choro dos meus povos' – National Council of Brazilian Bishops (CNBB), May 6, 1973.

wide enough for six car lanes there was no pavement – and Adelia's front door opened on to the dusty red earth and broken tarmac spewed up.

That morning four men arrived at the house. They drove up in a dark blue and unmarked caminhão. The very kind of van which made daily deliveries to the Vezes bookshop in São Paulo where Dermi and Darci worked. Dermi easily recognised this type of van. It had a sliding door at the side. Whenever a delivery van drew up outside the bookshop a boy would jerk back the door and toss out those sacks of books all in one motion. So quick was the boy the van's wheels hardly stopped. Dermi had always compared the dull thump thwack of the sacks to cadavers. They hit the ground, or so it seemed to him, with a flesh-like weightiness.

That morning, Adelia played in the yard with an orange box on wheels which her father had made. As for that caminhão outside the house, it was no delivery van for the Church bookshop Vezes. And there were no sacks of books, books weighted like blood, to be tossed outside Dermi's door, even though the caminhão looked like a delivery van, and even though Dermi was the manager of the Vezes bookshop.

Adelia stood in the yard and watched her parents talking to the men. She couldn't hear what they said. And the exchange was very brief. Dermi left first. Adelia saw Darci try to step out into the yard through the kitchen door. As if she wanted to say something to her. There was an urgency in Darci's eyes, Adelia could see that, her mother's eyes were wide and wounded. But one of the men led her back.

Adelia remembered she had left her doll on the sofa in the front room. She ran inside but her parents were already gone. The blue caminhão outside the window drove away quickly.

There were two men in the room. The other two must have gone with Darci and Dermi. The tall man held out her dolly. And it was this man who asked her her name. Asked her if the dolly was hers. Of course it was. Stupid question. But when he told her he might destroy the dolly, and when he wouldn't say where her parents had been taken to, Adelia burst out crying.

She stood very stiffly by the wall and felt the tears slide down her neck, wet tracers around her adam's apple. There was a certain coldness, hot as it was, and a fear, in her own home as she was, and her scalp tingled. Beyond the mosquito grill she could hear the morning cars outside stampeding into São Paulo.

Something different had happened today. Usually her mother walked her across to the neighbour where she played for the day. In the evenings Dermi and Darci fetched her after they had finished work.

It was going to be different today. Later she could explain all about it to dolly. But not now.

The sofa was made of an off-white plastic. One of those men took out a knife and ripped the plastic until the foam rubber underneath billowed. He lifted the matting to prise up some of the floorboards. The print on the wall of Guanabara Bay was torn out of its frame. All the drawers in Dermi's desk were tossed on to the floor.

Darci kept a stool in the corner covered with a white cotton skirt surround. She placed her rosary beads, a Bible and the crucifixion predella there. Each week she changed the cotton skirt for clean white. It was always a ritual for Darci. Dermi used to laugh because he never prayed. The men kicked the stool over they were in such a rush and they didn't stop to notice the holy pieces all over the floor and the water from the upturned vase and the plastic red roses lying there which were all part and parcel of Darci's faith.

The men reminded Adelia of the plumbing people who created such a shindig when the sewage pipe cracked beneath the road just by the front door. It was a standing joke amongst the neighbours that nobody knew they even had sewage until the men came to tell them it was broken and there was a health risk.

Even though she was still crying she could not stop staring at the men. And her eyes ached now. They were fat burly types. One taller than the other. They had pleasant round faces, rolly-polly bellies, and they both wore moustaches. How moustaches tickle ... Adelia remembered a kissing uncle who had one. She noticed too – how hairy and thick their wrists were, covered in black hairs, quite unlike her father's thin bones and pale skin. They each wore rings. Large ones with coloured stones set into the gold. But there was one uniformity about them, and Adelia's sharp eyes were quick to notice. Both men, on their left little fingers, wore a thin gold band which curled into a *figa* shape. They looked cheap the *figa* rings, as if they had come out of a slot-machine arcade.

She couldn't cry any more, and that was a good thing she supposed. She felt weak and trembly but she was brave enough to follow them from room to room. They wrecked and they tore, pulled apart and hacked away, as if ... she really didn't know what 'as if' ... it was even partly exciting, her curiosity at so many things being destroyed, even though they were her mother's, the sense of mystery, in her childish reasoning these adults must have an explanation for it. What had Dermi and Darci done? Who were these men? Why hadn't a friend called from over the road when all this started? Would Darci get back tonight? Well, perhaps, at a pinch, she could cook. She knew how to boil the feijão preto.

Eventually, the men stopped. They looked tired. The determination to find something, this hunting out was done with; it was midday and the sun stood at its worst. She wasn't going to offer them anything to drink. And that was a pity. Because it also meant she couldn't go and fetch a bottle of guarana for herself from the kerosene fridge. The men had seen the bottles she had heard them open the fridge a while back when they were poking in there searching, for whatever it was they wanted; but something told her they would not steal guarana. So she was resolved, no drinks for anybody, and this was no small matter of self-denial, her tongue and her throat were wool and paper.

Adelia was still afraid. It was a curious fear. It made her very alert. The smallest sound boomed. Time rushed by. Her eyes devoured everything about these men. And the tingling on her scalp had disappeared.

The men sat in the front room. They sat, as if to say – at last! It's over! And Adelia watched. One man was by the telephone. The other carefully rolled back the slit in the sofa where the rubber bulged. Perhaps he felt a little embarrased for what he had done with his knife. Dermi would go mad if he could see. The man tried to grin at Adelia. Very bad teeth.

"I'm Alcides ..." he said, "this is my friend Salles ..."

Salles held up Adelia's dolly. His fat hairy fingers crushed her waist.

"Now, Adelia ... remember I promised you you could have this doll back if you answered all our questions? Remember that?"

Adelia sunk her chin into her neck. Her face reddened. Salt prickles under her eyelids. She nodded.

She would have liked to ask, where is Darci? Why have you taken Dermi and she like that? Who told you you could kick the holy stool and smash the predella and all the plastic roses on the matting? It wasn't a fear which held her back. That had long since passed. Instead, she knew instinctively she was alone; no friends had come knocking at the door for her would she play with them; no Darci had rung back on the telephone I will be home before tea Adelia you are quite safe with these men; and Adelia could think of one thing only – how soon would it be before these men left? For they must have homes. A mother like mine. A daughter like me. Supper of sarapatel and tutu.

"Adelia, do Dermi and Darci talk in front of you?"

"Yes."

"When you go to bed can you hear them talking?"

"I close my eyes and pretend I'm asleep – but I can always hear them. It's a thin wall."

"Clever girl, Adelia."

"I will give you a list of names – if there is a name you recognise – perhaps a name Dermi has used often, you must say."

"I don't remember names."

"Pastoral Operaria?"

"No."

"Movimento Educação de Base?"

"No."

"RENOV?"

"No."

"FASE?"

"No."

"Acção Popular?"

She was growing tired of the game now. Perhaps the last name had a familiar ring. She didn't want these kind of questions to go on and on. All right, Dermi has mentioned that name. It was a simple enough name. And these men might go away if—

"Yes. I heard that," the men leaned forward.

"Acção Popular?"

"Yes. I heard."

"Often?"

"Oh yes."

"In conversation."

"That's right."

"Dermi and Darci?"

"Both."

"How often?"

"Oh, very," surely they might go away now.

"Think carefully Adelia ... remember back ... did they mention conscientizacão?"

"I don't—"

"Conscientizacão?" It was just one word.

"Conscientizacão?" repeated the other man.

"They did... I think... There was an evening and I fell asleep listening to their voices – yes that was it, that was the word. Are you going to go away now?"

"Dermi and Darci have lots of friends?"

"No. They only have the neighbours."

"Ever go out much?"

"No. We have no money. They stay in every night."

"And talk?"

"Yes."

"And that makes you sleepy?"

"If you like..."

"Adelia, what do they talk about?"

"About... books. Books and the bookshop. And magazines and papers. And people who read them. Buy them from the shop. That's all."

It was the familiar ring. Her heart leapt at the sound of the telephone. Darci was there. She was coming back any moment and these men would go away. Adelia you must keep very calm and sit quietly, and we will see you before your bedtime. I promise. Dermi promises too.

The man called Salles picked up the phone and hunched his shoulder up close by his neck to balance the mouthpiece.

Salles gestured to the other. It meant send the girl out of the room. Do it now. The man Alcides led Adelia out into the passage. She didn't like his fat fingers on her neck. She twisted away from him and slammed the door of her little bedroom against him. She waited for him to go back, then she climbed up on to the cot and rested her head against the thin partition wall. She was near to the table where the telephone stood. Her hot breath made the paintwork slippery she knelt so close.

"Yes... Yes sir..." the man Salles was speaking into the mouthpiece, "... just the daughter. She's a kid. No. No one... that's right... All done... no need there's an ónibus... I will ... tchau..." and he put down the phone.

She could feel the weight of his shoulders as the man Salles leaned back against the partition wall. He was quiet for a minute.

The scraping of his heel over the floor. That man Alcides was waiting patiently.

"That's that then..." Salles scratched his head and breathed deeply, almost a sadness in his voice, a resigned quality, "it's not going to be very difficult to make out a report. It won't be me who does it. That's a relief."

"What happened?"

"Nothing! That's what! Just waste! All shitting waste! And ... we're left here ... like wet mothers."

"What will the report say?"

"There was an accident."

"That all?"

"Found dead beside the road ... man and wife."

"I see."

"Hit and run ... esquadra alert for a large lorry ... no other details."

"The girl ... Adelia?"

"Fetch her."

She was standing in the front room with them. Although there was this silence between them, it was not strained; the air was charged with unspoken kindnesses, the men's eyes were soft and dark brown, they leaned forward and clasped their fingers. The man Salles clutched Adelia's dolly. But this time he didn't crush her.

In the men's hesitation, the way they moved shifting their body weight on the sofa, dry lips and perspiration beads on eyelashes, there was an element of lament, that untranslatable saudade of the spirit, a cry of grief albeit as puny as a wink in an ant's eye. These men Salles and Alcides...

"We have to go now, Adelia."

"Yes..."

"Here you are – you can have your dolly back."

Adelia could hear a rising tumult. It could easily be thunder the clouds had been so low all the morning. But it was not. It was not that tin sheet shaking reverberence the close of the rains hammered out in the sky. It was too contained, and too much inside of her.

The thunderousness was between her eyes, it roared inside her mouth back of her tongue deep behind a veil of sinew it pounded inside her skull.

Last year she and Darci and Dermi had played together on the Guanabara beach, and Darci shouted to her she could stand up to her ankles but no further for the current pulled so much it sucked and slid back leaving streamers of sound until another wave boomed and the spray pounced. That was what the noise in her head reminded her of. And as the sound grew in her, it wanted to burst between her ears, so loud was it now, she could faintly picture the Guanabara.

"You love your dolly don't you?"

"She's my dolly."

"Take her. Here ... You want her?"

She shook her head.

"Adelia?"

Hands to her ears.

"Here she is..."

"I don't want her!"

"Adelia?"

"No!" The booming...

THE OCTOBER HABIT

It is near enough five hundred kilometres from Cuiabá to the village of Villa Bella. In the old days of Brazil the capital of all Mato Grosso was this same Mato Grosso de Villa Bella. Two hundred years ago the town boasted a palácio de governador and a military fort of red sandstone which was hauled by African slaves from the Bolivian frontier across the Rio Guaporé.

Now, Villa Bella was nothing. The palace was a skeleton of stone, and the fort, or what was left of it, had retreated its arrow-slits deep into the enfolding mato. Ants built ziggurat towers of mud on carved red pedestals; and the main street the Rua Pouco Alegre (little gaiety) led straight to a field back of which lay the tiny walled cemitério. It was an aptly named street.

Sun and mato gave the concreted vaults of the dead a second interment. Wood crosses, dried to brittle grey, axed the air at obtuse angles. Indeed, there was little much at this end of the street.

Carlos the Italiano was once a lieutenant in the Duce's army. When the British arrested him he was very relieved, he always preferred the English to the Germans, they had such reserve such aplomb.

He was sent to a camp outside Nottingham for the rest of the war where he worked on potato crops. He liked Nottingham the little he saw of it during his imprisonment and he appreciated the farm girls who brought the Italians cigarettes, and he believed himself to be far away from the battlefields of Europe.

Sophie was a nice girl, she too worked the crops; she took a liking to Carlos' shrivelled onion face with his deep black sideburns and a mouth filled with generous yellow teeth. He was clearly a good man, industrious and honest, it appealed to Sophie's heart how he stood almost a foot shorter than her, and it was the mothering whimsy in her humour which grew accustomed to the fact that he weighed a good two stone less than she did.

At evensong in the fields, before the early to bed call to the prisoners, Sophie pressed her soft and loving breasts against Carlos' chest. Like all Italians she believed he wore his shirt steeply unbuttoned. Her ample arms felt the queerness of the taut muscles around his neck. She touched his teeth with her tongue and shivered a little, but quite deliciously, in the Nottingham night.

A year later they were married. Her family refused to attend the ceremony and an all-male choir of Italians sang for them in a Catholic church. It was rumoured everywhere soon the war would end.

They were sitting together in the kitchens behind the prison yard. The news told them Italy lay in ruins. When she switched the wireless off he did not stir. He was not going to take her to a home of rubble where burnt out tanks littered the hills like unearthly armadillos. He had other plans.

Carlos took Sophie to Brazil in 1946. He tin-panned streams in the serra on the Bolivian border for gold. They tracked with garimpeiros the length of the Rio Aripuana for diamonds. Nothing.

He built a shack on the Serra Aguapi out of liana and tree bark, and he formed a few hectares with manioc. And Sophie contracted malaria there. For ten days her temperature stayed at 104 degrees, it wasn't the pain or the isolation or even her mad ravings which destroyed her, it was her small fatty heart which gave her the lie, though it could never have pumped more love than it did, it just was not able to sustain her large body.

When she was gone, he sat beside her hammock and rocked the body all night; and he hummed to her those Nottingham tunes she had taught him when they used to kiss and laugh in the potato fields while they waited for the prisoners' evensong roll-call.

The Italiano went east to the shanty town on the edge of São Paulo. It was then 1951. There he found a desk job. He clerked for an Italian company, and by October each year he completed the accounts and made safe the trading profits correctly returned to the Banco Brasil. He always took a week's holiday in October.

The Cruzeiro do Sul service installed a DC3 flight between Cuiaba and Villa Bella. Two brothers always piloted the plane. Once every October the Italiano flew into Villa Bella. He stayed for a few days in the pensão on the Rua Pouco Alegre. Every day he collected flowers and strolled up to the cemitério. He laid them carefully on a black concreted grave. At night he sat alone with the rice and beefy and fried bananas he was given, and it was always noted how he relished the particularly hot sauce his table possessed. Before he left each trip, he borrowed a horse from the black boys by the river and was seen to ride up into the hills close by the border. He wouldn't come back until the sun had long tripped the horizon, and the grilos had commenced to shriek like an adze.

There was one October not many years ago when Carlos met an unlikely traveller on the DC3. An Englishman. They were the only two left going on beyond Cáceres. The Englishman had little Portuguese but he had a large number of questions to ask. Carlos quietly apologised for his lack of words.

"You see..." he began by shaking his head, "I have forgotten the English. I have not spoken the English since 1951," and for a moment the traveller thought that he discerned faint tears behind the dark eyes in the wrinkled skin, "Mister ... I have forgotten, you see."

Nevertheless the Englishman plied him with questions, and more questions, but Carlos just shrugged and slid deeper in his seat.

But he did say to the Englishman, while they waited for the canoe to skim them along the Guaporé to the landing stage on the townside of the river, where the water flows beneath wild white water flowers and butterflies as large as your hand trigger their wings in the air, and the humidity is like a bath in cold cream—

"Tell me sir, you know Nottingham?"

The Englishman shrugged, he replied he was afraid he didn't awfully. Carlos nodded and reached for his plastic leather grip as the transport canoe drifted to the bank by the air-strip.

The year after, Cruzeiro abandoned their old DC3. They had doubtless sold it off at a singular profit to a Japanese cane grower who had begun to *form* thousands of hectares. Perhaps the Jap was once young enough to remember the old DC3s he flew in the Korean war. Cruzeiro installed a more modern French twenty-seater which God only knows they picked up somewhere.

The younger of the two brothers who made this weekly trip to Villa Bella realised that new October how, strangely, the Italiano from São Paulo did not turn up for his annual flight to Villa Bella.

The brothers always referred to Carlos as 'the October habit', and on this particular month he was looking forward to showing the Italiano the new plane.

'The October habit' never arrived in Cuiaba the following year, or the year after, or the year after that. And on the fourth October of the new plane both brothers had almost forgotten about Carlos.

On a day the plane was passing over Villa Bella, they wouldn't stop, all they carried was the mail from Cáceres to Guajará Mirim, and the younger brother glanced back at the empty rows of seats behind him.

He remembered the little fellow with the shrivelled onion face and deep black sideburns who made the flight every October. It was a shame he never did get a ride on this new plane. He'd have enjoyed it.

Perhaps not, the younger brother reconsidered, the old onion may have no need of Villa Bella or his work has taken him such a long way off it is too far to come back here, he has simply forgotten all about it or he cannot afford the fare any more: perhaps old onion face has no more reason to come here in October, and that is that; or perhaps it is he cannot come cannot ever come again to Villa Bella, and that is that also.

ESQUADRÃO DA MORTE

A THIEF ROBBED *a bank and shot a guard in São Paulo. The police arrested a student and tortured him until he confessed to the crime. Meanwhile, the 'esquadrão da morte' captured the real thief. They put a magnum bullet in his head and cut their initials on his chest. Legally obliged nevertheless to press forward their case, the police presented the student to a judge. In the trial the esquadrão supplied the court with their evidence against the real thief – his confession. The judge accepted the fait accompli of his death. Presented with the student, the judge found him guilty of perjury and sent him to jail for two years.*

Last year Nerival was a student of political science in São Paulo. In a month's time he was to celebrate his nineteenth birthday. He was standing outside the CNTI building in São Paulo the moment of the shooting. A street cop lay dead outside a bank, and people milled around with the exception of Nerival. He turned and ran. There were no witnesses to the shooting there was only this boy who inexplicably hurried away from the scene, so Nerival Candido Adarias was arrested on February 2nd, 1972.

If you were a radical student in Brazil that year, like Nerival, your choices were few, you'd be a member of the UNE (União Nacional dos Estudantes) but you'd find its factions broken into a complicated tri-split – of pro-Cuba/Marighela/Ferreira national liberation by armed struggle support (ALN), of Prestes-inspired peasant revolt/workers' land reform/anti-Latifundia support (PCB), and of urban guerrilla/republic seeking militants/numerous successful kidnappings support (VAR-Palmares), but like Nerival you'd still run away from the scene of the shooting; you'd run because in the world outside of university agitprop the Acção Libertadora Nacional (ALN) has long been declared a clandestine body by the government, you'd run because the Partido Communista Brasileiro (PCB) is a victim of intense suppression and army brutality, and you'd run because the Vanguarda Armada Revolucionaria-Palmares (VAR-Palmares) is yet another outlawed group of the Left, driven underground (to ALA Red Wing) and they have become branded criminals: Nerival ran because he knew nobody would support him if he was netted in a chance arrest, his fellow students would only be victimised, neither his affiliations to these parties for they were all disbanded, nor his family who weren't wealthy enough to risk offering up bribes.

When the city police arrested him and discovered what Nerival's politics were, they charged him with the shooting, and they called in other departments. The government wanted to make the most of this ideological meal, and the political police arrived (the DOPS), the Communist Hunt Command arrived (the CCC), and the National Information Service arrived (the SNI) to interview Nerival.

Men force-flooded Nerival's belly with water and jumped on him. They drove an electric cow prod into his anus, and dipping him in cold water they attached voltage leads to his nipples and his genitals.

Nerival confessed to the shooting.

His father made a public statement, declaring university political life an evil influence, and he begged the State have mercy on his son's twisted ideals.

Nerival is not in prison any more now, he has been moved. They have locked him in a high security asylum on an Atlantic rock island outside Campinho; and when his mother comes to visit him, in order that she may reach out and touch him through the bars, even place a kiss on his forehead, they must strap down his arms and legs with leather bonds and stick surgical tape over his mouth.

BRAZIL NUT BUST

"There was this other one . . ." Luis hesitated, after all it was his younger brother.

"Go on," Jesus insisted.

"There was this big fat carioca woman real snob big hat on her head and this little Jap – oh you oughtn't to hear—"

"But I do!" said Jesus.

"Big fat carioca woman hundred husbands."

"And the little Jap?"

"Jap's new to Brazil, he says come for a ride, shuts the door and they're heading out into the country, she says where we going? Jap says igreja verde. Igreja verde he says to her and he's lived in this country for four years! She grin like an onça hundred husbands she buried so she shrugs. Jap a doido thinks he's a Brazilian after four years! But she don't care. After all, it's a new VW, her sons won't ever see her, and they stop in the sertão and lie down. He got some straw mats. Little Jap like a grilo on a jacaré snout he fucking and banging and doing it – you don't want to hear the rest of it . . ."

"Hands of God Luis, finish it!"

"She says I didn't know you had such a small organ! And he stop look down at her he sniff – I didn't know I was going to have to play it in a fucking cathedral!"

Jesus cracked up, he clutched his stomach and laughed so loud; he'd try to remember that one.

Until this year Cuiabá, besides being the capital of Mato Grosso, possessed the finest cinema in Brazil – the Tropical. Strange as it may seem it was a more magnificent palace of celluloid than anything Rio or São Paulo could offer.

The Tropical still stands near the corner of Barão de Melgaço and Av. Getulio Vargas, and no hot knees mosqu pit this you'd guess from the very look of it. And if you read the advertisements it has the works – air-conditioning under-floor vents, seats as deep as Wai Wai funereal urns, a bar back of the lovers' tandem seats, carpets like clouds and a screen as wide as the plate-glass wall of the Banco Brasil outside.

But advertising is such a deceptive art, and in recent weeks the amenities of the Tropical have not lived up to the hoarding claims.

Just not lived up to them at all.

Most of the State Governor's relations were in construction, and that was how the Tropical came to be built. The Governor liked the short walk to the movies from his palace behind the Praça Alencastro and to take his family and his influential friends to the finest cinema in Brazil.

But the Governor, like all his predecessors, hastily resigned, he and his family and his friends retreated to their kingdom farms in Campo Grande, all of them narrowly escaping long prison sentences, but it was not at all surprising to anybody for he was behaving in the time-honoured tradition of all governors around here.

Luis was the projectionist at the Tropical. His younger brother was Jesus. For many hours he taught Jesus the art of the machines in the back room above the circle. How to synchronise the sound and when to prepare a second reel. Jesus was getting the hang of it, he wanted his brother's job, the extra money would pay for his keep at home, and he could go back to day school.

Luis was in a hurry to pass the job on. He needed six months' field work to finish his courses in geology, he had saved enough money for this now, and there was the promise of a vacancy from a mineral firm in Cáceres, once he'd completed the studies.

After the Governor and his family stopped their regular trips to the Tropical, the Cuiabánas saw the kind of movies they really did enjoy. It was a diet of bangy-bangys (every time Randolph Scott or John Wayne or Clint Eastwood laid down a handful of ketchup corpses the Brazilians rise to stand on their seats with honking enthusiasm), and British costume dramas (nothing gives Cuiabánas greater pleasure than to see these piles of gloves and overcoats and thick sweaters and warm hosiery) and the diet was occasionally laced with ancient cartoons, but never was there a musical or a French 'new wave' film, nor any other kind of experiment no matter how minimal the obscurity.

Cuiabánas like their films realistic, a lot of blood and sobbing and as many women as you can fill a screen with getting their rough desserts.

The audiences didn't seem to care too much if Luis sometimes put the wrong reel on his machine, so long as the mayhem had some kind of recognisable reality they'd sit there all night through reels three, four, two, and one, in that order. So long as it wasn't a musical or any type of intellectual experiment.

There came a rupture in this diet of ciné pulp. Some peculiar films started to arrive at the Tropical. The manager put it down to distributor's errors in São Paulo. He was receiving the classier type of film you'd find up in Belém, and the Cuiabánas were pretty dissatisfied about it.

And they started to show their feelings. Everybody knows smoking is prohibited in cinemas, nevertheless that far-sighted Governor had installed imitation brass ash-trays in the Tropical. And the audiences had begun to rip them out. If that wasn't a sign of the times for a cinema manager, even in Cuiabá, nothing was.

Things got tougher. The audiences learnt to ask for their money back. One Cuiabána was so angry at a British movie, a gothic costume drama titled *Os Quem Chegam para Noite* starring Marlon Brando, he ripped his funereal urn seat from its mountings and took it home as a demonstration of disgust.

Truth was – they simply weren't getting the film fodder they were used to, and Cuiabánas didn't like change.

Luis rolled new movies three times a week at the Tropical. It was the Thursday evening change-over. Jesus couldn't stay with him that night, so there was nobody he could practise his Cuiabá jokes on.

The manager forgot to remind Luis to run him the new film before first showing. ('New' in terms of Cuiabá ciné diet was a matter of poker dice chance, new could be as recent as 'One Shot' Woody Van Dyke's *Andy Hardy gets Spring Fever*).

The film sounded like a French costume love story, and as far as the manager was concerned, if it had some big lipped Moulin Rouge prostitutes who fell to just and bloody Jack the Ripper retribution, it would go down fine.

The Tropical was always two thirds house full the first showing of any movie. It was no exception the night Luis rolled the first reel of Jacques Demy's *Les Parapluies de Cherbourg*.

It took the audience about ten whole minutes to realise the

entire cast was singing, and furthermore intended to go on singing right through until the end of the film, it took them these precious dawning minutes to compute these actors weren't just singing some of the time, but all of the time, and what was even more of a crime – everything looked real, the people the houses the horses the carriages, they all looked real until they opened their mouths. That did it. There was pandemonium.

Those who couldn't be bothered just to stand on their seats and whistle raced up the back stairs to Luis' projection room. Luis tried to fend them off the machines. They wanted to rip out the sound track. They wanted any bangy-bangy he had on his shelf left over. He didn't have one. They screamed and stamped and raced up and down.

The youths from the stalls beat him pretty badly. Twenty of them crowded into the little room and all he could do was beg them not to break the machinery. But they didn't stay long. They heard something crack in Luis' chest and he felt so weak he couldn't cry out. Blood lunged in his throat. The youths ran.

The manager ducked behind the cash desk and dropped the wood barrier before the first fist could demand his money back. A cleaner called the police and the manager lay on the box office floor until the last angry footstep faded away.

Luis woke up in a ward full of road-builders. He was in the Santa Casa de Misericordia Hospital. A nurse told him four ribs were cracked, a bone in his right leg was broken in splinters and it had pierced an artery—

"You will be here for a week."

The road-builders were nice to him, although they didn't show too much enthusiasm for his saga of the singing film; they patiently outlined all the various diseases and dangers a worker can encounter building the trans-Amazonian highway through the forest. And the cinema manager came to promise Luis he wouldn't have to pay a conto towards the hospital fees.

Two days later the Tropical opened. The manager asked Jesus to operate the projection and he found a particularly violent americano bangy-bangy to calm his audience down with. Jesus ran a trial hour of this very long western and it looked good and gory. Ketchup and dust and electric guitars and drum-cracking explosions.

On the Saturday, Jesus stood in the projection room for the first time on his own, with nobody to swap jokes with, and it was a peculiar feeling to watch the audience file in for the evening show. They were coming in all right, plenty of them, but this time there was a certain look in their eyes. As if they had tasted first blood. This cinema was no longer a palace to sit in with awe. They weren't baffled by the grandness of the building. The youths put their feet up on the stalls in front of them and they stubbed out their cigarettes on the cloud thick carpet, and nobody came to tell them smoking was forbidden. The youths had an instinct that, in the last few days, the building had somehow come down to their level. It struck one or two of the Cuiabána youths it wouldn't be long before they could piss against the brightly coloured walls, and other youths knew friends were working hard on the mechanism of the americano-style safety-exit doors, and soon enough they'd all get in for free, and the Tropical would be right under their little fingers.

Luis nodded to sleep after supper in the ward room. He knew Jesus would come by to tell him how the evening went. He felt so weak, Jesus could wake him later.

In the morning, Luis could hear a faint voice whispering his name. He opened his eyes. It was Jesus saying—

"Ssss! Luis – hey wake up!"

Luis looked up. "Where are you Jesus?"

"Here I am Luis!"

Luis turned. Jesus was lying in the bed beside him. His foot was pulleyed high above his head, the lower part of the leg was icing encaked with plaster-of-paris. Over his face and neck were numerous crosses of adhesive. But apart from some purpling bruises around his eyes his younger brother looked remarkably cheerful.

Luis twisted so violently in his bed, his ribs rattled like a bag of golf sticks.

"Hands of God! ... Jesus! What happened to you?"

"Luis I didn't want to wake you last night!"

"Did you get knocked down? In the street?"

"No no – I was in the projection room and there was another riot."

Luis groaned.

"Much worse than your riot," said Jesus with a certain amount of pride, "mine was terrible."

"What happened?"

"I was doing everything right. You don't have to worry about that. The reels were fine. It was a bangy-bangy and they were loving it."

"Well—?"

"Suddenly the film went insane – all of its own accord."

"You lost a reel?"

"No. It was extraordinary," explained Jesus, "this long movie, and at the end of it there's this gunfight – all these guys in a compound and the other guys meant to be the good guys though they were in fact the bad ones they take hold of a machine gun and start killing everybody women and children and everyone."

"What's wrong with that? That's what they like to see!"

"You don't understand, Luis – the whole audience sitting there waiting for this fantastic gunfight and suddenly it all goes wrong."

"You fouled up the sound tape?"

"I fouled up nothing. It was perfect. Suddenly the last twenty minutes of the reel goes dead slow as if the reels have snarled up. It just slows down. It wasn't my fault. It all slows down all the action slows down so it's like the projection has gone doido on me and they go mad down there in the stalls."

"They did?"

"Oh they pull out the seats they piss on the walls they throw beer cans at the screen and—"

"What happened to the manager?"

"The manager he just a joke he come running up to me in the back with all these youths hanging on to his hair and he say it's my fault! Me!"

"Did you show them the reel in the projector?"

"Of course I did. There was nothing wrong with the reel. It was still turning over and it was like slow motion on the screen and all those people screaming at me!"

"Hands of God, Jesus."

"That's what I thought!"

"Did you tell them the reel was right way in at the right speed?"

"Oh they just started to hit me."

"What about the manager?"

"They took his keys and opened the cash desk out front."

"How's the cinema?"

"Well . . ." Jesus paused, adding it all up, "half the seats are gone, some of them ripped out the carpet up in the balcony that's gone too, they taken all the fire hydrants and there isn't an ash-tray left in the house. And they took away the billboard for Monday's Big Feature" – Jesus looked remarkably cheerful about it, he added – "it was a bigger riot than the riot you had, Luis."

Luis lay back in his bed. His ribs jiggled inside his chest. He was looking forward to his six months' field work in geology, then there was that good job offered in Cáceres, he was glad he was out of the Tropical cinema. Although it was rough on Jesus.

"Tell me," said Luis, "what was this film called so as I will know to watch out for it—?"

"Called *The Wild Bunch* ... but I never heard of it before."

"Americano bangy-bangy?"

"Big director it say, Sam Peckinpah's *The Wild Bunch* ..." and Jesus lay back on his pillow, he swung his pulleyed ankle from side to side above his head, "I'd like to have seen it all," he added.

"You didn't?"

"They broke up the projector."

"Before it was finished?"

"They tore the last reel out and ran down the street with it."

"Just think of that ..." said Luis softly.

"Take some time before they open up the Tropical again," said Jesus.

"Some bangy-bangy that must have been ... cause all that trouble," Luis murmured to his younger brother.

"Hands of God," said Jesus crossing himself rapidly, "I'd have really liked to see the end of that film."

CUIABÁNA BLUES

"There was this Mato Grosso town well-known for its high standards of Christianity and quiet."

"Excuse me, Coronel, but—"

"There was this statue of a naked couple embracing to represent these ideals. One day God tells the statues they can have the day off as the town has been so good. They leap off their pedestals and dive into the bushes with joy. Shrieks of delight can be heard and the bushes shake violently. They make so much noise though, God gets furious. He tells them they must stop this dreadful uproar or it's back to the pedestal and no more days off. But the noises get worse. Nobody dares interrupt the statues. And God puts his foot down. He peers behind the bushes to see just what really is going on. There's the male statue saying to the female statue—

"OK now it's my turn. You hold the pigeon down and I'll shit on its head'."

Horst was close enough to seventy now. He was a sertanejo with a difference, he also possessed a government licence to look after a certain group of indians way up north towards Rondonia; and the authorities in FUNAI, the modern indian protection service, never quite saw eye to eye with old Horst. They said the years were defeating him now, and anyway, they didn't want estrangeiros wandering around the forest with missionario licences meddling with *their* indians.

His were big heavy hands, veins like rope, friends said they were large as his heart, and he looked like a character Victor McLagen might often have played. Underneath his gruff manner Horst was a bit of a soft touch, there was an old woman in him, a whiner, and given a situation a real crunch situation he'd panic.

Tall and dour, whenever he reached Cuiabá for a stay, he'd hang his hammock outside in the yard of Dona Schmidt's pensão on the Commandante Costa. The pensão is a ramshackle pile of wood huts, tin roofs, washing laid out on lines like a boat in full rig, and the yard was always packed with Volkswagens and grunt squint pigs and a heinous dog which never ceased yapping at the night sky.

He was an honoured friend of the Schmidts. Rudi Schmidt treated Horst like a loved older brother, and the Schmidt household kept an area of the yard always ready for Horst and his hammock. Against a wall in the passageway which served as a dining room stood a tall glass cabinet. It was a gift to the pensão from Horst. The cabinet was crammed with magnificent amerindian ceremonial head-dresses, the colours of the brightest cockatoos, and the Schmidts prized this thing. Visitors always remarked on the richness of the plummage but Dona Schmidt never allowed anyone to open the glass door, even try to. Indeed, the cabinet hadn't been opened for thirty years or so, and although she could no longer remember what she had done with her key, she was sure Horst had a spare one tied to his watch chain.

German friends, old pals, would bring Horst his meals, offer him Bremen-style home-brew beer, and they'd sit at his feet all evening to catch an anecdote of the forest. Trouble was – no anecdote worth hearing ever emerged, Horst was no story teller, he lacked so much humour, perhaps you'd call it spark of delivery, he had a weighted manner, and any stranger come by would only think big kraut bore droning into the night like ten grilos on a single string birimbau.

Nevertheless, Horst was a legendary figure amongst the German population in Cuiabá. Perhaps it was because he never did discuss politics. In truth, he hadn't been back to Germany since 1928, the year his mother died. And as far as Nazis were concerned, and all those rumours about South American Mengeles thugs hiding out in the forest, well, Horst was as clean as Dona Schmidt's new VW beetle bonnet.

More than a man of the forest or plain missionary, Horst took his friends on onça hunts up in the serra, sometimes he hired himself out to mineral companies; he'd find certain rock formations for them and they'd pay him to bring back samples and detailed maps of the land. Yet Horst had an integrity. He lived all those years in the forest of Mato Grosso, through those terrible times –

murder and man hunt of the indigenous groups – through the forties and fifties when it was at its worst, and he'd kept the faith with himself. He loved the isolation of the forest, he respected any one who understood this strange lifestyle, the passion for the forest some men feel (only pathetic Conan Doyle Englishmen ever referred to it as the jungle in Horst's presence).

He didn't break his back working for the indians. They weren't smothered with the Cross. He preferred to adopt the same lazy rhythms they lived by; if they were curious about our western gods they'd ask, if not ... Horst didn't ram it down their throats.

He was popular amongst his own kind because nothing from Europe had tainted him; nobody could accuse him of being a hide-and-seek mad dog Nazi or an indian killer or a land claim civilizado-style carpetbagger, he was just simple thick old Horst who liked to get lost in the Brazilian forest.

For the past four years Horst looked after a small group of Kaxarari, there were less than fifty of them, moiety of Aruak, they lived beside the São Miguel River south from Porto Velho, they were Horst's children, his little brown-skinned friends, and they doted on him.

A Brazilian rubber collector employed the group for toe-nail-eating wages on the headwaters of the Ituxi River. It was Horst's duty (if a rather self-imposed one because sure as eggs nobody else cared a fart in a pig pen whether they lived or died) to keep them in reasonable health, discourage them from taking cachaça in lieu of wages, and learn a little Portuguese.

He liked them to grow their basic foodstuffs, if they were idle about it he bullied them to smoke their fish for the rainy season, he pulled their septic teeth out for them, and even managed to persuade them not to jump in the river to cool off the minute they contracted grippe/fever.

A while back FUNAI, in an astonishing gesture of goodwill, gave Horst's group inalienable rights to land beside the São Miguel River: that is – once they were fully assured by speculators there was not one branco civilizado in all Mato Grosso who wanted this particular parcel of land. This was at a time when it looked like world opinion (i.e. indefatigable press and media coverage) would force the government to ratify a bill of inalienable rights for all indigenous reservations and parks.

But the trans-Amazonica highways started to cut through the forest with their World Bank Dollar loans, and people like rubber collectors on the São Miguel River soon discovered the value of their land multiplied in percentages of thousands once the minerologists headed their Wyllis jeeps down the highways.

The Coronel at FUNAI's offices in Cuiaba was said to be very smooth and smart. He kept a mistress in an air-conditioned room above a hair-dressing salon in Campo Grande, he was a first-name-base pal of General Bandeiro de Mello, he liked dirty Cuiabána jokes and the Governor of the State gave him a box of cigars for his last birthday. In a place like Cuiaba such prestige was this, it could only best be described by what the Peace Corps boys called 'scratch my back going ape right out top of the shit pile'.

The Coronel had it in for poor Horst. It is generally supposed Brazilians have a healthy respect for Germans, but – (Americanos =spit, Japs=little bugre yellow thieves, English=arrogant jokes no money/greed sense, Lebanese=bunch of Arab shoe salesmen) – there was something so very dull about Horst. He had no secrets never was a Nazi, and all coronels have a sneaking regard for a Nazi. He had no vices men women or boys, and beside that he was a dull fellow when it came to dirty jokes time this seventy-year-old sertanejo who looked like a crowd artist out of King Vidor's *The Big Parade*.

The Coronel fixed Horst proper one day this dry season. As it happened, conveniently for the Coronel, Horst was way up in the serra taking his flabby German friends on an onça hunt – nothing but crates of beer, garlic sausagemeat and stubborn masochistic Hamburg executives stumble-foot in the damp darkness of the trees sweating bath sinks of Brahma Chopp.

The Coronel sent a doctor to the Kaxarari group by the São Miguel. He gave the doctor careful instructions. If he could not find Horst he must talk to the indians. Eventually, when Horst made his way back to the little friends his children by the São Miguel River they were not there; they had vanished. Their employer was different, too. He had a new cockiness. The rubber collector told him of the doctor's visit. But little else. He didn't like Horst, old kraut interfering idle missionario, and Horst knew it.

He raced back to Cuiabá, that is if you could call canoe and donkey a race to anywhere. But Horst was bitterly angry. And when he slung his hammock in Dona Schmidt's yard his friends sat at his feet and urged him to fight for what he believed right. After all, he was their equivalent of Livingstone, yes that's right, he was their Horst of the Mato Grosso.

Horst breathed in deeply, the vein on his forehead stood out and throbbed. His friends at his feet – forever slapping at their fat red arms and legs – thought it perfectly natural how the mosqus never bothered their Horst.

The FUNAI offices down the Rua Ricardo Franco are in a colonial terrace building. It has a museum of amerindian artifacts which is prepared to sell you anything you want in the left-hand doorway, and myth says – some of this money in due course finds its way to the indians, or at least in kind, because FUNAI frowns upon handing cash cruzeiros to indians.

Horst hardly remembered what the Coronel looked like. They rarely ever met. And it was such a rigmarole, too. FUNAI employed two dozen secretaries to lie the Coronel is out. But on this day, anger and friendly German voices propelled Horst to the Coronel's office. In fact, he walked right in the door, brass bold without as much as a perfunctory knock, and found the Coronel polishing a desk photograph of his two children. The Coronel sat up stiffly, above his head the aeroplane size fan propellers whirred sibilant scissors in the fat humidity.

"I want an immediate explanation, Coronel!"

"My dear Horst."

"Why did you send the doctor to my indians?"

"FUNAI from time to time—"

"No doctor has ever been sent out to my indians in four years!"

"You'd agree then, it was about time?"

"I want to know why?"

"The doctor took tests for T.B., malaria and leishmaniasis, he took faeces, he—"

"They don't have anything like that, my word on it has been good enough in the past, yes – occasional grippe."

"These things must be written down," said the Coronel.

"I want to know what the doctor told them?"

"Horst at the time I couldn't contact you, the doctor told them the new facts."

New what?

"Between Guajará Mirim and Ariquemes there is to be a highway – the BR 421."

"So?"

"The Ministry of the Interior can no longer guarantee inalienable rights to land so close to this highway – such as your group's land – what are they called?"

"Kaxarari, Coronel."

"The doctor had specific instructions from me to inform you or your group of our new intentions."

New what?

"All indigenous south of this highway planned must move north towards Porto Velho."

"That's scrub land. They cannot crop there."

"It is better for them that they are moved away from the highway."

"Now let me tell you," Horst gulped at his breath, that thick vein on his forehead was throbbing, "since the doctor told my group this they have run away. I cannot find them!"

"Is that so?"

"I am their father and they trust me. I told them the land was theirs."

"It was. But now they'll be safer elsewhere."

"They will trust nobody now."

"I can send men to find them, if you can't, Horst."

"Once they are on the run they break up their family unit they become vagrants they are confused."

"They will be safe on new land closer to Porto Velho."

"If they get too near a town they'll become drunks in shanty suburbs."

"You must understand my position, Horst ..." the Coronel stood up, he buttoned his shirt, the silk strips of medals on his uniform had a laundered look about them, sheen as if they were newly dunked in soda suds. The Coronel walked around the desk, and, standing behind Horst, he placed his hand warmly on the old sertanejo's shoulder.

"You think I don't know I'm so stupid?" said Horst bitterly.

"My friend—"

"That rubber collector thief by the river got the Ministry of Interior sell him my indians' land."

"I know nothing like that."

"You think it's time old Horst give up his licence now he has no indians left."

"You know that isn't true."

"The kraut's too old now to chase around for idiot indian groups who have trusted him too much, because I'm seventy now."

"My friend Horst—"

The Coronel tapped the German's shoulder warmly. His

plump moist fingers smelt of manicure. The gold band wedding ring was studded with diamonds. They winked at Horst.

"My friend, all these years Horst, my friend!"

The old fellow paused in the intense morning heat on the steps of the FUNAI building. The Coronel's office door closed behind him. A strange trembling gripped Horst. It was unlike him, and his leather skin, to feel the heat like this. His knees wobbled beneath him. He felt so confused, he did not know tears from sweat beads when they dripped down his cheeks. The sun burnt the Rua Ricardo Franco, and Horst stood on the wrong side of the street where there was no shade.

Oh, they were clever all right. They'd rob him of his indians his little children. They'd file a report back to Brasilia about his age, his lack of evangelical zeal, his wayward fondness for taking those German buddies on onça kills. He couldn't win. One of these days they must surely revoke his missionary's licence.

Horst was alone in the pensão. The Dona was out buying the lunch salt beefy. He took the small key from his watch chain and opened the tall glass cabinet which had never been opened before in more than thirty years.

He tried to pull out the ceremonial head-dresses, beautiful extravagant dance dignities made by tribes he'd once contacted, now extinct, lost children in the civilizado's shadow of death, little brown toothless angel friends squat spirit eyes dark darting ghosts in the trees who never achieved the first puberty of manhood, hunted out of existence by the rubber tappers and diamond panners of the 1930 and the early 1940s, he remembered them – Ipotewat, Xipaya, the Hahahai, wiped out now, long rotted away in the liana slither cemetery of the forest.

The paint on the feathered shapes powdered at his touch, the plumage humming bird, macaw, rainbow tanager, king pica pau woodpecker, cockatoo, suddenly shaken across a tabletop fell apart and dropped like burnt butterfly wings. Within moments there was nothing left of the pride of feathers which did look so bold shuttered inside the cabinet. Termites had had their day.

Dona Schmidt's quick steps drummed down the corridor. The tin roof echoed.

"God in Heaven, Horst! What have you been doing?"

"I ..."

He couldn't speak, his big hands clumsily let slip the crumbled air-light feather fronds, dust ruins of nimble fingers, splintered hair pieces for shamans, he could only think of those friends who would sit at his feet in the evening and wait upon his sertanejo word, encouraging him to be their guiltless legend, time was once when the trees dark and wet were the wilderness only he could trespass, when there was an indian group who would trust him and no other no matter how lazy his mannerisms or careless his Cross, when his barrel-shaped Hamburg friends would follow him with beer and sausagemeat in search of onça high in the coldest serra and in his loneliness come this old kraut King of his kingdom forest, and Horst did not know what anecdotes he'd tell them tonight from his hammock slung under the stars in Dona Schmidt's yard.

THE CITY OF THE CAESARS

McCARTHY HUGHES WAS a language teacher from Wellington, New Zealand; both his parents died in one year, they left him a little money and a bungalow with a conservatory window which overlooked a lake. His hobby was comics, he kept mounds of this pulp in his garage, and it was in one of these papers he first read about the City of the Caesars.

His over-riding ambition was to go to Brazil. He'd find this lost city of gold, he believed in it, and one day he'd confound the archaeologists of the West. So McCarthy flew to Belém, on the Amazon, he'd mourned a suitable period for his parents, and now it was the start of his summer holidays.

In the Goeldi Biblioteca he discovered a book published in Lisboa in the eighteenth century. An ancient hand drawn map was folded almost hidden inside it. McCarthy was barely able to conceal his excitement. The map was the testimony of a dying man.

It was more than that, it was a graph of all McCarthy's dreams. It described a route to this legendary city in the forest, jewel-paved eldorado silver riveted roofs which Pinson, Cabral, Orellana and Raleigh searched for in vain; McCarthy believed the dice of gods had tossed him the answer to this riddle.

He took a steamboat up the ocean-wide throat of the Rio Tapajós to the most southerly port for large boats some two hundred kilometres north of the Rio Juruena, a Jacarèacanga. The Juruena was his destination.

At Jacarèacanga he bought a wood canoe, salted beefy strips, net and fish lines, and he placed his papers and brass compass and medicine bottles in a waterproof bag.

He made up his mind, whatever the outcome of this crazy trip, at least he could tell his grandchildren that he once hunted for the eldorado of the Amazon.

He paddled to a settlement called Aldeia do Rancheiro. It was a collection of huts on stilts at the side of the river. He had to tie his canoe underneath the case de planta and pull himself up by rope ladder to the front porch.

There was pinga to drink, and the rubber tappers kept parcels of animal skins and casks of cachaça, white rum, in separate corners of the room. At night everybody slung their hammocks in between poles, the slat walls were pulled away to allow for more air, and the sleeping bodies dangled above the brown swell of the river, crushed vegetation at its bank, cruising its weighted matter of mud and torn liana up to the Tapajós' great throat on the Amazon.

Napoleon and Ires were brothers. They worked the forest up in Rondonia for years, they were sertanejos, could turn their hands to anything, they lived on the gossip of the rivers, whispers of work to be had at a nearby fazenda, chance meetings with branco mineralogists who needed guides for their diesel launch; they dealt in rifles and saddles, and they were always ready to meet an estrangeiro.

They couldn't leave McCarthy alone. There was something so vulnerable about him. His wide sheepish grin, those electric blue eyes, the way he talked so openly as if he hadn't a secret in the world. The brothers poured a lot of cachaça down McCarthy that night.

"You tell us again. You want to find this city? Out here in the forest?" and Ires laughed until he choked in his beard. His stomach rose and fell and he couldn't control it. Tears streamed from his eyes.

"It's an ancient city, could be thousands of years old, but I don't have to tell you," said McCarthy, "you've heard the same stories before."

"Cidade antigo," Napoleon nodded wisely to his brother, "some hidden civilisation deep in the forest," and Ires blinked with confusion.

"Right!" emphasised McCarthy.

"Where you look for this fabulous place?" asked Napoleon.

"I think I know."

"How can you?"

You don't know anything, estrangeiro, thought Ires, paddle two metres in here, tell us these crap stories, I been working this forest twenty years, I heard all these stories, listened to the old men, been down every path, don't tell me no city is here, you born with a bee-hive in your skull you born.

"You see," said McCarthy, "I have a map. Old map. I have the directions. Everything."

Napoleon leaned across the table, he pushed the white rum towards McCarthy, he watched the New Zealander's adam's apple pump up and down as he swallowed steeply.

"It is there ..." McCarthy wiped at the rum spittle froth on his mouth, his eyes giddied in their sockets, "it is waiting there for someone to walk in – like that!" he clicked his fingers.

You some doido verrido, thought Ires, real americano skull full of dysentery, crato of the nut, disorder of the brain, I tell you.

"But we've been in this forest for years—" tried Napoleon.

"The secret is – where you'd last think of going."

"Forest people would have heard about it years ago – we'd have found it!"

"Where it is," McCarthy whispered thickly, "nobody would look. Nobody would want to. Not even indians."

Ires sucked in his breath with a snort of derision. He was the silent one, not too given to speech. Napoleon did the charming. He liked to talk things out. He liked people to make mistakes. Say stupid things. There was nothing else to do that night. Why not draw a bucket of laughs out of this branco?

If McCarthy had been rich he'd have been perfect plucking. But he was a kid. Barely twenty-two. Flashing electric blue eyes. He'd never tell a lie. He'd never recognise one, either.

McCarthy dribbled his tongue in the rum. Torrents of forest mystery came out of him, the legends, the men who had gone before, what they each mistook for the lost city.

"I have the map – have the map with the only answer!" he bubbled. The rum gave his legs a knee-less feeling. His fingers were caterpillars they couldn't lift the bottle any more. Saliva drifted down from his mouth. His lower lip hung out in a flap. Ires was laughing at him, loud and raucous. Stentorian bursts. Napoleon's sincerity flannelled along in his ears.

"Gerente," Ires loomed over the table, "if you find this place and they got a bar there, give me a call – I be first guy to buy you a drink on town!"

At night, McCarthy slept in his hammock strung between poles, rows of sleepers beside him, sertanejos of the forest, drifted in their net rêdes like pendulum worms; creak of damp rope, guttural throats snarled for breath, and he closed his eyes, the rum made his brain reel white, sinking dizzying roll, and the humid hand of night palmed him to sleep.

By five in the morning all the Brazils were gone. There was no sign of the brothers. The rifles stashed against the wall were taken, along with their belts of 404 shells.

The girl who watched over the tappers' possessions while they were away helped McCarthy down the rope ladder. She slipped his twenty-five centavos coin into the heel of her shoe and smiled; nothing but gum behind her lips, all her teeth atrophied away.

The canoe was awash. Provisions tipped all ways. A pair of socks floated in the brown water beside the stilts below the house. An animal, McCarthy guessed. Perhaps a coati, eccentric otter-like chaos maker, will tear open the smallest box or bag. He tidied up and slopped water out. Tied down his packets and found that nothing was missing.

The girl on the platform in her flimsy dress waved her smile at him. He dipped his paddle, and the nose of his craft lifted in the air. He pushed out against the north-seeking current. Not for a moment did he envisage he had been raided by anything larger than a wilful coati.

McCarthy was like that.

For four hundred kilometres the Juruena winds south to a flood wall in the Serra Parecis. It is forest all the way. The density of this mato is made up from the heaviness of the leaves, the water they contain, and the way each new season brings another fall of strangler through the boughs, mantle lace of decay, and so much height have the trees the dark in there dresses seed with mould, thin throws of light trap themselves in the slither green, all a dense limpidity.

There is one halt between the tappers' house on stilts and the flood wall in the serra, it is called Peixote. An American Protestant Jonathan Wells has a mission station for Aripaktsa indians. These are gentle indians, afraid of their fierce neighbours the Cinta Larga group, most hostile and vengeful of the indigenous, such gentle kind are they these Aripaktsas they have too readily succumbed to Jonathan's Bible. They fish for him and exchange gifts with him in the name of what he calls Greater Knowledge.

Nobody ever called at Peixote. Sertanejos looked on the place with contempt ... this americano priest spy shovelling New Testament down animal throats. Those first days Jonathan didn't take too kindly to the New Zealander. But he discovered it was impossible to dislike McCarthy for very long, his honesty, his enthusiasms, how his blue eyes burnt holes with determination.

"I can give you a dozen reasons why you should go no further south than this," warned Jonathan, "you have got to consider what you are risking."

"Oh but I have!"

"You have no relatives?"

"None whatsoever."

"There is no address you can leave me should anything happen to you?"

"Correct."

"Once you go south from here you are in Cintas Largas territory. It would take me weeks to arrange a search party. It would be an intolerable strain on the police to have to send a launch down here."

"I'm not going to die. Nothing's going to harm me. I know exactly where to go. I'll come out just the way I went in."

"McCarthy I've grown to like you so much. I want to help. But you've got to look at it from the Brazils' side – here is a lunatic teacher on summer holiday paddling hundreds of kilometres into nowhere in search of something that doesn't exist!"

"But it does."

Jonathan hesitated. He could have insisted on seeing the boy's map with its ancient secret. But he didn't want to know the exact location. He didn't want any more responsibility for him. The mission was difficult enough to hold down, the authorities didn't want him there; the least trouble – they'd use it as an excuse to send him home. He began to wish McCarthy had never set paddle in the Juruena.

"It's all right Jonathan – you don't have to ask me for the exact place on the map," said McCarthy with considerable perception, "it will only be an extra burden for you. I understand."

Jonathan breathed with relief, "You keep your secret. Whatever you find there – it must be all of your own making. I don't want to know."

The mission house was a hut built on stilts. Jonathan had a certain air of detachment, but there was also deep kindness. These were his last years here in Brazil, he was old enough to retire. Before he reached his fiftieth birthday he could ask his department in Ohio for an early pension.

He kept pigeons at the mission. Five homing pigeons, pombos

correios, in cages made from sugar cane beneath the hut. The birds were never pure white, and when they flew high enough in the rain season it was impossible to follow them with the eye. They became grey flirting commas against the sandbag clouds weighted ready to burst flood torrents. He fed them carefully and they were perfectly trained to return to the mission hut. If there was an emergency, indians cracking under a virulent grippe, his own health failing him, he could rely on the pigeons. They would always return.

It was McCarthy's last night. While they ate, the missionary was quick to notice the sudden tiredness in his friend, eyes which didn't shine so much, and how his hands shook when he reached for a glass of water. In a spirit of generosity Jonathan made an offer to McCarthy—

"I won't sleep unless I know I have been of some help. I want you to take the birds with you. You must take them. When you return – come back safe – you bring my pigeons back."

McCarthy was grateful. He smiled weakly. Sweat poured from him. Beads of moisture, veiled transparent molecules trembled on his forehead.

I'll do better than that. You say they cannot fail to come back?"

"They always return here."

"I'll send you a relay of messages. One by one. Like the Syrians' telegraph code, like the Romans – until you get all five birds back."

"I mean you to use the pigeons – if anything goes wrong – you can alert me by using them. But I can only move so fast. I have no outboard motor for the canoe. It's for your safety."

McCarthy couldn't eat. He gulped at the water, he poured it over his face and neck, and Jonathan could see the strange trembling in the boy. He shrugged. It could just be the anticipation, or the fear...

The missionary dowsed the lamp and prayed quietly on his knees in a corner of the hut. McCarthy lay in his hammock, the river water buffeted and snarled at the stilt posts below him. He knew Jonathan was praying for him, for his God speed and his blessed safe return, and he felt humbled by it.

"You didn't have to do that for me," he murmured.

Jonathan blushed in the dark, his cheeks burnt him.

"I think," Jonathan replied, "you'll need all the prayers Peixote can offer up."

The light in the morning sky was a soft stain of fruit, the sun hesitant beneath the spilling colour – more flushed than apricot half the spring rain rouge of caju – and the missionary helped his young friend to load the canoe.

Jonathan gave him extra provisions, mangaba fruit and rice, dried farinha. He lifted his pigeon cages on to the craft and packed a bag of seed for the birds. As McCarthy pulled out from the bank, Jonathan called—

"You must remember about the pigeons! Treat them kindly. If you frighten them or hurt them they will never come back!"

McCarthy waved reassurance. He skimmed along the muddy water. Soon trees married their upper branches over the river flow and the hut was out of sight. He was alone with his City of the Caesars. The noises of the forest chuckled. And the Juruena was so high when his canoe rounded a deep bend there were no discernible banks on either side, the water spread into the avenida of trees like a burgeoning sea. Light lay thinly apportioned beneath the arcade of green, and the blue haze of the sky was masked.

In the forest there is a paint bright yellow canary, it has a head of fierce orange and red feathers, long frowning tips at its eyes. Talk says it likes humans, and is the first to sing out a zippup zippup zip zip zip at the sound of voices.

Every early morning the children of the Aripaktsa collect beneath Jonathan's hut. There is always a blackboard prepared for them and they recite a morning prayer. Jonathan woke that early, too. But nothing rose like the canary.

Sometimes the parents came out of their aldeia ring of huts in a clearing a short walk away – to watch the small brown faces in a semi-circle, clacking and lisping their tongues around a Saxon language beside the thick flow of the Juruena.

Zippup zippup zip zip zip.

At the end of the week Jonathan stopped worrying about the boy and his pigeons. When he woke he didn't look to the sky immediately for a homing flight. Although he admired McCarthy's spirit, his zeal, the wide-eyedness, it was no good being sentimental about strangers out here.

He kept a bowl of farinha and dried egg powder on a ledge beside his door. It was for the pigeons. One day they would come back.

He was soaping himself in the river. The little Aripaktsas tumbled and splashed beside him. They were so curious about his whiteness, and the tufts of black hair he *wore* in certain places. Indians never had hair where the missionary had hair, and the children liked to take handfuls of the stuff, especially from under the arms, where they were convinced it was somehow sewn into the skin.

Jonathan never had to warn them about the river. They knew. They never swam more than a few feet from the bank. There was the fast current, the sliding jacaré, the paraque with a sting enough to knock out a horse, and of course there were the spirits of the river – sometimes they'd steal children and keep them up among the stars all through the hunting season.

Jonathan cocked his ears – noises reach you slowly in this humid bath air, liana cossets sounds and the river bends unaccustomed resonances into the skirts of the trees – he believed he faintly heard the phut of a motor canoe down river. The sound faded away.

And that moment, his eyes flickered across the sky. High above his head, a grey white lancing hover of wing, the first homing pigeon flew over the mission station.

He raced up the ladder to reach the food bowl by the door. He placed a mound of farinha and dried egg in his palm and called out a sweet wooing noise to the pigeon. The children grew silent. They watched with fascination. The bird made a sharp call. Its wing tilted, it brushed violent strokes of air into Jonathan's face before it settled on his wrist. Jonathan firmly stroked its back. The beak darted for the egg farinha. He held the warm liquid-dry thumping shape, all heart and cage and supple silk feathers, frail breathless span of milk-weed pollen made flight.

A strip of paper was wrapped around its leg. A thin wire clasped it firmly. Jonathan's fingers eagerly—

I HAVE LEFT THE RIVER AND AM CUTTING ACROSS TO SERRA, MCCARTHY.

Jonathan frowned. What serra? There were no mountains between here and the Aripuana River. Perhaps McCarthy was turning east. He must have lost the main thread of the Juruena then. By turning east the New Zealander was stepping into forest no one had penetrated.

Yes, he'd heard that sound, that phut phut of a motor canoe. Jonathan watched the two men ease their boat to a drift. Napoleon and Ires cut their engine before the shallows and swung the craft to the bank where the missionary stood.

Their canoe was covered with transparent yellow waterproof sheeting, beneath it lay guns, hides, machetes and tools. Smoked fish and salt beefy hung on wires the length of the boat. They looked like river trash. Cheap cangaceiros in search of a dead man's garimpo claim. Behind Jonathan, the children ran in panic. Napoleon, smiling black chasms of lost teeth, held out his hand—

"You the missionario?"

"What do you want here?"

"You see the americano? That one come down from Aldeia do Rancheiro?"

"He is a New Zealander not an americano. Why?"

"It is a small thing."

"If it's important enough for you to come up river all this way it can't be. I've seen him. He was here. Why?"

Napoleon said he and his brother were old friends of McCarthy Hughes. They'd fed him, helped provide him with stores for the trip. An ingratiating manner about Napoleon – tough, he certainly looked – but he whined and smiled and looked like a barrel of pig fat. He said they didn't want any harm to come to the young americano, they were concerned for him, it was a mistake to have allowed him to continue like that. How can he survive in the forest and the river? Ires barely opened his mouth. Jonathan noticed that. Napoleon was the one with all the far-falhar, the talk big. Clearly, thought Jonathan, Ires was the dangerous one.

Jonathan refused the cask of cachaça rum they pressed on him. But they got him to accept a huge chunk of rapadura – brown boiled sugar candy – he'd keep that for his indians.

And Jonathan relented. The brothers cooked a fine meal on the mission's fogão. They beat the beefy with river stones and the black beans were dipped in banana oil.

He still didn't trust them entirely. There was nothing they could steal from him. And as long as he was there no harm could come to the Aripaktsa. It was his bounden duty to give shelter to river people. Even the trash. And eventually, in the sullen warm evening, Jonathan read to them the message the first pigeon homed back with.

"Tell us, Father – how many birds did you give the americano?"

Jonathan told them.

"There'll be four more to come?"

"Only if McCarthy needs to send them."

In the morning he was given no time to search the sky for the second pigeon. It fluttered above the hut and perched on the planta roof, until he could coax it down with a fist spread full of farinha. Ires was by the canoe. Water seeped into the petrol pump over night and the outboard motor must be stripped. Ires straightened, he could not take his eyes off the pigeon. Jonathan barely glanced at him. He was so eager to open the message tied to the leg—

WITHIN STRIKING DISTANCE. VOMITING ALL DAY. LEGS BAD. HURT. MCCARTHY.

Jonathan remembered how ill the boy looked the day he left. The perspiration on his face, the peculiar way his eyes shrunk inwards, a slight yellowing there – if he was lucky it was severe grippe, if not, then malaria.

Napoleon was behind the missionary. When Jonathan turned with surprise the bearded sertanejo beamed at him. But he had his hand held out. He expected Jonathan to give him this message.

"What does our friend say?" Napoleon asked.

Jonathan hesitated. There was a definite change in the sertanejo's expression, in the way he glanced across at Ires who climbed the river bank to join them.

But Jonathan read them the message. Napoleon still wanted that scrap of paper, he wanted to hold it, and without exactly snatching it he deftly plucked it from the missionary's fingers.

You can't read it, so what good is it to you? Jonathan asked in his mind. He hurried away towards the indians' aldeia. There was work to do there. Those branco brothers wouldn't follow him.

"What are we going to do?" Ires asked his brother a few moments later.

"You know ... you know, all right." The fat trash sertanejo's voice rolled like blood in the black of night.

Napoleon's humour was river dirt. Jonathan cut the supper as short as he could. He lied, he said he had little oil left to burn. Your little indians, father, they animals, they good just for shooting, nothing else, I even seen rubber-tappers cook an indian and eat it—

"—I'm told they taste like frog shit!" Napoleon continued.

A sense of duty held Jonathan back. He couldn't demand they leave. Perhaps he felt he owed something to McCarthy Hughes, an indefinable debt, and the brothers were the boy's friends. At least, according to them. But the boy never spoke of Brazils he'd met.

The missionary slept fitfully. Many times he woke to listen to their snores. Their hammock swung in the clamorous limpid dark. Beneath the stilts the flow of the river shone like the moisture in a drunk's eye.

Jonathan was up last. By the bank outside he found the brothers in rapt contemplation of the sky. They were watching the treetops on the far side. Streamer clouds licked the green horizon and the sun climbed slowly.

A pigeon, cloud grey, eyes could only make out its black beak, settled on a high branch against the wall of cloud.

"Missionario!" yelled Napoleon, "there it is!"

Jonathan raced back to the hut for the farinha. The wings waved with a slow stroke and it drifted over the river towards the mission. Jonathan held out his arm. And Napoleon ran to his side, he stood so close to him, it was as if he wanted to grab the pigeon out of the missionary's hand. Jonathan unravelled the note on the leg—

AM VERY WEAK NOW. IT IS A DAY'S MARCH AWAY. THE ROOFS AND THE WALLS BURNING LIKE THE SUN. MCCARTHY.

"Read it out to us!" Napoleon's voice was a shout.

As angry as Jonathan was, he still could not refuse them. Afterwards they stood in silence. It was true, it seemed, this city does exist, this place of so many men's dreams.

Napoleon moved quickly. He held Jonathan's arms twisted back, and he tore the note out of his hand. Both brothers stepped away almost apologetically. Jonathan knew them. They were the river trash he first took them for. What an idiot he'd been to trust them like this.

"You were never any friend of the americano!" he screamed out, "you lied to me – both of you lied!"

They smiled. Fat bland smiles, like kids, strong with the knowledge they at least would always forgive themselves, whatever they did. Jonathan tried to ignore the revolvers in their holsters and the bullet belts they carried.

"You're not welcome here at the missão. You must go from here!"

The brothers barely changed their expressions. He couldn't force them to scratch ticks. Fake CIA americano gospel seller Prostestant indian sucker what you come here to Brazil for what you come to steal from us? Got dollars? He got nothing.

Napoleon said they'd take their belongings from the hut. But they'd camp by the canoe for a few more days, and there was nothing Jonathan could do about it.

"In heaven's name why stay!" Jonathan demanded.

"I tell you," Napoleon began, with the recall of a hundred yankee movies, "because, all of a sudden, we like pigeons!"

The indians were warned to stay away from the brothers. Napoleon and Ires fished in the river and made a great show of cleaning their guns. Jonathan calmed down. He could reflect on trash like this. These river men put great store by mad dreams in the forest, they thrived on the fantasy of the interior, it was a drug and a lore and a justification for their existence.

And the days were quiet. Jonathan ignored the brothers. He hoped to God McCarthy would send no more pigeons. Although he still had two left, perhaps, Jonathan hoped, he won't need them, perhaps McCarthy will stay out there in his city of dreams and never come back. He'd be safer to.

Two Aripaktsa women called on him. Their men were trapped in the forest with fever. They couldn't get back without Jonathan's help. Jonathan organised the expedition. He didn't want the brothers to learn about it. They might follow they might think he'd lead them to McCarthy. Four young blood Aripaktsas went with him. They took blankets and medicine, and they slipped away in the night.

Ires grew tired of watching the sky. At the edge of the aldeia he found a group of Aripaktsa children playing with a wounded pigeon. The children shrieked and fled when he fired his revolver in the air. Napoleon came racing up from the river bank. They carefully unwrapped the message tied to the broken leg—

TOO WEAK NOW SO PLEASE HURRY. YOU HAVE EXACT LOCATION AS DRAWN. I AM HERE PLAZA OF GOLD AND EMERALDS WILL WAIT THIS IS THE LAST BIRD. MCCARTHY.

The brothers placed the americano's note which they couldn't translate on the table in the hut. It was peculiar the way the missionario disappeared these two days. Ires laid his revolver on the table. They waited there until long after dark.

Jonathan waved to the indians. They stood below and watched him climb the ladder. As he stepped inside a match flared to light a lamp and hands held him in a vicious grip. Below, the indians could hear the stamp and skid of the men's boots, and the muffled shouts.

Blood slit Jonathan's lip where the ring on Ires' hand crashed against his chin. He crumpled, and read to them the words on the piece of paper. Napoleon's fat bland won't-convince-nobody-now smile—

"Which bird is this, Father? Which one?"

"The last! The fifth!"

"Ires and me want to know – what you do with the fourth? The fourth one got the exact bearings – right?"

"It can never have arrived!" the missionary gasped.

"You seen it! Yankee fucking liar you seen it show it us!"

"Of course I haven't! Otherwise I'd go to help the boy! It's lost it's died how do I know!"

They slapped him about the room. He fell easily. He was a weak man. Soft stomach muscles. Neck like a chicken. It was easy. The stilted floor creaked and shook. Ires wanted to shove his pistol down the missionario's throat. The Aripaktsa collected together beneath the hut, it was the home of their friend, and they huddled against the bottom rungs of the ladder, not daring to climb up. Napoleon watched them. He didn't want that kind of trouble. He pulled Ires away and they backed off. Don't want to shoot up a pig pen of indian animals. Perhaps this idiot missionario is telling the truth. He so scared now.

The brothers were gone in the blink of first light. Jonathan never heard the phut phut of their motor. All morning he thought about McCarthy. He could only assume the exact location of the city was attached to the missing bird, the fourth pigeon.

He was desperately relieved at the departure of the river trash, and, almost as if he wanted to follow in the wake of McCarthy Hughes, Jonathan took out his own wood canoe, and skiffed it away from the shallows. Gently, he paddled it upstream.

The trees twined over his head like the vaulting of a green church. Matted liana love branches into snakes, boughs trespass sky, strangler sequestrate of darkness...

Redbreast thrush the sabiá tiny waltzer in green mesh tree-tops, dying fall of notes, burnt pathos...

Leaning melancholy torpor, flute wood hearts of fifty metres, pau de ferro, jacaranda, sapucaja, white laurel and silk-cotton, myrtle bark beading blue black damson warts, dying fall through mato roof, sweet sadness of saudade, this sobbing sabiá cry, infinite yearn, mirage made holy, soul wrecked against sorrow, forest lorn—

hui u hui u.
hu u.
hu u.
u.

He was studying the liana fold over him. There it sat. There on a branch see-sawed the fourth pigeon. He waded the paddle deeper and swung the canoe beneath the branch. He was so careless he stood up in the boat until he toppled.

He whispered to the bird, he clicked his tongue as if to say you home now you safe and he pushed his open palm towards the branch. The pigeon gave out one shrill note and flapped clumsily on to his arm.

A thread of wire neatly snared a folded white slip of paper against the leg. Jonathan breathed in deeply. McCarthy would be all right now. He would get to him.

The brothers eased their canoe out from the shallows. Faint sunlight through the curtain of green unveiled their presence. They had been waiting for him. The missionario would lead them to this city of gold. The brothers were great believers in jeito, and this was their fortune day.

"Missionario! ... Ay – missionario!"

Jonathan slipped in panic to the floor of the canoe. He clutched the bird so tightly its heart convulsed, as if it might burst out of skin and feather.

"You give that bird and no harm come! ... You hear!"

"Give it now!" Ires added his voice, intense anticipation gorging his throat.

Jonathan spun the canoe around. His paddle spewed back the water. Napoleon sighted his pistol and fired. The bullet stunned into the missionary's shoulder. A corridor of pain tunnelled his body. Jonathan collapsed in the canoe, his paddle fell away and sloped half submerged in the river's current.

Napoleon yanked the outboard starter. The rope was slow to fire it. Ires fired over Jonathan's head. The noise started the forest into quiet. Jonathan ducked low. They'd soon start their motor. He couldn't attempt escape. His arm lay limp beside him. Numbed weightlessness in his shoulder.

"We don't want to kill you missionario!" Ires called out, "Just the bird just give us it!"

He could hear the desperate lunges at the outboard motor.

The pain ate into him. He could not help McCarthy either way now. If the brothers found him what chance would he have? River trash seeking cities of gold they'd kill McCarthy they'd kill me for it. The pigeon popped its black eyes at him. The little heart pumped against his fingers. Unless—

The outboard motor stammered into life. Jonathan flooded with new pain. He opened his fingers, he released the pigeon. It hurled in the air. It vaulted up. Jonathan, if he twisted enough could lie on his back and see its flight.

The brothers pulled out their rifles. The motor skidded their boat wildly forward. Brown water waved ditches. They fired again and again at the bird, but it still gained on the bullets. They reloaded. The firing again. The crump echo in the trees.

Blast. Blast. Blast.

But now diving up into the blue lake of the sky, piercing green strangler, love liana falling below, fingers stubbing trigger hairs behind it, lift little heart plunge vertical at the azure surface of the lake, higher and higher go, strike the searching sights blue blind, razor the light...

I met Kim Yat Sun at Beto's one evening. That was when I told him the story about poor McCarthy Hughes, from New Zealand. Kim listened politely, then he laughed a lot and said I must be kidding!

Kim was drinking alone at a table when I joined him. Beto's is the best bar in Cuiabá. It stands a little to the west of the Presidente Hotel on the opposite side of the Avenida Getulio Vargas. There is a broadwalk of sloping concrete and the two hundred or so scattered tables are never emptied until long after three in the morning.

On this trip I was trapped in Cuiabá for a week. No bank would change my traveller's cheques and the chartered flight I had been promised was five days overdue. The next week I intended to take a mule across the serra west of the Guaporé River, there was a pass between twin table mountains which led to Bolivia, and the plane was to drop me by the river.

Nothing in this town works very efficiently. The fan in the hotel bedroom bled sparks when I plugged it in, and I blew the lights the length of my landing. Last week a bank manager gunned down a customer in the street, the man's overdraft was twice the value of his worldly goods. Rumour has it – when the authorities dynamited the ancient cathedral in the Praça da Republica in order to replace it with a modern one, nobody told the nightwatchman about it. The wreckers pulled the plunger. The archbishop crossed himself and the entire priceless gem of eighteenth-century colonial architecture hit the sky like a shower of broken dog biscuits. At the time, the nightwatchman was asleep inside, he'd swung his hammock behind the altar piece.

Cuiabá has been the capital of the state of Mato Grosso for two hundred years.

Not an efficient town at all.

You get used to sitting in Beto's night after night pouring ice cold Brahma beer until the sweat drips off you like the freezebox globules on the beer can.

Kim Yat Sun was north Korean. His family came to Brazil when he was nine. He was a dapper man, very crisp black hair peeled back with oil, he always wore spotless American army drill pants. There was a scrubbed quality about him, for example, the shirt on his back never clung glue bath to his skin, unlike the rest of us out here. He liked to affect an American accent.

I don't think he was forty. He looked young and alert and he weighed about 110 lbs. The Brazils called him chines- Kim the Chinaman. If you were remotely yellow, and relatively free from malaria, as far as the Brazils were concerned, you were chines and that was that. Kim didn't give a fart what they called him.

He was a US-trained pilot. He'd flown everything from DC3s to fighter jets. When I met him he'd just finished a job for a German mining company. For three months he flew a Caravelle jet back and forth over the whole of Mato Grosso in twenty-mile-wide swathes. An automatic multi-spectral camera with videotape linked to the aircraft's inertial guidance system made a minutely detailed infra-ray survey map of the entire State.

"And you come to me with this McCarthy Hughes story," Kim grinned mischievously at me, "just how old is this tale?"

"Perhaps ten years."

"You writer guys come out here this far and all you find is crap lost City of the Caesars bull – couple of ex-Nazi war criminals turning honest buck out of soapflakes made into ice-cream – role of film showing some doubtful bum indian being knocked off – go back to Europe, Paris magazine pays you big sum print up Amazon massacre," he took a breath, "you guys won't look for *Brasil real!*"

"What are you saying?"

"It couldn't happen."

"The man existed – McCarthy Hughes never came back."

"Thousand nuts a year disappear in the forest."

"He wrote the messages."

"Brain full of malaria."

"He found the bloody place!"

"He saw gold walls and emerald pavements?"

Right!

"He saw towers and palaces and giant statues?"

He did.

"He wanted see dreams. That's all. He saw a hole in his head!"

"He found the map in the old book in Belém."

"A con."

"He died for it, Kim."

"Plenty guys want to go in there get lost they don't ever come back. Don't want to."

"What reason did Hughes have to stay there?"

"Listen – little England man you are – I seen with my own eyes biggest bestest fucking map ever made of the Mato Grosso inch by inch of it shows serra shows pantanal river rock and ditch, it shows for bauxite and copper, for zinc and casserite, for tin deposits and oil, so good a map it shows for the mosqu on a bald man's head!"

"OK."

"Whatever it was McCarthy Hughes thought was there – it never could have been there in the first place – and I know I seen the biggest map in the world!"

"But—"

"Don't tell me!"

"Kim—?"

"No don't!"

In 1920 a discovery was made by an inland lake stem of the Rio São Francisco in the state of Minas Gerais; bone in stone fragments of men and horses carbon dated to 8000 B.C. The first horse to set foot on Brazil was brought here in 1500 by Alvares Cabral.

Kotosh, curiously built on the eastern wall of the Bolivian Andes, is the ruin of a city which pre-dates the Olmec at La Venta and the Oaxaca-Zapotec at Monte Alban.

On the Ilha de Marajo at the mouth of the Amazon long barrows of piled earth have delivered up after excavation numerous figurines of Phoenician-style pottery.

The Chaco is a flat waste land between Brazil and Paraguay. An expedition in 1964 found the remains of a stone wall a thousand years old. It stretches for fifteen hundred kilometres.

Freak theorists ask what happened to Atahuelpa's brother who disappeared with a large army from the Vilcabamba valley in Peru? He led them down the Solimoes to the Amazon flood rise. He took with him a legendary gold chain, seven hundred feet long, links wide as a man's wrist. Where did he settle?

The town of Santarém stands on the widest lip of the Rio Tapajós where it flows into the Amazon. Over the years people have accidentally unearthed pottery of an extraordinary quality. Four-foot high funereal vases, intricately shaped in a profusion of curled and fluted patterns. So detailed are they they can only be the end-result the final sophistication of a once large civilisation. Three or four hundred years old they are decadent examples of a society which has already attained its zenith.

In Rio there is a document in the Biblioteca Nacional. It was written two centuries ago by Francisco Raposo. Raposo describes a journey west of the Rio São Francisco to a city in the forest of huge proportions. Raposo describes an architectural style he could not possibly have invented. So closely does it resemble the ancient empires of Peru; cities and buildings and ceremonial complexes archaeologists exhumed long after Raposo's death.

In the nineteenth century the explorer Richard Burton, a retired Irish Consul O'Sullivan Beare and an adventurer from Guiana Françesa, Appolonario Frot, all searched for Raposo's lost city.

There is the fame of Colonel P. H. Fawcett who perished with his son and a friend in the Xingu area in 1925. Percy Fawcett looked for this city.

> "For example, I'm the kind of man who looks for cities in the forest because I could not live in a society within which I have no control anymore."
>
> *O'Sullivan Beare.*

"And this is how I sometimes think of myself, as a great explorer, who has discovered some extraordinary land from which he can never return to give his knowledge to the world."

Malcolm Lowry.

"Yage makes you see cities."

William Burroughs.

"According to many of these messages, the explorer [Fawcett] is not only safe, but he has reached his lost city, of which the residentual amenities are considerable."

Peter Fleming.

My friend in London is the poet. He called one day to describe a dream. Thousands of years have civilised us. We are so advanced stars are colonised. We have devoured every perimeter of our understandings. Only chance in games and the familiarity of love concern us. The rest is satiety. The new is tired.

Our final resources are spent on space ships sent to the edges of the universe. Now all our ships but one have returned. Their news is no different.

Save for this one lone time traveller, final captain galactic skater of light, who has the power of suns to reach one hitherto unknown corner of the universe.

The waiting is eager. His news must be different.

Our perfectly adjusted human heirs chariot him home with time capsules. We cluster around him with the impatience of chance in games. He tells us he has searched to the end of the universe, in space he reached the point where a circle reverts to its first radius, and there are no tangent lines left to follow.

His news is no different. He tells us, yes it is true, we are alone in the universe. We have measured all space and there is nobody out there. No humanoid. No planet with life. We call out our names amongst the stars and there is no reply. We are singular. One. And that too is our chance in our games.

DOIDO

BOSCO LIVES IN the streets of Boca do Acre. At night he sleeps in the rodoviária on the concrete gutter with the day's garbage. They call him Bosco doido, a doido is a crazy one, and he plays all the time with the children if their parents will allow. He plays the games the children invent, and they don't seem to mind he is thirty years older than they are.

He has a peculiar way of walking. He lets his slippers drag in the dirt behind him, they make a sherslep sherslep noise, slow and purposeful, as if he knows where he is going. Bosco doesn't know anything. He is doido.

And the Brazilians feed him from time to time, like they feed their own dogs. They give him scraps, and if the prefeito comes by, he huddles in the concrete gutter, because Bosco is afraid the man will notice him. The prefeito likes to kick Bosco, he likes to pull him to his feet by his balls and shake him until the saliva rolls down the doido's fat lips, and Bosco trembles so much his shirt and his pants fall away and others come by to laugh when the prefeito bends the doido over a bench to goose him with his pistol.

Peter and Jenny are Paulistas. Very few big city people come here to live. They are so gracious, they play cards at night, tell jokes about each other, (and that's a thing the people of Boca do Acre cannot do), and they never discuss the land they own.

But they are young and rich in a place like this, they talk about the estado novo, and the threat of Chinese communism, so when people glance at them in their new German car they nod to each other and say they won't stay long in Boca do Acre.

Like everybody else, Peter knows the doido, he sees him every day in the street, dragging his feet, sherslep sherslep, crying out incomprehensible sounds, grinning broken teeth at a girl with a skirt above her knees, tugging at his cock until a wet discharge shadow darkens the cotton pants and the girl runs down the street fast as she can.

Not long ago Peter bought a farm with an arab. Soon after, the arab sold his half of the fazenda without Peter's permission. Peter went to the courts. They froze the arab's money from the sale, and refused to allow the new owners possession of the property. Meanwhile, the arab remains low in funds, and no bank will give him a loan.

Peter despises the cheap bungalow they rent, it has no class, the air-condition ceiling fan is twisted and the tap water runs brown. It is so different in São Paulo. They must sit it out here and wait for the trial, which they assuredly will win, and then they can sell the farm at a great profit. The courts will force the arab to give up his portion of the land at cost price and – (all courts in Brazil give arabs really bad time) – as for the arab, he will go to jail.

Everybody in Boca do Acre knows the arab. Children run past his shanty hut and throw firecrackers at him. He sits in a sprawl on the verandah brooding on his misery. Nobody wants to talk to him. They'd rather speak with the doido. The arab knows he must go to jail. Unless this Paulista, Peter, this accursed easterner were to go away. Then everybody would forget. And things would return to normal.

The arab looks for Bosco in the night. He finds him in the gutter of the rodoviária. Bosco shrinks from him, thinking it must be the prefeito. But the prefeito is not in town. He is in Porto Velho with his wives. The arab smiles at the doido, his hook nose is the shadow of a great banana, and he has a kindly voice.

Jenny is asleep. She has the cot bed. Peter will use the rêde in the open doorway. There is no electricity tonight, nor has there been any all this week in the whole town, the generator is broken, and the German engineer is away. He is somewhere down the Guaporé on the steam-boat from Guajará Mirim.

Sherslep sherslep.

Peter is half awake. He knows those footsteps. He sits up in the open doorway. Bosco is standing on the porch. In his hand is a snub-nosed Japanese revolver. He points it carefully at Peter.

"Bosco?"

"Gerente."

Bosco's fingers, he has both his middle fingers around the trigger, tighten their grip.

"Who told you to come here?"

"Oh you know who told me."

"The arab told you?"

"Yes gerente – told me to kill you."

"Put down the gun, doido."

"I must shoot you first."

"Put down that gun, Bosco doido!"

"I must kill you before I do that."

Bosco pulls the trigger, all the weight of his middle fingers behind it, but nothing happens. Peter sweats with relief, the safety catch is still on.

"Bosco – listen to me—"

"It's all right gerente, nothing has gone wrong, I forgot about the safety catch. I can do it now," says the doido.

"Bosco! I will give you twice what the arab gave you – if you'll go back and shoot him!"

The doido pauses. His fingers lie still.

"Bosco, tell me what the arab gave you?"

"He gave me one hundred – no – two hundred cruzeiros, gerente."

"Then I'll give you four hundred."

"Is this a trick?"

"No Bosco, it isn't."

"But what do I do about this gun?"

"After you have shot the arab you can keep it. The arab won't want it back, will he?"

Bosco smiles. Well, that isn't such a bad idea.

"Will you tell the prefeito?" asks Bosco.

"Of course I won't. Would I want to hang myself?"

"Will you tell the pretty wife you got?"

"Nobody."

Peter reaches in his pocket and unrolls four hundred cruzeiro notes, from a wad of money. Before Bosco can say anything more, he shoves the notes inside the doido's pants. Bosco squints at the Paulista with a puzzled expression. Saliva dribbles. It hangs from his chin like a necklace of glue.

"Will you go and do that for me, Bosco?"

"Yes," the doido replies, with a confused frown.

"Then hurry! Go!" Peter shouts and claps his hands in a loud burst. The doido runs.

The *Folio do Sol* is the daily newspaper in this region. It is printed in Porto Velho; but after the censors have read it, it never reaches Boca do Acre until six in the evening, when a truck collects the mail from Rio Branco.

Peter and Jenny drive away for the day. They visit the half of the farm they still own. They look at the ring fence which cuts off their land from the arab's. And they have a picnic beneath a giant angico tree. Peter claims the tree is taller than the spires of Cuiaba's new cathedral. Jenny cannot believe that, but she laughs, and kisses him, and they make love in the hottest part of the day. Paulistas are peculiar in that way. Afterwards they must rub lighter fuel on the ticks in their skin to kill them off. It is so cool in the car, driving back, the wind whips their hot faces like sleet.

There is an unusual quiet about the town, Peter notices, when they reach Boca do Acre, there do not appear to be as many people on the streets as usual. When they step inside the bungalow, Jenny has to flop down on the rêde by the open door. Peter reaches for the folded copy of the *Folio do Sol*. It is just under the door. He cannot find any mention of the arab's death, not even on the back page. Perhaps the killing of a foreigner, bit time shoe salesman Lebanese with a broody look in a place like this is of no importance. Peter looks up. He does not know why.

Sherslep sherslep sherslep.

He is on the porch, a foot in the doorway, a paralysis grips Peter, Jenny sits up in the rêde her mouth is frozen wide, wide enough to take a whole bacu fish, Peter is turning to say something to him but the doido just walks straight in and places on the cane table in front of him a crumpled roll of eight hundred cruzeiro notes; a scream of panic in Jenny's throat chokes her to silence, her hand flutters like a signature on a piece of paper you want to dry in the hot air; now they see what Bosco is holding in his other hand, holding out in a steady grip his middle fingers so firm there and that doido smile of apology on his lips, broken black roots in pink gum, and the front of his pants wet with the dark discharge shadow of come as if he has been watching that girl with her skirt above her knees who runs down the street fast as she can.

BACHIANA BRASILEIRA

SINGING RIB OF *saudade inside the Brazil. Sulk carelessly weaned beneath his smile. Insouciance made rapture by rivers of mouths carioca carnival laughter. Love welcome you but shit disgust behind your back what you want to steal from us what you want here to make yourself rich, chefe? Fear of his colonial past black African blood thousand time removed legacy, cafuso cum black indian, mestico cum black white, caboclo cum white indian. The darker yau are the closer you come to panning the dogcrap on Leblon beach. Nobody likes to say it is a sick scheming for a whiter soul. Forest paradigm of nostalgia he won't walk into the interior terror tells him. Waiting with a patience longer than any anticipation for the estrangeiro fall prat on your face and beg him for help, you dying there in his gutter and no mistah credit card fly me thousand dollar safe one signature, the Brazil make a gorge of chattering macaco laughter, you the idiot now you feed his saudade a craving for malevolence he see you fucked you robbed blind and it féria scream funny.*

But leave the Brazil alone with his fond remembrance saudade, if all these tourist spies were to go now (after all the Brazil he only borrowed three thousand billion dollars), and the rest – Japs disguised as missionaries trail mechanical bleep instruments searching for oil ... Peace Corps boys with chicken necks throbbing adam's apple innocence making tapes of sabiá shrill but survey rockfall for bauxite and zinc findings ... barbershop deals with Paulista lawyers mouthing gold capped desenvolvimento rustle of 500 cruzeiros notes, 'you keep ninety per cent chefe I keep sixty per cent we screw Brasilia for total per cent MEC-USAID/SUDENE subsidy and index-link-write-off one hundred per cent loss, no problem' ... at building site white German crepe silk-lined blue suits under yellow steel helmets leap out of helicopters pay favela trash ten cents an hour make million dollar a week profit, no problem Herr Krapps ...

Oh if these bugre tourist spies were all to go, all these americano coronels retired from Cuba Korea Cambodia CIA agents (the Brazil know they agents for certo he hear tranni news radio censor speak he read billboard comics hear pinga talk in fat nights under corrugated roof bars), oh but he'd miss their presences, for what is there left to talk about if one is not allowed to talk about the government? And out come his infinite surge saudade again.

But they don't go away. They steal from him again. He look forward to it now, he need them, it become a drug. He reliant on theft now. The singing rib is a lament for the loved hated out of pride, hand help held out with embrace after embrace but he yearns his saudade and it is salt in septic greed orifices, saudade yearns like seeing countless eldorados in other men's eyes, saudade lacklustre awareness his Europe-sized country has never been his own, cash capital flow pillage gold-bust/rubber-bust/land-bust in history book create slave of sadness.

Saudade—

—a passion, faithless cry of pathos, never once claiming first rights, land trod venereal waste for mindlust profit singing rib saudade, soul sound, sabiá notes fall in trees, careening pitch, death sob for longings lost.

Then, of course there are other kinds of eldorados. If they aren't all dreams, or made of man's greed, indefinable yearnings, then they are made up of black hearts behind white faces.

And you can't button down the Brazilan spirit in one word like saudade. So much else, besides. But of all the truths of the forest the Brazils make a habit of one. That is – most people who go into the interior never to come out, those who close behind them the walls of silence and distance and no contact do it in order to forget. And that is why in the Amazonas when you stumble across an Englishman reciting Dickens you are not so very surprised. All right, it's a bit of a shock when he asks you how that shilling Algerian plonk in Fortnum's is standing up, but on the whole the romance of the green desert fades fast beside the approach of the big yellow cat excavator.

You can still go in deep and nobody find you (because that is what you want) and though you might be dreaming of W. H. Hudson's white indians or Orrellania's Manoes, it would be a shame you can't hear that radio report or read that newspaper account of Claudio Villas-Boas big trip up Rio Iriri with the chairman of Volkswagen Brasil because he actually found them. Six feet tall with blue eyes and heavy pubics, that's right, sure; all of a sudden you don't need that dream any more, that role of lost longings, something much more subversive has crept in – the bare want.

So, lets not demorara around; inside saudade don't doubt it, you can find this new want.

Frei lived in Belém. He worked for a mining company, JAPOCHEM. The company explored for gems. But Frei was bound to his desk in the analysis department and all he had to explore were sample stones beneath his microscope. And it hurt him to think about the enormous profits JAPOCHEM were feeding back to Tokyo. He'd look at those skinny yellows who employed him, bunch of thin-lipped Japones, to him they were just bugre pirates. And Frei had saudade. Not the romance longing that sounds good in a folksong, his lament was for envy and strike back. It was true gut Brazilian resentment, and you can't cash that in the Banco do Brasil. Perhaps this envy only comes out of a Brazilian from the north-east, like Frei. He had no illusions about church or politics. If you'd been born in the north-east in the thirties like Frei, where you were amongst the poorest and least employed, you wouldn't ask the State cow for milk either. Frei wanted.

In the state of Pará, a little above the town of Marabá, beside where the Tocantins pours its body north into the Amazon's atlantic swell, there is an area of high stony campina. There are rock formations where minerals are explored for. In recent times Marabá itself has been overrun by the new trans-Amazonica highway, which crosses the breast of all Amazonas south of the great river. For years, between Marabá and the Rio Loutra, a hundred or so indians called Parakana kept themselves hidden from the civilizados. They hunted undisturbed, stored up for winter rains, and were by repute rather shy. The itinerant seringueiro up in the campina liked to weave fantasies about these discreet indians. The Parakana would offer you a woman for the night if you stayed with them. The Parakana could wash precious stones out of the rivers and they found emeralds the size of your thumb. Of course, the fantasy continued, all you have to do is capture one of their women and exchange a bottle of cachaça for the stone around her waist. There had been a number of unconfirmed reports – a rubber tapper bought a necklace of jade from a Parakana, another man discovered a bag of emeralds buried beside the Parakana winter stores. Recently stranger things have happened. White trash field workers have disappeared in the campina. Upon investigation, someone always claimed he saw the indians in the vicinity. Word was out – the Parakana were making random killings. Then the trans-Amazonica highway boomed into Marabá. The indians were forgotten. There was work and a new period of prosperity. But for the Parakana the highway spelled disruption and chaos. The hundred or so indians split up. Some turned to the road to sell artifacts, in due course they were selling their bodies to the motoristas. But a hard core of the Parakana retreated up into the campina. There was a place there where they could feel tolerably safe. Where there was a Capitão Parakana who protected a sib grouping of four families. They had been up there for years. This Capitão indian was a wise timbu (opossum), he had a little Portuguese and he understood how the civilizado could cheat and lie. He knew what the white trash from the fields down below around Marabá called the indians – bichos da mata. And he hid himself away in the campina with his family groups. He knew, too, all the legends and fantasies the branco weaved around Parakanas. He was a timbu.

Frei worked for JAPOCHEM in a wood and asbestos hut. The walls were lined with glass cases, each filled with various mineral finds. Apaje was Frei's assistant. They sat at opposite desks in the mineral analysis hut. Frei did the chemical breakdowns and his assistant kept a close record of all the stones. There would be certain weeks when they were inundated with finds. A man would pan a glassy object in a stream and send it to Frei's office at JAPOCHEM for analysis. It seemed like every man who owned a strip of land in the state of Pará believed in priceless gems hidden underground.

Frei's job wasn't such an exciting one. He might find one sample out of two thousand of any value. Day after day he raised his eye and focussed the microscope, but it was always glass rubbish.

In truth, Apaje wanted Frei's job. He was half his age and the Japones liked Apaje. He treated them with a certain respect. There was none of that ... you yellow bugres come to steal from Brazil nonsense from Apaje. The younger man had been sold the miracle of development.

Each day the mail brought Frei these curious-shaped little packets of hope from all over the State. He never hurried, he spent the morning on his notes for the JAPOCHEM samples, and the little packets were put aside for the afternoon. It was a bone of contention between them that Apaje had to wait half the day to index the new deliveries because Frei hadn't opened them.

On a morning Apaje arrived early. The usual pile of assorted parcels lay on Frei's bench. There was no Frei. Apaje opened the packets and took a note of all the names in order that he might issue receipts. He laid the various quartz and glass samples on the desk and tied numbered tabs to each one. Apaje was pleased with himself. He would keep to this new procedure in future.

"You've no right to touch these packets," Frei snapped when he came in later, "it's my job to open the mail."

Apaje shrugged. What did it matter anyway Frei reasoned to himself. Green boy like that and he think he can step into my shoes. He so thick about stones he'd bend down and try to pick up a cat's eye in the middle of the road. Frei sorted the samples in front of him. He held one up to the light and weighed a couple on his delicate scales out of curiosity. All rubbish. Not a hope.

A small box the size of a thimble shoe was wrapped in yellow newspaper. Apaje hadn't opened it, he'd just taken the name of the sender. Frei prised away the paper and lifted the lid. Shyly indented on a pad of cottonwool lay a green stone.

A chill ran through Frei. He didn't need to pick it up. It had been a long time since he'd last seen that depth of chromium oxide. That green vitreous lustre. It was as perfect a rough-cut emerald he had ever looked at.

Frei glanced behind to see if Apaje had looked. No, he was still working, his head bent down over figures. Frei folded the paper over the thimble shoe box and slipped it in his pocket. He walked outside. Apaje was unconcerned.

Nobody had posted him a gem like that before. Frei had to breathe in deeply. He looked up at the blue sky and rubbed the clamminess at the back of his neck. What was he doing here? There was no need to stay on. The pay bad. Frei had no wife to support. No mother, now. His sole responsibility was the room on the top floor of the King Hotel.

Frei drew the package out. Yes, there was a note attached. It was from a porceiro up in the hills near the trans-Amazonica, south-east from Belém. Something scribbled there in between the perspiration sog from his fingers. I would be grateful if JAPOCHEM identified this stone. I find many here like this. Is it valuable? Signed, yours respectfully, *Melio*.

He felt afraid of himself. Jesus o Senhor Cristo it was a miracle. Everybody else had them, those Japones had, those branco americanos had, now it was Frei's turn. His estado novo miracle.

Apaje was calling for him from inside the hut. Ah yes, there was his assistant to deal with. It was all right wasn't it? He hadn't shown the package to him, Frei reassured himself, he always gave Apaje the samples after the morning work. Apaje had no idea of the existence of this ... Frei grinned quietly and stepped back inside the hut.

Melio lived in the Morro Boa Vista. This high land, rugged red rock and in between the seca mata clumps of cheeky vulture-nettle-trees harboured wasp nests just in case those black urubus took the trees' name seriously. Nothing seemed to work so quickly on vultures as wasp nests. And it is something to remember – the sight of urubu caught crazy in the air with half a mil wasps beneath its wings. The Morro was campina, and it lay a hundred kilometres north and north-west from Marabá. But Melio never referred to it as that. To him it was his high scrub planalto retreat where the civilizados wouldn't dare to climb. Melio felt truly mean about the old people, those people in the cities down below, for he'd made up his mind about them. They had cheated him too much in the past. Their lies. Their untrustworthiness. He hated contact of any sort with those city bugres. Not quite true ...

Years ago Melio lost his savings in two business ventures north in Belém. One was a restaurant. The other was a tyre import and retread company. Because he was an immigrant Italian in those days, couldn't understand the language well enough, he was fleeced by the business partners he chose.

The tale gets worse: Melio lived with a woman who cheated him out of all else he possessed, and that broke this Italian camel's straw back. He had no money for the boat home to Italy. His woman died in mysterious conditions and Melio received the blame. And he – like so many others before him trapped in the very littlenesses of all his foundered schemes self-righteous victim of hapless incidents – he turned to the interior. That was where he could survive. Without anybody. And Melio knew of the Morro Boa Vista.

He squatted on a patch of scrub and rock fall. In the wet season there was a plentiful stream, and over the years he encouraged the dry forest to envelop his perimeters. The greener it became the easier it was to exclude the outside. And in due time Melio (not without some hideous pratfalls) learnt to survive up on the campina.

His only neighbours were a family group of Parakana indians who, for reasons safe only to themselves, took a liking to Melio. Their Capitão, said to be quite a wise timbu about those brancos, never looked closely at Melio and said to himself this white nut is as mad as a snake which chews off its own tail. And the Parakana taught Melio to fish with a wild bracken which stunned the bacu in the stream. The bracken gave off a powerful drug when thrashed through the shallows. They showed him how to hunt by laying bait-traps and deadfall pits. In time, Melio's patch became a regular homestead. He had wildfowl (fat perus, twitchy thin feather-skin chickens and seriemas kind of long-legged bustard bird taste of turkey) and his manioc and salted fish and maize was enough to keep him in stock through the wet.

The Parakanas were always around him. He'd never admit it but he could feel the twinges of prison in every tree; they were watching him. As if he was there courtesy of the Capitão Parakana. When they came to him, the indians never entered his little lean-to planta thatch structure, sloped at a forty-five-degree angle against posts. They showed themselves by standing in the shade of the trees at the clearing's verge. They had a delicate way with them. He was expected to cross the chicken strip to them. And they had a curious but charming habit of taking a pace back from him, just one odd step of retreat into their green corridors. Melio never could persuade them to come any closer.

The group guessed at Melio's hatred for his brother branco civilizado below the campina in the towns. They knew Melio would never invite any more of branco up here. This the Parakanas took as a compliment. It meant that the rubber tappers and seringueiro gem panners would never penetrate. Their Melio would see to that. They were safe with this man and his hatred.

One year the Parakanas brought Melio an ancient Mannlicher Carcano. Melio didn't ask them how they came to possess this 6.5 carbine. He thanked them and took the damp cardboard box of shells. What did they want in exchange? He asked. A couple of perus the Capitão shrugged amiably pointing at the chicken strip. Melio wouldn't have it. He took them twenty of his best perus, fattest turkey cocks he kept in the wicker strip and he threw in a sack of black feijão.

Now the indians became accustomed to bartering with Melio. Fish for maize. Wild pig for manioc drained of its poison sap. And the Capitão liked to tap Melio on the crown of his skull with his fist and gesture to him – *you my son* – it meant and – *I like a father to you* – notwithstanding the fact that Melio was hardly a year younger than the Capitão.

There were times when Melio was forced down from the red rock planalto. His gums bled so much he had to see the armazém dentista at the Jatobel trans-Amazonica junction. Another year he feared he had caught leishmaniasis. The flesh began to boil and supurate beneath his nostrils. The hospital truck which carried sick highway workers to Marabá stopped for him on the road. It was nothing as bad as he imagined. Always he was asked about those indian animals up there on the Morro. Did they really give their women away? Are there secret catches of gems buried in the Parakana aldeia? Limpid sneak tongues sweating favela trash dreams last sad revolt of the senses operatic pinga nights porceiro whispers. Or rubber-throated bull worker straddles his hammock remembers tale of motorista who plucked a Parakana fifteen-year-old out of red dust road and drove her two thousand kilometres. Makes imitation fuck of this little girl in his hammock she impaled on him skinny legs stroking the night with palsied shudders, fist rammed down her throat dream, and he coming like dirt conquest, secret laughter shared; later, piss on her face when he's finished in the daylight she just litter like discard kero cans you don't have to feed.

Each time Melio returned from one of these trips the indians were slow to show themselves. You could go as far as saying – they wanted the dust of favela branco contact to wash away before they spoke to Melio again.

The Capitão stood on the verge waiting. Beside him was a daughter. Well, to be precise, she was his brother's daughter. And the Capitão couldn't afford to keep her any more. He'd made too many rash promises to the other women. He was forced to give up this one. He already had too many wives. He smiled at Melio and pushed the girl forward.

"Pei Pa," he said pointing at her. That was her name.

"Pei Pa," he repeated.

A round face with moon lips and pretty gaps in her front teeth where she balanced the tip of her tongue. It was clear to Melio, all right. If he refused this offer the Capitão would be intolerably compromised. Melio was conjuring through his mind all sorts of remonstrations ... what I need a girl in the hut for? ... At my age? ... What good is she to me? ...

He saw the stone placed in her navel. And he paused. It was a perfectly gleaming green gemstone. Moss dark shafts of warmth keening knife light lunges in its innermost heart. The Capitão could see his expression.

"She brings the stone with her ..." the Capitão's Tupi-Portuguese stuttered the sounds, mouthed hiccups with plenty of signalling, "it was her Spirit gift when she was born ... you must not lose it ... or sell it ... it is a sworn word of mine – she will come back to us immediately."

Pei Pa was giggling. Melio felt uncomfortable. His beard seeped with perspiration. Cristo O Senhor! What I done to deserve a wife! Pei Pa scuffed her tiny brown toes in the stony ground.

The emerald, at one stroke, was both lock and key to Pei Pa's white heart behind her smooth dark face.

In the beginning, Melio thought hard upon killing Pei Pa. But how could he escape from the Morro? And why should he? She, in her turn, grew to love this bony branco with a vicious heart of loathing. She allowed him to keep the gemstone in a tin box of nails and assorted screws, and Melio kept his eye on it placed on the shelf against the wicker wall to the moment he fell asleep at night. He was so transfixed.

The indians didn't visit the chicken strip very often. Melio heard talk that a government agency was trying to round them all up, keep them away from the new highway. Pei Pa never learnt much Portuguese from Melio. She didn't seem to care. She liked this old skinny devil and she trusted him enough, in all truth she trusted him so much she never once asked to look at her Spirit gemstone for months on end.

Six seasons passed. Pei Pa kept away from the casa de planta when ever the occasional branco found himself lost by the chicken strip. She knew Melio gave these strangers brief welcome. She'd wander off in the mata seca for a couple of days. Later she would return. And the stranger was no longer there.

Pei Pa and her branco Melio swung their rêdes into the receding light. She could glance up at the wall and see the tin box with her Spirit gemstone. She never asked about it now. She knew it was safe. When it got completely dark she might persuade her branco beard to make love to her. But he was a lazy one, just like her father.

It wasn't easy to climb up the Morro on a mule. Frei didn't kick the animal too hard. Perhaps it was much further than the man said down below on the road. You going up there? The man asked him after he sold Frei the mule. You find onça up there, bugre indios up there, doido guys believe they found diamonds and emeralds. You must be crazy too!

The man indicated a path up the Morro. You might find Melio somewhere along there, he said. Watch out, gerente, he got a gun.

Frei had packed a hammock and a sack of black beans. He rode five hours up the Morro to reach the chicken strip beside the wet season stream. He was a little surprised to find Melio so unconcerned at his arrival. Frei stood at the open door and Melio was in no hurry to get up from the floor. Frei explained he was from JAPOCHEM. He had been sent here specially to...

"I could hear you coming a kilometre off," Melio nodded roughly, "could see you even – mule's feet kick up the dust behind you." There was not much of a welcome in Melio's tone, but Frei could detect something else in the old sertanista's eyes. A bright flicker of eagerness. Melio was pleased enough all right to see this city branco.

Pei Pa hid herself on the verge of the clearing. Now and again she appeared, somewhere beside the chicken wicket strip, and Frei caught sight of her out of the corner of his eye. But he and Melio had much more serious matters to talk over.

"Where did you find this stone, Melio?"

"Up here..."

"Why did you send it to us at JAPOCHEM?"

"Everybody knows – big yellow firm like yours. Find a gem deposit in my rocks like this – more money any of us ever dreamed of. I'm poor trash – can't you see...?"

Frei could.

Melio was full of questions like what kind of terms you going to give, chefe? We split it down the middle, right? And pretty soon they were arguing over Melio's non-existent deeds for his land. They had a plate of feijão together and Melio pulled a cork out of a Fanta bottle with his black teeth. It was a fermented banana juice, nut rum flavour in it, and Frei let the thick liquid roll around his tongue.

"All you have to do – you show me where you found this stone..." Frei tipped the thimble sized box on the table, the uncut green eye trickled translucent edges as it rolled in front of them, "And ... I can arrange the rest. Just show me the place."

Words won't sweat. But Melio heard a kind of breathlessness in the civilizado's voice. Too much of a hurry about him, the way the promises tumbled from his lips.

"You want see the rock where—?"

"All you have to do – I do the rest."

"And you find more like this? Huh?"

"That's what we'd hope at JAPOCHEM."

Suppose I tell you the whole rock got a seam in it deep like a cave it's a kind of hollow and this seam the same colour as my stone?" said Melio.

Frei wiped the perspiration from his chin. That banana had too much acid in it, it clawed at his throat.

Melio took Frei across the chicken strip; cashew wood and oil-palms leaned against an outcrop of red stone. Beneath an over-hang, Melio ducked his head low to lead the way. The darkness inside was suddenly cool. As Frei's eyes got used to it, Melio was pushing ahead of him and he hugged the cantilevered rockface. The face was pitted with cave formations. But they were shallow and it was possible to kneel beneath the over-hang and reach the back of the hollows. Melio stopped. He drew Frei closer. Melio's banana aguardente breath creeper fetid—

"Look close, chefe...ne?"

Frei blinked in the damp green light.

"Reach out your hand...touch it...ne?"

Frei leaned in towards the hollow. The porceiro's hand guided his arm. Frei could feel his heart bumping. The shirt lathered wet against his ribs. Lips sand dry. Moth tongue.

"You see it ... ne?"

Frei pulled out a tab of paper matches. It was difficult to light them. Once he could – it took him seconds to take in the rind of green stone in the rockface. He touched the thin rind which shone with a brilliancy a laughing brilliant macaco scream in Frei's mind, gibbering useless brilliance ... Frei hurriedly withdrew. Melio turned to watch him. Frei had to stand outside the cave, the breath was crushed inside his lungs. Suffocating closeness of rock wall and oil-palms and liana and forest drip. Frei gasped out loud.

"You see it now?" murmured Melio, "what you think?"

Frei coughed and gestured that they must go back. It wasn't easy to talk in that airless place. As they hurried towards the bluer light through the trees at the chicken strip Frei shook his head in bewilderment, he had to analyse the situation. For that rind of glass stone in the cave was just rubbish bugre quartz. Fool's emerald, it was called.

There had to be an explanation. The old posseiro clearly didn't trust him. He had found that true emerald in another spot. Melio was trying him out. A test of some sort. There must be a perfect source for such an emerald. It was here up in the Morro strip of Melio's. The problem was – how to shake the truth out of the secretive musk-pig with his fetid banana breath and little indio whore. Frei would.

The men sat round the plank table in the little planta thatch hut. Pei Pa prepared beans and fish and chopped mangaba fruits for them. Whilst the men talked she kept in her corner by the fogão, the stone and mud bake oven, she crouched on her knees.

Frei sipped at the banana brew and plucked up courage—

"You ... never had any intention of showing me where you found that stone ... right?"

"Maybe..." Melio said softly, lowering his chin into his beard.

"Why, Melio?"

"It's lonely up here ... it isn't easy to trust a stranger ... so quickly," Melio's pale eyes watered beneath the swaying oil lamp, "and perhaps ..." he appeared to hesitate, "I wanted to see your face when I showed you that cave."

"And—?"

"I wanted to be sure you really were from JAPOCHEM. Sure you were an expert and that ... you'd see through that bugre glass in cave."

"You trust me now...?" asked Frei, and there was an unmistakable tone of relief in his words for he knew the old posseiro was coming round to him.

"I trust you..." said Melio.

"Sure you do!" Frei puffed up his own confidence.

"I only wanted to test you," murmured Melio.

"Test my knowledge of stones?"

"Not just stones, chefe..." Melio blinked nervously, there was a shy quality about him, a certain vulnerableness, "...greed, too."

Frei let it pass. What did it matter what the Morro squatter meant? What about greed? He was half insane, by any normal standards, reasoned Frei.

Pei Pa was pulling Frei's rêde, his bargain price hammock, across the open door. That was the customary pride-of-place hospitality all strangers receive out in the forest. For it is by the open door you get most breeze in the insect milk night.

Melio said something to Pei Pa in her own language. She stopped shock still. The porceiro turned to Frei—

"You like her?"

"What?"

"Like the look of her? She pretty, ne?"

"That's right. Yes, very," Frei had to answer.

"She'll stay with you tonight. She yours."

Frei had to roll with that one. I don't even want the indio whore. Those diseases they got. Then he remembered the rumours down on the road. These Parakana have a custom. They hand you their women for the night. Frei wasn't going to give up all grip on reality. Perhaps Melio was about to put him to another test. Frei glanced at Pei Pa. Trim little brown nothing shape, more bone than anything, and her wide black eyes boring into him. What did they tell him? Frei argued with himself – would he hurt Melio by refusing? Would he hurt himself by accepting? Whatever ... it would be a good anecdote to spin back in Belém.

"I mean it..." Melio was saying.

"I..."

"It's the custom up here on the Morro with these Parakanas ... think nothing of it."

Before either of them could move, Pei Pa suddenly rushed out of the hut. Her soft heels soundless in the blue starry night outside.

"You go!" Melio shouted out.

And Frei – not really knowing why he did it – followed her out across the chicken strip. She was running up an incline and he was able to close the gap. He was just behind her now. She ran across the stony serra surface above the incline towards a fringe of low imbauba trees fledgling and scrawny in this high land.

He gestured to her. Frei could see she was unhappy. She didn't want to sleep with him. No matter what Melio said. Indian wives don't become sex wrapped gifts over a plate of feijoada and bacu to any passing estrangeiro. Favela trash libido night talk, that's all it was.

Frei tried to explain to Pei Pa. It was fine by him, he had no intention of touching her. She was crying now and rubbing dust into her eyes with her knuckles to hide the tears. He tried to walk with her. But she kicked at him and yelled, and he couldn't understand.

She was standing by the imbauba fringe, skinny branches winded by the high air. As Frei approached again, his feet stumbled on the ground. In the blue star light moon riding crescent over black clouds he could see three burial mounds at his feet.

Pei Pa was pointing at the mounds and crying. She sat down in a heap, very distressed and shaking. He couldn't understand what she said. The Parakana words stuttered in short soft syllables. They tumbled off her tongue incessantly.

Later, when she had calmed down, Frei walked back to the planta hut. He couldn't fit it all together, but from the expression in her gestures and the meaning he believed he found in her eyes – those burial mounds were her children's graves. Children she and Melio had born. Well, any rate, that was Frei's guess.

He called to Melio in the hut, but the old porceiro was either asleep or too drunk to answer. Frei climbed into his rêde and rocked it with his shoulders. It was pleasant, Frei had to admit, up there on the Morro, you did not have to wait for the mosqus to descend, there was a coolness in the night air a certain stirring breeze which caused the planta roof to rustle like marching forest leafcutter ants, and pium mosqu even bloodsucking borrachudos retreated on such a starry night.

Frei woke in the morning to a strange noise. It was like a wind instrument without its mouthpiece unharmoniously showering an audience with spittle. He sat up.

Melio held the Italian carbine between his legs and blew with all his breath down the barrel. He wiped the length of the barrel dry with a cloth plunger, pulling it back and forth violently.

Pei Pa was outside. Somewhere on the verge of the chicken strip. Delicately treading the soft green liana underfoot, face and arm just a shadow's step behind the veil of trees, like her family used to be when they came to visit their branco porceiro friend, and she was apprehensive; for this stranger who arrived up on the Morro was no friend, and she did not like Melio's peculiar kinship with the civilizado.

Melio and Frei shared a pot of coffee on a bench some distance from the hut. Melio kept his carbine close by. He repeatedly practised with the bolt action and he checked and double checked the efficacy of the safety clasp. The old squatter was watching Frei out of the corner of his eye—

"You want me to take you to the place where I really found the stone, ne?"

"You trust me enough now ..." Frei said softly.

Melio snorted and shrugged his shoulders. He patted the carbine with the flat of his hand. Maybe ... maybe not ...

Melio pulled the emerald from the button down pocket on his shirt. He rolled the large uncut shape in his palm. The bright stone splintered the rays of sunlight. Frei was mesmerised. Melio still watched him from beneath his shaded eyes.

"I show you then..."

"There's nothing to fear from me..." Frei smiled. But Melio had walked away. Frei needed to move swiftly to keep up with the older man. Melio's wire legs ate up the clearing.

Pei Pa saw enough. She had watched the men pass the green stone between them on the bench. The stranger had touched it. Held it up to the sky. Now that was wrong. It was Melio's promise never to show that stone to anybody. Particularly to branco trash. Melio had let her down. He was going to sell the stone, all right. Perhaps to this new stranger. She had to hurry.

When the chicken strip was quiet, and the men had vanished in the trees on the far side, Pei Pa ran back into the hut. She had to jump to reach the box on the high shelf where the Spirit stone was kept. Now she held the box. It was empty. And Melio had sworn never to move the stone from the tin box.

She walked with the box to the verge. She felt so angry. She would take the box straight to her father the Capitão Parakana, and she would show him the empty box, with the green stone missing from inside it where it always should stay. Pei Pa didn't hesitate, the forest swallowed her brown little figure. She knew where to find her father.

Certainly, Melio was taking Frei another direction. They were far from the shallow caves beneath the overhang rock. As they stepped out into a clearing Melio stopped still. His nose lifted in the suffocating green air. His eyes were bright and shiny.

"What is it?" Frei asked.

"Can you smell?"

"No. What?"

"Smell donkey?"

"Of course not..." Frei murmured.

"We're very near the path you took yesterday. But you tied up that burro by the hut. Somebody else is here."

What was the old beard trying to do to him? Frei wondered. Is this another test?

"Did you tell anyone you were coming up here?"

"No. Of course not," said Frei. The old beard nodded. Frei had given himself away, but Melio didn't blink.

"Not even your business friends in JAPOCHEM?"

"Eh no... you see – everybody else down there is on holiday," Frei stammered, "I had no time. And this was clearly such an important discovery – this stone."

But Melio wasn't angry with Frei. He didn't turn on him and accuse him of doubledealing his own company JAPOCHEM. The beard motioned to Frei to walk low behind him, his head and shoulders went down in a stoop.

The undergrowth gave way to an invisible path. But Melio knew it. Both men stepped out on to the stony track Frei had taken yesterday. Frei couldn't tell a thing. But Melio unslung his carbine and held it at half port. Around the corner the hot track started to wind down steeply towards the slash of red highway in the distance.

Then Frei heard. It was a chink. Then again, more clearly. A burro slowly climbing the track towards them. Melio crouched in no uncertain manner. Frei stood to the side. As the brown and grey burro jogged round the corner of the track Frei let out a gasp. He called to Melio not to shoot. It was all right. He recognised the rider. It was Apaje, from the mineral analysis office in Belém. His former assistant...

Frei was white with anger. Why? Why? What unearthly motive had Apaje to come here? How did he know of this place?

Frei reasoned with himself. He still might get away with it. Apaje had no control over him now that he had thrown in the job. All right, it was a minor untruth that he still worked for JAPOCHEM, but the old beard trusted him, and Frei had told Melio he could make him rich. There was no disaster. They would send Apaje on his way, soon enough.

It wasn't easy to persuade Melio to allow Apaje on his chicken strip, even to step inside the casa de planta. But the old beard relented and put down his carbine. But Frei was in no hurry to describe Apaje as a splendid fellow to the old beard. Apaje had to leave. That was all that mattered to Frei.

He waited until Melio was out of ear-shot—

"Apaje I want the truth – what are you doing out here?"

"I came to check up on a point—"

"What in hell are you talking about? You followed me, right? Tell me why?"

"Not at all," said Apaje, "how was I to know you'd be here?"

Apaje explained that days after Frei had left his job, there was a discrepancy in the books. You know how scrupulous we must be in JAPOCHEM over receipts and names and addresses, he told Frei, então – all of a week's samples that we got in the post were returned to the owners, but for one sample. This sample had no record of return.

"What are you talking about?" Frei blurted.

"In my records book I had Melio's name down for a stone which was never returned to him. That is why I had to come out here – I keep my books clean and up to date and I don't want to be sued for expropriating a gem that might be worth a fortune!" said Apaje.

Frei was laughing now. Just as Melio came back from the stream with a can of water. Frei pulled a greenish quartz gemstone from his pocket and held it up. The old beard recognised it well enough. It was a piece of the seam in the shallow cave Frei had broken off yesterday.

"There is no mystery about it..." Frei was speaking expansively, extravagant relieved gestures, "I knew all along I hadn't returned this gemstone. Out of a whim I suppose – I decided to come up here. But Melio doesn't want it back. I've seen his spot where he found it – it's worthless. Worth about as much as a piece of green glass. Isn't that true Melio—?"

Frei was taking quite a gamble. But the old beard appeared to trust him. He understood what Frei was saying. Keep quiet on this, old man. We'll soon get rid of this interfering kid Apaje. You and I know the truth. Keep it between us.

"It true..." Melio spoke out clearly, "you can see the cave yourself, gerente," looking Apaje right in the eye, "...nothing but green glass not worth an ant's crap."

Apaje needed some reassuring. He was quite prepared to admit that he had it in for Frei. He mistrusted his former boss from the mineral analysis office. It did strike him – suppose Frei had resigned because he had stolen an incredible stone? The blame for the lost stone might well fall on Apaje. So the younger man believed he must protect himself. He needed to follow his theory through, in order that he might cover his own tracks; and Apaje was a very thorough type.

Melio took him below the over-hang and showed him the shallow cave where the green glass rubbish seamed in the rock. Apaje came out shaking his head. He didn't know as much about samples as Frei, admittedly, but even he could recognise that seam for what it was – worth not a conto.

"You satisfied...?" Frei challenged his former assistant.

"I suppose so."

"Course you are. What you think I am? A thief? Now you can go back to the office fetch out the file and mark it down in receipt, ne?"

"...Well—" Apaje paused. He wasn't quite convinced. A bicho itch clung to his brain. It ticked away there. He could feel the resentment steaming out from the old beard's ears. And Frei, too, made it clear – he wasn't welcome there a moment more.

Apaje dithered and demorarard. He suggested he ride Frei back down to the highway. They could hitch an easy lift from a caminhão to Marabá.

"No thanks..." said Frei, "I'll stick it out here for a day or two. I like it here. It's quite a change from civilizado-wage-work routine, ne?"

"Frei..." Apaje halted beside the burro, he made a game effort to tighten the girth but the burro kicked back, "Frei ... you up to something. Swear to God I don't know what it is – but you up to your throat in big trouble."

"Tchau, Apaje! ..."

"Tchau, you bastard!" Frei waited until not only was the squat brown and grey burro out of sight, but until he could no longer hear the sweet chip chip jog of its hooves. He looked back at the planta thatch hut. He still had a lot of explaining to do. His mind raced ahead.

Melio was pretty quiet that evening. He made a kind of tutu out of bananas and manioc stumps and black beans topped with a shovel-full of farofa. Farofa like a mince Frei's city diet was quite unused to, it was mixed with red dust and wood shavings God knows how they got into it.

Oh yes, there was a change in Melio. A cruel gleam lit up in his eyes. And his silences – they got under Frei's skin. They ate alone. There was no Pei Pa around. And if this worried the old beard he didn't give it away any.

Melio chomped his teeth on the manioc stump, he spat out the pap. Unlike the river bitter growth, this was sweet manioc and it held no poison sap. Melio lit the oil lamp above their heads and casually moved his Italian carbine nearer to his side of the plank table.

"You know what I want . . . ?" the beard murmured.

"I'm sorry?"

"You tell me – why you come here, Frei?"

Frei blushed. The roots of his hair prickled. He had to clear his throat a couple of times. He didn't like the calmness in the old beard's voice.

"I . . ." but it wouldn't come.

"You don't work for JAPOCHEM now, ne?" asked Melio.

"True."

"You resigned, that right?" calm voice, steely sound.

"Yes."

"You saw that stone I sent the company – put it in your pocket and come straight out here. That so?"

How could Frei deny it?

"You don't want anybody from JAPOCHEM learn about this. It may be – you found the biggest emerald claim in all Pará, ne?"

Frei nodded.

"And you come out here to see me . . . maybe think you fix deal with trash poor porceiro no gold teeth forty perus in the yard and prostituta indio, ne?"

"Melio – I thought you said you trusted me?"

"Yes, I did . . ."

"I've done nothing wrong. I haven't cheated you have I? You want me call back Apaje from JAPOCHEM you want them to come in here with big machines and see then how they cheat you. You'd be down on that highway begging contos if they came here . . . know that?" Frei had to work hard.

"What you offer me instead?"

"I offer . . ." Frei picked at his words carefully, "I – we look at this place you found. We – you I mean – you come with me to Belém lay legal mineiro claim all fixed up in front of the lawyer – and I get rich beside you. It's your claim your land – but you need help. You need a guy who can fend off those JAPOCHEM and AMERICAN ZINC and HANNA CORPS civilizado business operators ... I know them, sure I do."

The old beard stood up. He pulled his carbine against his legs. There was a distinct sadness in his face, more of an apologetic quality as if he couldn't quite bring himself to admit he had run out of table napkins. A hesitant manner...

"You with me?" Frei asked, after a moment.

"Yes, Frei..." Melio lowered his chin into his beard, "I show you now. You come. You come. You want to see the place where I found the emerald?"

The old man shouldered his carbine and led Frei across the chicken strip to the incline which Pei Pa raced to the night before. The sky was darker and Melio carried the oil lamp which swung garish white slithers of flame from side to side. Something like exultation gripped Frei. A certain feverishness. A sense of longing and desperation entwined in true saudade style. He was confident, he had engineered for this miracle to happen, his miracle, and nobody was going to come between the dream and the discovery. It was to be his black heart behind a white face, and he was prepared oh Cristo o Senhor to go along with that. If God is a Brazilian and if he understands my longing I must be forgiven.

Melio stood at the exact spot Frei stumbled beside the night previously. Beneath his foot lay the three burial mounds. Melio placed the spluttering lamp on the ground. He leant against his carbine and studied the younger man, this civilizado who had come up on the Morro to return him the beautiful green stone.

"Pei Pa brought me here," Frei said.

"What she say to you?"

"I could hardly understand what she said..."

"Did you ask her what these mounds were?"

"I tried."

"She told you?"

"I don't know ... perhaps she said she meant that they were your children. They had died ... died young ... I'm sorry."

Melio bared his teeth in a mirthless grin. He put all his weight on the carbine and shifted his ankles. He was in no hurry. His eyes were filled with cobra intent. This civilizado says he is sorry ... ah yes ... so he would ...

"It – is this the place, Melio?" Frei glanced about him. It was all hard red earth. No rock formations on this ledge. No place to find precious uncut stones.

"It is..." the beard murmured sadly.

"Please – Melio – don't be absurd you didn't find any stone here ... now did you?" There was a rising panic in Frei's tone. This was no time for any more tests stupid trials or forest tricks.

"In a way," Melio said evenly, "these mounds are my children."

"They what?"

"But in truth, friend – they just graves of three men I killed."

"Why?" Frei tried to sound calm.

"Each season – for the past two years – I send my emerald to a mining company. They send a civilizado – just like you – up here. And he – just like you – wants to cheat me. I kill each one," Melio took a step away from the younger man, the carbine lifted itself easily between his fingers, "...each greedy little civilizado who comes looking for the emerald strike."

Frei, in the sullen damp warm night felt silk sweat beads furrow his eyebrows and channel behind the lobes of his ears. His teeth had a sweet ache in them. As if he had just that minute swallowed a mouthful of rapadura.

"I send the gem to the mineral analysis office of any big company. In a matter of days someone like you comes up here – kicking a burro – with his money deal and his madness about riches and big claims...just like you, my chefe, just like you."

"Why...?" Frei's knees were sponge. Strength like water seeped out of his bones. Dream melting brain flash smashed his skull. He could only whisper...

"Want to know why? Look at me. You tell me, ne?"

Frei told the old beard what he knew now. Yes, nodded Melio, that's it. Frei said – you despise people, you loathe us down there so bad you'd kill for any excuse. The rub is – you got the finest excuse in the world to prove to yourself what bugre greed trash civilizado we all are, right Melio?

Melio smiled, mirthless crack of lips.

"Now you know...chefe," old beard murmured.

Melio gestured with the carbine for Frei to head back towards the hut. The old porceiro held the oil lamp high above their heads so that he could clearly see Frei climb down the incline to the chicken strip.

"You see..." Melio motioned with the rifle for Frei to step

inside the hut, "I understand people like you, mistah . . . I know who you are . . . I seen you before . . . plenty times . . . out here."

Frei could not feel the toes in his own boots. Wet cloth dripped against his flesh. He sat opposite Melio at the plank table. His heart was drumming in his ears, a distant booming more of miniature waves on a Lilliputian shore, nerved pump and blood rush yes, and still live in him. He had to find a way.

"That stone Melio – the good one, where did you get it?"

"I found it, all right . . . right here."

"You sitting on a fortune . . . you understand that? Don't matter what you do to me!"

"I not seeking fortunes . . . you do that bugre."

"I don't believe you any more, Melio . . . there's no rockface you can find an emerald like that around here . . . on this Morro."

The beard lowered his jaw, ". . . Perhaps that so," he whispered.

"Sure, I know that!" Frei regained some of his lost strength, "I know minerals! There is no secret mineral source! Nothing there is!"

"But you'd kill me to find out, you'd come here and find out and then cut my throat for it, ne?" said Melio.

Frei was silent.

"Answer me!" Melio shouted, "You'd kill branco trash like me for it! If you had the chance! If that source existed, ne?"

". . . Yes." Frei's confidence seeped back into him, he felt a carelessness, an unearthly type of abandon, "Yes I'd kill to find the source of such a stone."

Melio sat back and gave out a prolonged sigh. He laid the rifle across his knees. There was an unopened bottle of banana aguardente beneath the table. He reached for it. Frei was amazed at his own temerity. At least he had told the truth. He'd be forgiven. Whatever happened now. He'd never said so true a word in his life before. The honesty made him blush. The old beard pushed a tin beaker across the table at him.

Outside the ichor melt darkness streamed insect rivers, for there was no breeze to take advantage of a guest's favoured position slung across the open door of his host's casa de planta up in the Morro. Melio spoke—

". . . Well then – we can sit and talk of honest things for as long as you like."

Frei could see the madness in the beard's eyes. That waking riot of hate and killer resolve. How could he have been so stupid to let himself fall into such a trap? Why didn't he take Apaje's invitation up – go back down to the highway with him? Too late by far. In deep now. Melio spoke again—

"...talk all we like for – one of us tonight is going to die..."

The old beard said he wanted to sit the night out. Fine by me, answered Frei. Melio wanted his younger guest to dangle before him hang slowly in the Morro breathlessness. Both had a sense of longing and of waiting, and whatever the outcome you can be sure, by light fall, they each would have made a good saudade meal of it.

The younger man studied old beard with his carbine. Perhaps, though he had years on his side, he couldn't match Melio for strength. The porceiro was made of piano wire and chicken gristle sinew. But he had dull eyes, as if with sleep, and they slunk away from Frei when he tried to ambush them. Frei was a civilizado, he was young and flabby compared to old beard; and the banana aguardente trickled too easily on his tongue. But Frei understood the odds. His heart drummed.

Melio was not aware of anything more immediate than his finger on the carbine trigger. He wanted to see this bugre civilizado sweat until blood dripped from his ears. And he was confident, he knew how to stay awake all night waiting for an onça to crash through an earth trap. Melio could sit like a stone in the forest and the bicho climb up his legs and arms until they dug so deep no amount of alcohol could stir them – he wouldn't move a muscle. Perhaps Melio was too sure of himself. The idea of a death, somebody else's death you look forward to is simple enough; but the reality of it, its life cry struck into oblivion heart in panic screaming mind is a different matter. And Melio failed to notice the cana handle machete on the earth floor beneath the plank table. It lay close to Frei's foot.

Ride down the Morro towards the red streak new highway in the distance and it looked like a child's paper ribbon thrown across an overgrown garden lawn. And Apaje had to kick the burro to make any headway. Serra and sloping sertão melted together beside a crashing stream, and when the burro pointedly came to a halt beside the swift water and stone step falls, Apaje gave in. The night was early enough for the mosqus to descend. But they did not cloud around the very edge of the little waterfall.

He unpacked his rêde and slung it between trunks as close to the running water as he could get it. The burro's sack was stuffed with salt meat and there were peach soft cajus tumbling down the waterfall, all he had to do was reach out his hand.

Without a blanket for night cover, at first light he woke shivering. The stepped stream cascaded with a wide leaf covered with a strange green lace substance and broken orange blooms fat as bromelias. Somewhere upstream, during the night, a flame acacia had tumbled into the water; perhaps a victim of rock fall, or the shallow slide of lateritic earth layers vulnerable to the fast flow of water.

Apaje climbed down from the hammock and jumped about to rid the shivering. Close by the stream, even in the barest sertão borders, all around him where he jumped and larked, lay clusters of violet bell-flowers. They were tiny plants only the first of morning sees, come the stetson sun across the Morro ridge and these mini blue hyacinths Brazilians call fleabane (fleas at first light are believed to flock to sticky deaths on the petals) exude a delicious cedar-like fragrance.

Apaje stripped and lay in a stone basin beneath a metre high cascade. He kicked and splashed and shouted out loud with the initial shock. Then the blood began to rush, and he shook his head beneath the waterfall and flame acacia broken blooms barraged him. He'd dry himself with his shirt.

He slung the sheepskin pad over the burro's back and made the animal stand while he girthed it. He kept a caju or two in his pocket and for no other reason than sheer curiosity he wheeled the burro round back up the steep track towards the casa de planta of Melio.

There was something very mysterious about the hut on the Morro. Perhaps Frei's life was in danger. That little wrinkled branco beard with his carbine looked bugre mean.

It took two hours to get back up there and the burro hated every step. Apaje kicked it good and hard up the worst slopes, and even slapped it on the snaffle with the flat of his hand. The burro blinked and skidded from side to side.

Now it was morning lemon light. The sound of *hoi hoi* from whistling frog in a petanga bush, and *zlit zlit* knife the soft air from hairy headed bough perch caboclinho little indian finch; mornings in a high Morro before the humid sun melt are filled with leaves and tall grasses which look as if they are made of sheen steel sheets and painted gloss lacquer.

Apaje was close to the chicken strip. Dazzling reds, lemons and pinks rode the Morro saddle like a burning rider, vengeful espirito santo evil ghost rider pouring vitriol heat colours, clarion of death; flower, fruit and water made victim; morning cavalier armed with the sun shield, merciless steaming scythe, a sabiá scream hiccups and paper darts among low liana finds heat safety there...

Apaje tethered the burro by the track. He climbed to a ledge above the chicken strip. He could lie there and see the entire quinta favela.

At the far end of the strip, where the trees verge a group of Parakana indians stood silently a metre or so inside the forest wall. Apaje shook his head with amazement. He cupped his eyes to see them more clearly against the glare. Yes, there they were ...just standing, quietly watching the hut at the near corner of the strip.

Apaje followed their gaze. As his looked at the shaky little casa de planta, there suddenly came a rifle shot from inside. Apaje rose on to his knees. He craned his eyes.

A moment later a small figure emerged. She was a brown squirrel tall indian girl with a bone tanga across her pubic regions and she was carrying a carbine in one hand. Her other hand was clasped finger tight shut.

The girl ran across the chicken strip. The fat perus bolted in front of her. She handed the carbine to the oldest indian of the group. He had grey frizzled hair and the nipples on his chest hung flat like deflated brown envelopes. He took the gun and broke open the bolt. He raised it high in the air and smashed the carbine against a great oval stone. The open bolt buckled and the stock splintered with an ugly snap.

The other indians scuffled the earth with their hands and made a shallow deep enough to bury the carbine. They quickly kicked the earth and mato verge back over the weapon.

The girl opened her other hand and held up a gleaming green stone to the older Parakana. He took it from her and placed it carefully inside a leather strip he wore tightly wound around his wrist.

The other indios stamped the verge mato undergrowth until the carbine could no longer be detected. The old Parakana gave a word, and they disappeared behind the veil of trees which edged around the chicken strip.

Apaje was terrified. He lay stone stiff still like those giant cellar toads whose golden eyes weep at the first hint of sun, bufo maximus, and they never stir until the light has cooled, the danger evaporated.

He began to shiver again. Even with the heat rising so rapidly. He would wait. He would not twitch for fear of those murdering indio things down there come back. In time ...

Apaje had fried long enough on the ledge. He climbed down an incline and gingerly stepped across the strip. He paused by the door of the hut. It lay half open, and the deep cool shadow the interior created was no welcome to him. He could sense the evil. It whispered and permeated through the planta thatch roof, as the sun's rays twisted the fibres.

Yet he had to go inside. He made himself. He moved quietly, as if that would alleviate the fear. He perched on his toes and leaned closer a step within the doorway. Now his eyes seem accustomed to the gloom.

The old beard Melio lay with his head bent in sleep on the plank table. You'd have thought it was sleep, had it not been for the machete edge which half buried itself into the scrawny neck. Blood streamed in a thick mantle, and flesh gave way to glass pointed bone chip where the blade had come to rest.

Frei sat upright, stiff and poised with his back against the wall, the bullet hole started in his cheek and it emerged somewhere back out the top of his head. He looked quite surprised. As if, perhaps, everything had been going to plan until one minor incident, not even worth considering, had taken it all away from him.

No, that was not being entirely fair to Frei. More in his expression of – hurt child last toy taken from – or – prize winner robbed at last moment by second cheat – or – certain unmistakable sadness in the flat eyes, a singing there, a pained yearning and mellifluous unfulfilment; saudade, again.

Apaje hurried outside into the chicken strip air – a sound of flapping fat perus cock combed hunt for maize. They'd get little this particular morning.

He had to shade his eyes to find the pathway which led back to the track where the burro was tethered. He strode across the clearing, each step felt like a mile walk in deep mud, because all the while – from tree and leaf shadow which made up the wall of green around him from each liquid drip of liana and crease of forest substance in the mato floor – he could believe those dark and truculent indio eyes were watching his every stride. For so many eyes were there, he thought, they were stripping the skin off his body, literally eating into bone, uncovering the marrow of his mind. They knew his thoughts. Branco trash tales told him what the indio could do. The torture they'd inflict if they took him ... there was no escape from a place like this if ...

Apaje knew what to do. He found his burro and kicked it hard down the stony track. He'd empty his mind. If those indio animals were tracking him, he'd forget all he'd seen, and they could peer all they liked into his mind, they'd see nothing. He'd make his mind a hollow. He'd think of nothing. They'd spirit read inside his thoughts, but he'd be safe. (Fear seeped.)

He was kicking that burro like a striker's hair football. (Fear still seeped.) Apaje had heard all those stories about what indians can do to you if they find you – they eat your entrails while you still alive watch them – make you watch make you live while you see them eating you part by part – oh Apaje knew those favela branco trash pinga tales about indio animals.

Burro heave and hand smack on the snaffle, Apaje jog trotted along the track. He filled his mind with such clarity, mould blown into transparent nothingness, void of innocence he prayed it to be not a memory not a flicker of what he had just seen, his being clear as that caju and flame acacia floating waterfall, and if those animal things were close by in the veiled green wall waiting for him watching they could drink his mind until it spill their cup.

Kick that burro.

Ride sun shield.

Only fear vengeance.

And Apaje longed for his civilisation. His analysis hut in Belém. Fantasy tiled Belém houses, royal port town of rubber Kings and mansion river launches rust tilted in jacaré shallows – or Pará as it was called in colonial boom history; avenidas of Fortnum & Mason booted Englishmen, Bates, Wickham, Wallace and the Booth Shipping Line agents for red velvet opera seats and the *Central* on Avenida Presidente Vargas the original English tea shop.

Apaje remembered the antique nostalgia phrase for, if not his Belém, old Pará – quem vai para Pará para.

And the burro skiddled head down in the dust like a pregnant goat. Apaje jounced.

They'd make it.

S.N.A.F.U.

TWINS OF GREEN, light and dark, play in the forest on the banks of the rivers where the red brown mud yawns as if idle with heavy river flow and liana drags graceful wedding train rot in the mato molhado.

Our little skiff of hollowed out wood was knifing the shallows.

Way back, early as 1946, Colonel Bandeira Coelho had already discovered the true source of the Rio Verde, this lonely trib of the greater Rio Guaporé on the Bolivia/Brazil border meandering through the flat-topped Ricardo Franco mountains liquid helix even now quite unpeopled red sandstone slake shores for the rarely found black cat onça, night serra panther but made a little smaller, so ... what was I doing there?

For weeks now, Coffee and I had taken off into that marsh river area of many branches which lay between the Guaporé and the Verde; we stole softly along the sleek brown waters from first light to the height of each day's sun when then you just had to halt. Take shade. Put the lighter to the leeches. Pray the Acriflex tube lasts out. And wait for the soft mosqu descent of early evening when we could go on for a couple more hours.

Coffee was a river man. Take you anywhere, so long as you got the sack of beans and the dried salt beefy and a decent hammock. Perhaps we have all got too soft these days. Coffee boasted that the first estrangeiros he took out for weeks (but this was ten years ago or more) – they had ordinary cheap rêdes without any extras, just net hammocks to throw between trees; now, both he and I were careful to bring these new hammocks with a built-in sleeve of mosquiteiro netting.

Coffee used to shrug when I poked fun at him. I told him – look now, Coffee, listen, you the same as me, you ain't the tough barqueiro you once said you'd been. He looked up at me as if to say – when last time, chefe, did you let an onça jump you out of nowhere, ne?

Coffee smiled—

"Maybe ... the mosqus got bigger in the last ten years, you filho da puta, hah?"

Out here, of course, what we had been doing was none too legal. To the east there were two groups of Nambiquara indians, one on the Rio Sararé, the other on the Rio Galera; I had wanted to make contact with them, and I knew FUNAI, the new Indian Protection Service, wouldn't take me there themselves – they were so terrified of what I'd find.

Out here, these two groups had had a very bad time. The small missão service employed a German priest who simply never went near the indians. And FUNAI liked to imagine they didn't exist any more. For these Nambiquara, of recent times, had been decimated by measles.

I had already been to the coronel at FUNAI in Cuiabá, the capital of Mato Grosso, and when I told him I wanted to go up the Galera and Sararé he smiled and said – oh, yes, tell you what I do; I write to Brasilia for permission for you, I not give it, and you wait ten months for them to reply, you want to wait ten months?

No thanks, I said. I knew what the reply would be anyway, I said.

Coffee took me up the rivers. We always packed sacks of sugar, maize, good black beans and plenty of cardboard haberdashery boxes of coloured glass beads.

The Nambiquara groups were very small, the Sararé was down to eight (although they said others were hunting), and the Galera was down to nineteen indians. Once, there were two hundred. Less than four years ago there were eighty. Time dies doesn't it?

Coffee never liked them. Said they made him itch. Made him take up scratching something quite chronic. And – Cristo they smelled! he complained.

The groups got used to us. They often stood on the river bank, brown waif skin and bone not one more than five foot three inches tall, mouthing chattering whispers yellow whites of their eyes crinkling in the play of sunlight from tree to tree.

I used to tell Coffee that it was crazy they so much liked white sugar. That kind of sugar sends you to the dentista quicker than any sweet natural cana stick would.

"What the hell ..." Coffee liked his americano style drawl, although he only spoke Portuguese, "... they nothing but bunch of cracky bugre indios ..." and he'd seen a lot of John Wayne bangy-bangy movies in a mosqu and tick pit Sunday nights in Bom Futuro down river, "... that all they are, chefe, they ain't got no teeth anyway to worry about, they lose their pearlies long before they reach age of twelve, little Englander guys like you make me piss in my pants talk about dentistas load of nationalised communista never pay nothing free health bullcrap you got! No wonder all you guys in Great Britain so fucking broke. A bugre indio don't get nothing free man if I can help it ... he just pig-shit bottom of the list of the bottom of the list, ne?"

Coffeee used to grimace when I gave sacks of food to the indian groups. You could see the bile rise up in him. He just couldn't believe it – there's this stupid motherfucking britisher come all this way and all he can do buy white sugar sacks for a couple of animal indio things who don't give a fuck one way or the other you live or die! Cristo!

But there was a bright side to all this. Coffee and I liked our cana fermented pap liquor bottles which we could fill up at almost any river-side halt where there was a casa on stilts, and mosqus nothing! – I could tell him all the tales in the world about Europe and cities and friends, and he dreamed of our old world, of our spires and our decadences, our wars and our museums, and almost anything else that sprung to his mind—

"Take girls, for example," he said.

"Fine ..."

"They say – go to England – ask a girl out – and she hit the sack with you so quick don't even need ask you if got clap or not, ne?"

"Untrue."

"You lying to me, son! I know it! I been told! I have!"

He screamed away at me like that, and even if you are thinking the rhetoric is indeed John Wayne mannerism gone crazy, I swear to God that was how Coffee spoke, how a lot of Brazil nuts spoke, all the time, and although it was in their native Portuguese – this was the only means of getting their inflections across.

"Now look here ... chefe, wake up, Cristo, wake will you ... ain't it true? Never need spend money on a Great British girl take her out once she lying in the park with her legs wide open, ne?"

But I was already fast asleep cana pap soaked and God aid me that I do not dream about Coffee's mad brasileira pig chauvinism, that was all!

We had strayed upstream a long way past the Galera river, but there was not a chance of reaching the porto on the Rio Cabixi meeting with the Guaporé before evening mosqu fall the speed we paddled at: when, we were suddenly and agreeably surprised by the sight of a lonely hunched figure potter putt pooting his outboard motor towards our wood craft with such accuracy Coffee thought the guy was trying to ram us.

He was Chino. Cambodia-born missionario lived all his adult years out here, confirmed Protestant, manic and possessive indian lover, he demorarared some distance north nearer to the highway up Vilhena and on to Rondonia with his own group of indians, Nambiquara certainly, and if he could help it he never emerged from the forest and the trees he and his indians saturated themselves with. Word said Chino could run and commune and sing and play with his group like he was born an indio toddler. And they worshipped him. And Chino was famous among the river people in this corner of Bolivian Brazil.

I had met him quite often before in this region. But if the company I kept became too much the bugre branco white river trash and if the cana pap fermented stuff was flowing too freely he would express his disdain and slide off into the river with a hasty apology, muttering something about how late it was; can you imagine a river person in these reaches paddling into the blue night brown water talking about time!

In the past, Chino had chided me for my liberal humanitarian nonsense. If I mentioned the word *ecology* he would crack up: shouting at me – nothing but an indigenous groupie you are. And I raised the cana pap bottle to my lips and told him what I thought of yellow-coloured missionario carpetbaggers of indio souls, masochistic swagmen burglars with nothing better to do than take away their moon and sun spirits the forest gave them and instead thrust God and Jesus novo tales when all the while this Vilhena/Rondonia highway coming through to destroy these indios and make them twice as confused as they were before. At least, that was how I saw it.

Chino cut his outboard motor and drifted beside us. Coffee looked at him and sniffed as if to say – whole rio full of nothing but estrangeiro indio lovers, soon it get so crowded out here there'll be more indio lovers than indios whole damn Mato Grosso State, Cristo!

"You been up that Galera river where you shouldn't?" Chino grinned at me.

"Sure ..."

"Feeding indios like they pigeons or etcetera, ne?"

"Right again ..."

"FUNAI know you here?"

"No ..."

"You running terrible risk. They find out they send the river police out for you. You get arrested. Take you one hell of a pace up to Guajará Mirim that the end of your visa out here, Take you across to Bolivia frontier and you never get back no how!"

"FUNAI go crawl up its own ass ... !"

"No way talk about Ministry of Interior."

"Don't be such a creep, Chino – what they ever done for you?"

He stopped. He casually rolled his outboard wire over his fingers. I think I had made my point. There was something wrong. Something had disturbed him. He wasn't too keen on FUNAI either. But I wasn't going to get it out of him unless I took him to the river's edge and insisted we brewed green leaf chá de mato out of my saucepan, and stretched the rêdes for a while between the trees. He shrugged solemnly. Fine, he said. Coffee snorted.

"What is it, Chino ... ?"

"You'd only laugh ..."

"I'm in stitches, what is it ... ?"

"Something serious has happened to my group."

"Your indians."

"I had to go up to Arenapolis. By when I got back last week – they'd all gone!"

"What all gone?"

"Every damn Nambiquara I got gone!"

"I don't believe it ..."

"Not a trace not a mark!"

"Incredible!"

Chino looked at me hard to be sure I wasn't laughing.

"Just incredible!" again.

I could tell Coffee was having trouble. He wanted to double up collapsing with giggles. And I too could have done so. But I kept a straight face. Here was this famous manic encarregado sertanista spent all his life with his indians now telling us he lost the whole group don't know where in hell they gone to! I could have died.

"Where were they last, Chino?"

"Up by Ruy Barbosa."

That seemed to me to be dangerously close to the Vilhena highway.

"How many did you have?"

"Twenty-eight last count."

"A capitão with them?"

"Capitão Luis."

"He like you?"

"All I ever told him you must cut down marrying your own son's daughters. He can't afford them all. Too old. Otherwise we're bosom."

"You made them crop enough this season?"

"Absolutely."

"No fazendeiro offered them slash-and-burn wages?"

"They seen six brancos all their life. Except for the Capitão Luis – I took him to Porto Velho once."

"My heaven ... Chino, you got a problem!" I said unhelpfully.

You don't often cruise down the river in your little humble wooden canoe meet up with a missionario supposed to be ace dog of the hard soul racket and he tell you he suddenly lost all his lambs don't know can't think and how on earth, they ...

"What'll you tell FUNAI?"

"I'll murder them!"

"They anything to do with it?"

"Wasting my time make me demorara up in Arenapolis all those days."

"What was it up there?"

"Conference."

"What about?"

"Indian control/protection/care ..." he had to smile. And that was my cue to burst out. Coffee joined me. We rolled about on the ground in hysterics. Eventually Chino stopped using the cha straw as a laugh strangle and he did join in.

After we sobered up, Chino asked me—

"Got any ideas?"

"None. What I know about indios?"

"Neither have I."

"Up by Ruy Barbosa?"

"Five river kilometres further north."

"They heard about the new highway?"

"The Capitão Luis told them."

"They heard it government policy to move them north of the highway beyond Vilhena?"

"Luis told them."

"And that the land bugre rotten north up there by Vilhena?"

"They been told."

"And it your duty c/o FUNAI take them there end of this dry season?"

"I never had the heart to tell them."

"But Chino – don't be so stupid, maybe the Capitão Luis already guessed. Maybe he saying chefe Chino fucked us, ne!"

"I had thought of it."

"Course you had. Stands to sense. So don't pretend to me it's a big mystery!"

"I been a fool."

"Sure . . ."

"I should have told them first—"

"Not let river trash tell the Capitão Luis. I can hear the river trash talk. You know – one of these days big yellow steel claw caterpillar cat coming to chew up all you bugre indios end of the world coming you shit brown animal things!"

Harsh as it all sounded, there was room for a lot of heart; Chino was wounded, and he knew – though we were at opposite ends of the integrate-or-make-zoos-for-them argument – I was not like a FUNAI employee coming out in all sneers spots and grease grimace with his so fuck you missionario innuendoes.

Chino cried. And Coffee insisted he drink the cana pap do him world of good. We ate a lot of salt beefy that day. And come the mosqus descent in the early evening Chino was quite drunk. Very funny when he was drunk, too. No control of his legs. He said he'd try both the Galera and the Sararé in the next few days. But for all he knew his group could just as easily have slipped south into Bolivia. What he do then? He asked. Misery faced looking at me.

If all else failed, his last resort was the Rio Verde. And that was no easy task. There were few river huts. And groups like semi-contacted Nambiquara had a strange respect, a caution made out of forest spirits for valleys filled with onça and high serra sides. Mountains gave them an uncomfortable feeling. They were afraid of the presence of high mato walls like the Ricardo Franco plateau peaks.

In the darkness picking ticks Chino told me certain things I already knew about his Nambiquara. And I was falling asleep. Then he leaned across and kicked me and said—

"I ever tell you about that amazing americano woman up at the Chácara outside Cuiabá?"

No he hadn't. My eyes prickled every time I heard a jacare splash sound below us in the soft liquid river flow. Coffee snored out loud. And Chino told me about this americano woman – I'll call her Patricia although that was not her real name – who came to Brazil to look after indians. And as it was Chino's account, albeit with the aid of fermented cana, I wanted to put it down exactly as he told it to me.

"You never heard tell of Patricia and the measles?' he asked.

"No ..."

"Jesus God it was amazing!"

"If it is pornographic I'm interested."

"Filho da puta, you limey fucker indige groupie listen to this ......"

The Chácara Ambulatorio is a clinic for indians. It stands on a bald scrub corner of the Rio Cuiabá some twelve kilometres outside the capital of Mato Grosso. There is a fazenda-like dwelling and a few sheds in the compound. To reach the Chácara you must take a difficult winding route through a neighbour farm of bananas. The Chácara has neither a telephone nor a radio.

Basically, this was the second clinic solely designed for the indigenous in the south-west of Brazil. It was controlled, naturally enough, by FUNAI the new indian protection service who, in turn were controlled by the Ministry of the Interior. FUNAI's offices were in the capital Cuiabá. This Chácara (which means rural homestead) posed many problems for the FUNAI employers in the capital, too many perhaps.

To begin with, although the safe at the Chácara was stocked with medicines, the key to the safe was kept in the Cuiabá offices of FUNAI. The safe was only opened when a visiting Red Cross dignitary for example turned up on a goodwill mission. The doctor – who naturally preferred working for big business company commissions – avoided going up to the Chácara as much as he could. He collected his stipend from FUNAI, but that didn't encourage him to drive out there twelve kilometres to dirty his white jacket on these indios who were going to die off no matter what he did. And it was a common joke in Cuiabá that, soon enough, there will be more FUNAI employees in the whole of Brazil than there are indios. And you know . . . sometimes those indios, sick but still fit enough to make it, would travel four hundred kilometres to get to the Chácara for treatment. And there were problems no chemist could precisely explain – why, a case in point, do some indios react very badly to the vaccines? – or perhaps could explain if time and money enough was provided for a field study. And problems FUNAI themselves had to honestly tackle, though the final decisions seemed so cruel: suppose an indio has got a type of leishmaniasis – slow rot fungus of the mouth and the nose and the throat difficult to cure even with concentrated doses of antimony injections – he comes to the Chácara with three-year-old advanced lesions of this disease, it would cost five hundred dollars to start the victim on the vaccines, the pain could be resolved a little, but nothing could check an inevitable death. So the five hundred dollars could be better spent elsewhere. If the victim was lucky a death in the quick shape of pneumonia might strike.

Patricia volunteered to work in the Chácara, outside Cuiabá. She wanted to help the indios.

She had lived all her life in one State – Idaho; her husband had been a successful insurance executive; and the family of four, they had a son and a daughter, lived fatly in Idaho. After her husband's sudden death, Patricia looked around at herself, saw her children married and happily settled, saw the big white wood frame house which was home, and she made a decision. It was the first decision she had truthfully taken which involved more than domestics since she had been wed. She sold the house and traded in the two cars. She put all the furniture up for auction and she gave away her clothes. Patricia took a course in lower grade home nursing, and shared what money she had in the bank with her children. She applied for a work visa in Brazil on an American exchange compact with the Brazilian Government, and, as luck would take her, she was offered a post as nurse-in-charge of the Mato Grosso Chácara, outside Cuiabá.

The white-coated doctor told her that, in effect, he was in charge, but he was too busy to keep coming up to the Chácara, and she mustn't waste his time with petty errands; so, really, the Chácara became Patricia's kingdom. She ruled it her way.

Within a year her Portuguese was a mud rambling kind of lingua anything you like to call it American slang indio garble talk and High School influenced *portanhol.* But she could get her point across. She had a violent temper, and sometimes she tore such strips off those secretary girls and clerks in the FUNAI Cuiabá offices – they ran for cover.

Only her great friend Dona Cecilia, in the FUNAI offices, would stand up for Patricia. The Dona knew zeal and crazy americano spirit was the only way of getting anything out of FUNAI, and Patricia had all that.

And Patricia worked so hard. She slaved her guts out to heal those indios who managed the journey up to her clinic for the indigenous. Sometimes missionarios brought in very bad cases for her. They flew their Cessnas and Pipers and Comanches in and drove the sick brown animal things up to the Chácara. But that slowed down when FUNAI became increasingly reluctant to pay missionarios their gasoline overheads for these trips. Sometimes a guy would wait a week arguing with the coronel at FUNAI for his expenses.

It was two years ago now. The Chácara had begun to run down. FUNAI hadn't paid any wages to the clerks for three months. A *delay* in Brasilia was the excuse. An unfortunate red tape confusion. Then, when the coronel himself discovered his wages had been cut off as well, things got really serious. And he departed for Brasilia. He stayed away months, and with the exception of Dona Cecilia, FUNAI's offices in Cuiabá began to fall apart.

The white-coated doctor never went out to the Chácara. The electricity was cut off in the Chácara, FUNAI hadn't paid its bills for the month. The kerosene container for the icebox was returned but the dealers refused to send out a new one until their bill was paid. It was one of those indescribable Brazilian events. Everybody hung on knowing they would get their wages in the end, but nobody could explain what had gone wrong. And the coronel was nowhere to be seen.

It was a February. The rains still coming. And a truck arrived, driven by a gibbering Brazil nut guy who was in a great hurry to dump his load and drive out fast. Jesus, he was all ants in his pants red ass terror.

Patricia had two assistants. They were girls in their teens who lived in Cuiabá. They had less medical knowledge than Patricia even had. The three nurses helped the truckload of sick indios down from the open caminhão. The gibbering driver jumped back into his cabseat and accelerated away. An epidemic had come to the Chácara.

All the indians were semi-contacted Nambiquara. They came from a maloca close by the Rio Sararé. There were eight women and six children between the ages of three and ten. The Nambiquaras had an advanced stage of measles. They all showed red to yellow flaking of the skin. A fierce dry cough. And a stream of mucous membrane catarrh poured forth from each one. The children dripped a continual diarrhoea, and most of the women were so weak they could do nothing but lie prone in the hammocks Patricia slung for them under the shed roof.

There were a number of other indios staying at the Chácara; various Kadiweu, Yanomami and Kalapalo (Patricia loved all the Kalapalo, she said they had the sweetest disposition of all the groups she'd met) and they were terrified at the sight of the new arrivals. These Nambiquara were highly contagious and within two hours most of the other clinic inmates had fled into the forest along the Cuiabá Rio.

Worse still – Patricia's assistants took one look at the fleeing Kalapalos and they too decided they had had enough of the Chacara. They walked out. Patricia was alone. Well, almost alone; for she didn't know it, at the time, but there was one old indian, a Bororo Capitão from Gomes Carneiro, who was making his way towards the Chácara across country with a strange swelling beneath his armpit. He was Capitão Pedro.

It was a Friday evening. And the two girls had taken the only jeep at the Chácara. Patricia was trapped there. She could not get at the medicines in the safe for the office in Cuiabá had the key. The icebox was dead. The electricity was cut off. And she had fourteen shapes swinging in their hammocks in the shed outside dying on her.

She walked five kilometres to the banana fazenda. The fazendeiro allowed her to use the telephone. And she called the FUNAI office in the capital. She got through, by a stroke of luck, to the white-coated doctor.

"I want to speak to Dona Cecilia, quick!"

"She left. She's on holiday. She'll be back in a fortnight."

"This is Patricia here!"

"Hallo Patricia."

"I got an epidemic.I got fourteen Nambiquaras here and they'll be dead by Monday if you don't come up here with the key to the safe so I can get the vaccine out! You understand!"

He didn't. He asked her to describe their condition. She was emphatic.

"Then, it's too late," he replied, "the vaccine won't help them. Nothing will. They'll have to die. I'm sorry."

Patricia screamed and raved down the telephone; the old fazendeiro on the porch who had been listening scuttled down the wood steps.

"I want that fucking safe opened! Hear me!"

The doctor tried to reason with her. She wouldn't listen. She explained how everybody had deserted her. How she was alone with no electricity with nothing to cook with and on and on. The doctor was looking forward to his evening tennis game. He put the phone down on Patricia.

The farmer warned Patricia he didn't want her on his land if she was contaminated with bugre indio grippe. She had best not come back again. She swore at him. She advised him where he could stuff his bananas.

Capitão Pedro was a canny old wrinkle. He walked, canoed and hitched lifts from Gomes Carneiro south-east from Cuiabá on the Rio São Lourenco, where the main Bororo maloca lay, to get to Patricia's Chácara. He wanted that swelling under his arm looked at. A few days' rest at the clinic would suit him fine.

It so happened he got to the Chácara when Patricia was away telephoning. The Capitão hunted about until he found this groaning snivelling shitting shed of near corpses of Nambiquara in their hammocks, and he felt concerned. Concerned for himself. He knew death rattle of indio grippe. And these Nambiquara were threequarters on their way to meet their forest spirits.

Patricia was hurrying back to the clinic across the banana plantation when she stumbled into this dirty old indio who appeared to be retreating from the Chácara. The indio told her he was a Capitão from Gomes Carneiro, he had come for medical aid, but when he saw the state of those other indio inmates, the Capitão Pedro shook his head, he had no intention of staying there to pick up death grippe too.

"Now wait a minute ..." said Patricia. "You hold on there. I could use you out here."

"No you can't. I'm not going to die in your clinic, I came here to get better."

"I'll heal your arm – I can give you something for it."

"No thanks."

"Big old Capitão like you speak Portuguese like you do – you afraid of a little grippe?"

"I certainly am. I'm sixty-five. I'm the oldest Bororo Capitão whole State of Mato Grosso. I aim to continue being the oldest Capitão."

"I'm not afraid of the measles."

"Don't worry me."

"So why should you be? I'm only a woman."

"Don't care."

"You come straight back with me and I'll give you a hammock in the main house where I sleep. You'll be safe."

"No thanks . . . you want to see me you come out to me here and bring me my medicine. I want my medicine. But I'm not going in there die with bugre Nambiquara grippe."

What with the fazendeiro and now this scheming wily old indio it just seemed everybody was against her. And she was powerless to help the dying little brownskin mellow eyes with soft groans and dry coughs and hammocks covered with diarrhoea.

That night she cried. Tears bucketed down her face. She could hear the moans from the shed across the compound. She made one last walk over to the shed. She stood by the open door. She studied the shadows of the hammocks. Already certain hammocks had ceased to sway. The smaller rêdes where the children were. The dead have no need to swing from side to side to allow for a little breeze.

In the morning she discovered four dead children and two adult women dead. She ran across the fields to try to persuade the Capitão to help her. But he wouldn't touch the bodies. Single-handed, Patricia washed the bodies and sealed their orifices. She laid them out on a plank table inside the main house and covered them with palm leaves.

She was dizzy with fatigue. She could only wait for the others to die. By the afternoon, three more Nambiquara succumbed. And the old indio out in the fields was persuaded to help. She had gone back to him again—

"If you don't help me – so help me God – I'll tell the police. So help me I'll strip you of your *Capitão*. I'll fill your swelling with more poison. And I'll give you no food no water nothing will I from here!"

Capitão Pedro washed the bodies with reluctance. He cut down more palm leaves and Patricia allowed him to cover himself with a whole bottle of disinfectant, because he was under the delusion this tart smelling liquid was a kind of measle preventative. In the evening, the Capitão followed Patricia to the corner of the open door and they looked in on the five remaining hammocks. Yes, they were all swinging faintly. But the groans and the dry coughs like mato seca beneath burra hooves chorused little hope. Bugre death moon rider spirit of the forest was fast approaching.

They both sat up late into the night talking, Patricia, if only to keep her mind off the horror of the measle epidemic in the shed outside, plied the Capitão with questions. She was curious about him. He was unlike any indio she had met before. His canniness. His obvious desire to preserve himself in the face of insuperable measle odds. The near branco style determinism he had.

"You speak good Portuguese, Capitão."

"I speak good."

"Speak Bororo too?"

"No."

"No?"

"I forget how to speak . . ."

"But you don't forget the customs, the rituals?"

"I forget . . ."

"And dances?"

"I forget . . ."

"And Bororo tales Bororo stories?"

"No no . . . forget."

"Aw come on . . . ! What the hell is it with you Capitão?"

"I got a lighter I got a wristwatch – it doesn't work but I got a wristwatch – I got one pair of trousers and a pair of sandals – and I can walk into town like any branco in the day time and I can buy cafezinho in the Avenida Presidente Vargas, right centro in the avenida buy a cup of coffee I can. I don't want to remember Bororo tales."

"But you ain't got any means of identification?"

"One day will have . . ."

"You nothing in the city – police say all indios must leave by nightfall."

"One day I stay . . . spend night in a hotel."

"That what you dream about?"

"That what . . . yes."

"Driving a car?"

"And too ..."

"Buying a house?"

"One day too ..."

"Taking a wage holding down a job?"

"And that too – even at my age and I'm the oldest—"

"I know I know you the oldest Bororo Capitão all Mato Grosso State."

"True ..."

"Capitão – what do Bororo say when you die what happens in Bororo myth?"

"I forget ..."

"The hell you do! You just too lazy. I won't feed you tomorrow. I won't mend your wound."

"I suddenly remember ... !"

"That's right your sweet ass you do!"

"When a Bororo die – it is never a natural thing – for when you die you migrate to Arara. But your death is a wound. Your death hurts the world. Hurts the living. So those left alive must hunt the mori in the forest. The mori has done the killing to Bororo and the mori must be hunted down before the dead indio spirit is happy again. I forget the rest ..." the Capitão's voice trailed off.

"Can you recite to me a Bororo poem?"

"No ..."

"You just put your goddamn lazy mind to it Capitão!"

"I can't recite ..."

"In exchange for one poem I'll give you all the empty Coca-Cola cans down at FUNAI's office next week."

"All right. I recite. I recite poem my father used to say. He said it at night when the sun go down and there is no more red reflection on the river surface. I recite that, yes?"

"What is it called?"

"Not called anything. It is a questions poem. It asks questions."

"Go right ahead."

"My father did it every night and we all listened to him."

"Off you go."

The Capitão dramatically stood up and leaned out of the open doorway which looked across the compound towards the shed where the dying Nambiquara lay. He breathed in deeply. His chest grew. He raised his chin towards the humid blue black.

"... Are you there cera (ibis)?
Are you there ki (tapir)?

Are you there boro (lip plugs)?
Are you there ewaguddu (buriti palm)?
Are you there arore (caterpillar)?
Are you there paiwe (hedgehog)?
... Ho ho ho."

The Capitão beat his chest with finality. He stepped back inside with a sheepish grin on his face. As if to say – my goodness my Bororo relatives must have been real idiots to do all that rubbish.

" ... Thank you, Capitão."

"I forget anything else." He sounded adamant.

"I want to ask you – oh, just one more thing."

"Yes?" with no great enthusiasm.

"What are the most important things in the world to a Bororo – like things, I mean – objects—?"

"Most important objects in the world are – you must remember, that it is only those things – the very first of things and the very last of things that matter. And you must live your life trying to collect those things – when you find them – those first of things and those last of things. You collect those, and you will think like a Bororo thinks ... or anyway, that's about all I can remember about how a Bororo thinks."

On the Sunday morning, there was not a single rêde swinging in the shed opposite. And the Capitão was frightened. because now the last of those Nambiquara things had died, and the very last things made him nervous. He hid in the fields. Patricia washed the corpses and sealed their orifices and laid them out under palm leaves.

She'd have her revenge on those people down at FUNAI. She stood in the shed watching the lifeless and empty hammocks so still and shrunken without any body to carry. She cried to herself. They were my children, she told herself, and I let them down. They were my babies, and I could do nothing for them. And even the Capitão can see how weak and useless I am beside an epidemic like this. The hammocks hung very still in the heavy air. The diarrhoea was caked and smelt pungent sweet. She would have to bury them. Indeed, she would have to bury more than the hammocks! Those bodies had to be dealt with immediately.

Patricia armed herself with a bottle of green fluid. She approached the banana fazendeiro's porch. She held up the bottle and shook it at the old farmer.

"Don't you dare come nearer," he shouted at her, "you got indio disease. You stay away! No telephone!"

"You don't allow me use the telephone I'll drop this bottle on the porch. It's got enough indio germs in it to kill you and all your fucking bananas off in half a day!"

She got to the telephone.

Patricia knew the white-coated doctor's home number. She spoke clearly, and without a trace of emotion. She wasn't going to show that creep money greedy Cuiabána sloth any tears.

"All the Nambiquara are dead. What are you going to do now?" she asked.

"I won't come up. I'll send you fourteen wood coffins by special delivery first thing Monday morning. The motorista will bring them straight down to the cemitério."

The doctor's voice was angry, but distant; he sounded as if he just didn't want to know. Everything was now becoming too much trouble for him at FUNAI and he was beginning to hate the commission. He might throw it in. Wasting his time with indios dying of measles. Much better things to do with his time. There was novo Brasil to work for.

She walked back thinking of all those analgesics inside the locked medicine safe, all those vitamins she could have saved those indios with, all those antibiotics and vaccines. Too late now. Something bled and died inside her.

She remembered a phrase her son often used in his letters from Korea to her, years ago, in the fifties, when he was barely eighteen. *There's only one thing you have to remember out here, mother, and it goes like this – Situation Normal All Fucked Up.*

"... S.N.A.F.U.," she said to herself. Yes, that was it. That was it. That was how you described a situation like this. She'd try and teach that to the Capitão. Patricia was smiling.

But she never did see that Capitão Pedro again. The old indio sloped off through the trees on the edge of the Cuiabá Rio. His toes patterned the red brown mud banks where he walked. He'd had enough of modern medicine. Crazed americano women doctors. This Chácara where you were meant to get well was a sort of mortuary for Nambiquara indios who had been silly enough to go bathing in rivers to get rid of the fevers they had contracted. He was going home to Gomes Carneiro. Tell them tales about talking all night long to branco americano women. That would suffice for him. He was still the oldest Capitão.

The caminhão arrived at eight o'clock on Monday morning. The motorista – after a considerable amount of protestation – helped this angry americano woman to dump the fourteen indio bodies into the plain wood coffins. Best funeral any indio had for a long time, he thought.

Patricia sweated at it. She wrapped each cadaver up in one of the filthy hammocks as a kind of winding sheet. She lifted every box and piled them up on the caminhão. She tamped the lids down with nails. Oh, she worked at it. The anger in her drove her to do it.

"Where you want me to take them now?" asked the nervous motorista.

"I show you," she replied.

She stood in the back of the caminhão as the motorista turned off Aveninda Presidente Vargas towards the offices of FUNAI. The coffins slid over the damp vegetable floor of the truck. As the truck stopped outside the front steps of the FUNAI building, she ordered the motorista to back the caminhão as far up the steps as he could. A small crowd formed to watch. Heads popped out of the FUNAI windows.

Patricia tripped the hammers on the caminhão wood flap and she jumped down. She banged on the door of the truck. She shouted to the motorista to operate the automatic lift.

As the entire back portion slowly rose in the air, all the coffins tumbled on to the marble FUNAI steps. They made an almighty clatter. People shrieked out aloud. Those Cuiabánas really panicked. Girls and clerks ran out the back exit of FUNAI's offices. Cars came to a halt in the street. Children ran forward.

"S.N.A.F.U.!" murmured Patricia.

It took a few days to right everything. But life at the Chácara did return to normal chaos. The coronel returned from Brasilia with the wages. The electricity was switched on at the Chácara. And there were a further sixteen measle victims among the Nambiquara on the Sararé.

The loved Dona Cecilia was not yet back from her holiday, and Patricia felt alone and isolated. She was told not to return to the Chácara until further notice. The inevitable occurred – the coronel demanded an explanation from Patricia for her conduct. She really blasted him. The safe which was always locked. The doctor who would never go up to the clinic. The callousness and the inefficiency of the whole goddamn place. The coronel sighed. You see, he said, he had been so busy with the problem of the wages in Brasilia.

He told her that there was no excuse for the coffins episode. He would write to Brasilia. She would have to leave FUNAI. Anyway, he said, there were lots of Brazilians who could take her place.

Like hell, she told herself.

"Now Patrisha I am sad about this, but this is final between us, this is end."

"Fine by me ..." she lied, the tears welled up.

"And Patrisha – until I hear from Brasilia to the contrary which I won't, you are forbidden the Chácara. No going up there, at all. Ever again. Understood?"

"Understood ..."

"Next week I put the icebox back, and I send the doctor up there, and I have a proper butane stove put in."

"What in hell for? President goddamn Richard Nixon paying the Chácara a visit?"

"You don't joke, ne? Two very important British people coming here. Friends of Brazil. Friends of FUNAI. From the Primitive Peoples' Fund in London. They are visiting the Chácara."

"The Primitive Peoples' What—?"

"Robin and Marika from London."

The coronel made it clear to Patricia she must not go up to the Chácara, on any pretext; and if he, the coronel, could see to it he would make sure she was kept away from Robin and Marika. He was tough and uncompromising, and he made no bones about it. Patricia had had her day. Now she was finished. She must go back to where she came from. There was no place for her left in Brazil.

Goodbye Cuiabá. Hallo Pocatello, Idaho. Patricia smiled wanly. In three weeks she's celebrate her sixty-fifth birthday. America the Brave I still love ya! Take me!

...... the damnedest thing happened to me. I was demoraring about in Cuiabá Airport doing my best to look insignificant, and that is a difficult task for a foreigner out here, when I bumped into Patricia. She was waiting for her plane out. It was her last few moments in this bum town. And I quickly introduced myself.

I don't think she was too impressed by my appearance. Anyway, the short of it being – there she was, nobody to say goodbye to, (where was Dona Cecilia?) alone, no thanks from anybody for her work at the Chácara, and me asking a stream of stupid questions.

I remembered the tale of the coffins, and Chino's boozy account of it that night on the river with Coffee. And I had heard since quite a lot more about the famous visit of Robin and Marika Hanbury-Tenison. They never did, in fact, get to meet Patricia. But when they were taken up to the Chácara they weren't fooled one little bit. The electricity was working, so was the icebox, and the medicine safe was unlocked, and there were a few indios in the sheds in various stages of repair. For both Robin and Marika could read between the signs, and when they completed their tour under FUNAI auspices they produced a very hard hitting report, and it was no whitewash of the whole indio problem.*

It was just my bad luck to bump into Patricia in this ironic fashion at the airport. She was chilly, American matron style aloof, and who in hell are you whippersnapping at me minute I'm alone and trying to leave this snafu country! But she accepted a soft drink from me at the bar. She had a quarter of an hour or so.

"Was all that coffin tale true, Patricia?"

"Some of it."

"Did you really unload those boxes on FUNAI steps?"

"It's been a little exaggerated."

"Chino told me. A while back. I always wanted to meet you – never could catch up with you."

"Chino told you?"

"Right . . ."

"Well . . ." gentle drawl, humorous glint in her eyes, kind of nodding condescension, "you shouldn't believe all those cracky tales sertanistas tell. Chino – I know Chino well – he got too big an imagination. Lets it run wild. Too much living in the forest pretending he's a damn indio. I always tell him that."

Patricia was guarded with me. She was distrustful. She hadn't known me long enough. And, anyway . . . what a time to choose!

I was saying goodbye to her. Bon voyage and all that. The boy took her trunk and her two suitcases. She had no trophies I

* *Report of a Visit to The Indians of Brazil*, by Robin Hanbury-Tenison, on behalf of the Primitive Peoples Fund, January-March 1971.

could see, no mementoes, no souvenirs, there was a tough quality about Patricia, a strength lacking in all sentiment, perhaps she'd call it hogwash; so neat and tidy in her grey cotton suit and white sneakers, streaked hair pulled back and age, years, the passing of days too soon too sudden to ever account for measured on the backs of her hands in brown dimple spots. She was going. I followed after her.

"Excuse me ... Patricia – you think you ever might come back?"

"Nope ..."

"Never ever?"

"You right there ..."

"If they let you come back – what would you say?"

She hesitated. She looked back at me. Careful worry crinkles edged her eyelids. You do ask the damnedest most irritating questions whoever you are!

"I say ... ?" she asked.

"Yes."

"S.N.A.F.U. I'd say, I'd say S.N.A.F.U.!"

I watched her cross the blue grey tarmac to the waiting plane. She never once looked back. And I smiled, for those would be her last words. And there'd come a day, better than this, when I'd meet her again. Certo.

WITH THE BORORO

CAPITÃO JOSÉ AND his family group of Bororo have been separated for some years from the official Bororo Reserve at Gomes Carneiro. The Capitão was not keen on the isolation of the Gomes Carneiro land, and he resented the neighbouring branco farmers who tried to recruit cheap labour from the indians down by the São Lourenço. The Capitão and his group lived like white trash in favela shacks close on the BR 158 highway. The Capitão had no shame or self-respect, all his ancestors since the eighteenth century had been drawn to the promised world of the white, to the diseases and the alcohol, and it was the norm to be cheated and frightened by the civilizado. Well, that's how the Capitão thought.

For the Bororo were – in the anthropologist's terms – seventy years old; that was how long the tribe had endured intermittent contact with branco. The Capitão's group, two wives, fifteen or sixteen children from a rather confused family origin, and certain others who claimed kinship, often quite dubiously. There were friends who called themselves brothers, and there were uncles and cousins the Capitão gloomily discounted as hangers-on and, believe you me, to fall to the level of freeloading into Bororos was about as low as you could get.

The Capitão's group was weak and tired. They ate what they could grow in the dustbowl red earth, sometimes they begged on the highway, and inevitably there was prostitution. The Capitão shrugged it off to me—

"If she didn't do it they'd lie and say she did, and another would come by and want to take her ... so? You see?" he murmured.

This group of Bororo were decaying people, the older ones were already discarding their language, and they had forgotten the myths and forest stories of their young manhood. It gets like that on the highway BR 158.

I don't think I ever quite worked out the moiety web of the Capitão's little group. His first wife was definitely Angelica, and she was brown and crinkly like José, they both moved slowly, and they lowered their heads when I talked to them as if they were afraid I might not like it if they spoke up. Their feet shuffled like ashamed feet, the land wasn't theirs, I wasn't a real friend coming here like this and living with them with my cheap Goiânia hammock and my Minister brand cigarettes. But their sons/cousins/nephews/God wot had a liking for me. They admired my teeth, the way the teeth were still there in the front, you see they had huge gaps in their gums because the teeth simply fell out. They collected their own teeth and kept them in tin boxes.

There was Geraldo and Orlando and Vel Devino and Valentin, but all said Geraldo wasn't a son he was a freeloader. There was Elseario, Concepçion, Ceçilia and Madeleina, but they all swore little Madeleina belonged to nobody, she just appeared one day on the highway. It was possible, she wasn't Bororo at all.

The Capitão grumbled at me all day when I tried to squeeze a myth story out of him. He'd tell me if I found him a bottle of cachaca rum. I said we were fifty kilometres from anywhere. No chance. José shrugged.

They kept bald skinny dogs who yapped hopelessly all day, and somehow or other the excrement always got wrapped up in the warm dust fire they always kept going, and the young toddling Bororos like Apareçida and Guraçe would eat the dog shit in the dark by the embers and cry all through the night clutching their round bellies.

The Capitão and Angelica were in their late fifties, and that was real ancient for a Bororo out here on the highway. And little Madeleina was around ten years old. I spent most of my time with the three.

Well . . . you see, Madeleina was such a funny little creature – she never left the Capitão alone. She was a wise one, she liked to keep on his right side, just in case he turned and kicked her shouting – you don't belong! You go back where you came from! And poor little Madeleina was not too sure where she did come from. She could have got here from any direction. So how could she say who she was? Or whose she was? Anyway, she had a bad memory. Madeleina clutched the Capitão's hand tightly and told him she was his Spirit daughter. José gruffed and snorted and lowered his head from me. He knew I was looking.

One day, in the late afternoon when the swell of the heat had faded, I followed Angelica down a slope through trees to a marshy strip, a kind of watery pantanal, no good for man or beast or indio, and she clumsily shifted herself on to a rock and sat like a stone. The marshy land was very flat and smooth, and it appeared to stretch for ever beyond the eye. Angelica was watching the grey vastness of the sky, the clouds so uniform up there, and if she felt anything like I did she felt like an ant on a giant's sandwich, placed somewhere between a butter bread sky and the pasty smooth lining of a gentleman's relish or such.

The clouds, though they protected a thin skin branco like me from the sun, produced a pretty murderous damp heat. Air closed like a tired fist. But Angelica seemed to be enjoying it. Her heavens were low and blue slate grey, great upturned scapes of smooth vapour heat. And so low were they over our heads they met the flat marsh horizon almost at our fingertips, as though earth and cloud were rushing to meet each other.

Angelica was studying a white ring-necked urubu vulture. How it balanced on a cashew bough. It needed but one lift of its great wing span to pierce those clouds. Angelica knew the urubu was about to take off. The black bishop preen swayed on yellow talons—an eerie silent creaming light—

At the edge of the world
        the sky lies
flood fill fields to tree hips
        urubu wait
dogs of light monger miles
        the eyes die
lunge of wing like a breath,
        it open
humid lips of closed air
        it lift heart
the head wait it lick air
        in cold cream moist,
urubu pour feathers.

There was another day I caught the Capitão inside his hut with a soft Cola bottle of pinga a motorista dropped from his caminhão on the highway. So now you are pissed, I told him, you can try digging into the past. One of those myth stories. One you have almost forgotten. I give you a cigarette.

And he was spitting and grumbling, brown toes stubbed into the dirt, fish eyes hiding from me, trying the who cares about my ancestors routine, and I reminded him of the anthropologist who paid him his hired taxi fare all the way to Iguaçu one summer and so ... with the pinga pouring and the shamed toes wriggling ... hide from me his wet mouth—

"I tell you about ... you bugre americano rubbish full of questions ... what good it do me to remember what I want to forget? ... ne? ... huh? ... all right então—

"*The dancers of the living and the dancers of the dead* ... good enough for you?"

I nodded. The pinga seeped into the red earth.

"... I remember a day when half the village (aldeia dos indios) were the *dead*. And the other half were the *living*. The dance began after we called the tapir, after we called the hedgehog, after we called the ant-eater. Ne? It went on for hours. By the first light of morning the dancers of the living grew terribly tired. Some of them were bored, and others began to fight amongst themselves, and there was endless demoraring about. But the dancers of the dead could not stop. Fits like doido fits attacked them. Spirits out of the forest came to see them. And the *dead* danced and danced and danced and danced until they dropped. The *living* were already deep asleep. I forget the rest ..."

Angelica liked to tell stories about herself behind the Capitão's back. She liked them to be funny anecdotes, tales which made the Capitão less pompous. Because for an old trash indio who was ashamed of his every word the Capitão could get remarkably up yours I'm the chefe wipe your nose, lick my feet; and Angelica's best account was of how she allowed her son-in-law to make her pregnant while the Capitão was in Iguaçu, meeting with a learned anthropologist, to explain his family genealogy. (This famous trip by taxi had all come about through a rumour. Americano Protestant missionario anthropologist heard the Capitão say he was related to the great Marechal Candido Rondon, who was indeed part Bororo; and our Capitão at the time who was indeed stupefied with pinga.) Angelica told me the story several times, when we were alone, and she asked me if I would write it out for her in my own language, and leave her a copy before I left—

My husband José is in Iguaçu
to meet his friend the anthropologist, he'll be gone a moon.
I don't know why but in Iguacu there is a missão
which wants to study us. In the morning I am uncovered
and dogs roll in my ashes. I am asleep when
Geraldo and Concepçion decide to marry.

I am angry I am alone
I have no husband to tell my husband how José has
gone to Iguaçu. I dream I can find him,
going in a room with a white bed, to interrupt
him with the wedding of his relatives.

He is not here my Capitão.
Without him home we are poor Bororo who forget.
Though he could remember – what it is when
we have a wedding, how those were the old ways,
and how long it is since I married José.

Nobody else knows how it was.
And Geraldo is so determined he will leave if I do not help.
I tell him that, in custom, a night before the wedding,
he must run in the sertão and find onça and kill it.

Geraldo doesn't like to hear that,
And anyway, he says – the sertão is no place
to look for jaguar just suppose he kills
a deer by mistake?

If he does that, the deer's soul
will be hurt and someone – as stupid as Ignaçe –
might have to go hunt for shrew-mouse
to forgive us the deer.

Once . . . we did not live here.
The old Indian Protection Service moved us on
from the forest which was ours before.

I grow so unhappy and Concepçion
is my daughter, I have to tell her I like Geraldo, too.
And Geraldo, not wanting to go risking his neck
in the sertão (where it's well-known you won't find onça)
now decides he will marry us both.

José came back from Iguaçu with cigarettes
in his pocket and a tin lighter which he flicks
up and down in my face. He said 'I explained to the
estrangeiro just who we all are, how we are related
and whose everyone's child is . . .

'I waited for him to write it
and he wrote it word for word, as I spoke. Look –
he gave me 300 cruzeiros.' The Capitão flicks
his lighter in my face like a crazy cucujo. I refuse to blink.

I said to my Capitão—
'You return him that money and tell him
to give you another money because that 300 cruzeiros
is now wrong!'

'What! ?' My Capitão screamed.
You see . . . both Concepçion and I were now pregnant.

Apart from these occasional twists into self-parody, the life of the Bororo is a sad one; their pitiful situation, in many cases accentuated by their own passivity and laziness, is past helping. They will decline and in our lifetime they will simply disappear. They are the rotten dross of the indios, like the Parecis up on Rio Verde, like those enslaved indios on Bananál . . . what can we do for them?

You cannot read to a Bororo from Article 20 of the Universal Declaration of Human Rights; adopted by the UN December 1948.

There is no Brazilian Assembly decision on the 1970 Statute of the indian. No inalienable rights for any indio.

A Bororo must be out of town before darkfall because he has no legal identity papers.

A Bororo cannot get a ride on an ónibus, either the motorista is afraid the indio has no money (most often he hasn't) or the other branco travellers will move to the back of the bus and complain bitterly.

A Bororo is nobody a nothing a no document little brown shadow in borrowed vest and slacks on the highway hoping for a hitch from a caminhão, a lorry . . .

That was how I last saw the Capitão and little Madeleina, when they strode off, hand in hand, saying they were going to

Goiânia. I don't believe either of them knew how far it was to Goiânia. How far and how difficult it was to Goiânia for a Bororo—

There is a brown tree of dust on the road
from Xavantina and he will take me to Goiânia when he stops.
I cannot tell if it's an ónibus but even so he will wait
to ask if I have the fare. I know he won't let me sit down
on a bench but I can stand as far as Goiânia.

It is a caminhão on the road from Xavantina,
and his wheels make a trail like a swarm of red bees, he must
give me a ride when I show him my arco de fleché. He will have
a son he must buy it for.

Up on the planalto there I can see him,
he has twenty kilometres before he comes past. I will put
Madeleina up on my shoulders she waves so hard he cannot
mistake the smile on her face.

Now there's the sound of his engine, and when
I use the stick like a crutch to hobble towards him he will
slow down. He must pass me so close if I raise the fat sack
of feijoada and manioc and dried meat above my head he shall
see I will make a gift of it.

The back of the caminhão is filled with branco.
Each one has on his head a yellow helmet. If the palmira tree
hides me behind, Madeleina can stand on her own in
the road and open her eyes wide.

They are throwing and shouting and whistling
at her. Dust pours over Madeleina like urucum when she cries
in the night for fear the pium. I must lie down on
the highway and pretend I am hurt and they will certainly stop
to take me to Goiânia...

...After they have gone it is so quiet
I can hear her breathe. That dust settles like a shower of swift
wings on the road to Goiânia. To pretend she is not drying her
tears Madeleina rubs the red from the eyes with her hair.

She wants to tell me – *there are caju floating in the stream Capitão, we can stand on the stones and pick them with our hands, you know how soft and sweet they taste, and how you like them.*

'Vamos embora, Madeleina.'

'Vamos ver, Capitão José.'

PETAL AND FIST

THE PANTANAL IS a flat serra which stretches five hundred square miles to the west of the town of Poconé. For six months of every year most of it lies under water. The rains and the river floods bury the termite mounds, and the tall white, black and red tu-yu-yu birds cling to the trees, and the alligators – not the jacaré you will find in Mississippi – these are small and black with pink eyes, and they never make more than four feet in length, well they slide in the grass which strangely grows at flood level in the water. It is peculiar grass; as if it were a new cousin of the serra drowned beneath, it clings somehow to surface sediment, and shines a sharp yellow green glint across the high watermarks. The horses are different here in the pantanal, they are never shod, and they can somehow survive in all depths of water, against all snakes and jacarés, and in the April spring when the water slips back, and the alligators bury their pink eyes in the red mud beside the newly showing dirt-tracks, these horses wallow and roll on their sides in the brown water.

Certain fazendeiros swear by pantanal land, though it is only above water half the year, they say their beef is the best meat on the market, and if they cannot make six bois for one hectare, by the land roster, well, there is so much of the pantanal, and it is so easy and flat in distribution, there is no real counting of how much land you own, or where are your perimeters. As you ride across the land in the summer, it is as if you are galloping across a large meadow on the Kent/Sussex border, in England, there are thick clumps of oak-like trees, and lovely grass which sways up ahead of you; but whereas, in England, this meadow would run out of distance in a quarter of a mile, this pantanal land just goes on and on for fifteen or twenty or fifty miles – for as long as you want it to, or your horse can take it. Being such flat land, you know the heat, it seems to skid and shimmer in low invisible clouds of burning moisture for some three or four feet over the ground. But on a horse, you don't ever need to worry about that, and if you are on a horse, it is likely your mind is on many other matters than that.

For there is a lot to hunt in the pantanal – there is a fat feathery ostrich with a yellow spoonbill, he runs like the wind. There are black, short-necked wolves that carry behind them a trailing fox-like tail, there are three if not four kinds of antelope out there, from the fragile daughter of hart to a long-nosed galloper which you would imagine only lived up in the north. And there is the onça. A scruffier version of the lemur. A little thinner, too. And he swims fast and well against any kind of current. It is said that if an onça and an African panther paced themselves side by side to see which was the fastest, the panther could get closer to ninety-five m.p.h. but before it was finished, the onça would have killed the faster of the two. Smaller than a panther, with larger paws, it uses the pantanal at any time of day. It uses it for wild pig, antelope, the big badger-like roedor, it can kill, and any tired ostrich or plumed tu-yu-yu unlucky enough to come by the tender nostrils which smell fear so quickly.

Jen had never had time, in a strange way, to decide whether she liked the pantanal or not. She came from Milwaukee, and she was now married to Richard Eason, and it seemed that all her time and energy was consumed with him. Richard had been a Korean war veteran. He could not settle in America and he stayed in Africa for ten years as a mercenary. Richard was very tall, and wide, and the same strength he seemed to carry in his shoulders he held in his waist and in his long legs. And it was generally supposed this was why Jen fell for a man, in such a big way, although he had twenty years on her age, and although most of her teens were spent in the back of dark cars in drive-in movie-houses, and before her teens in those sullen childish churlish years, most of her nights were spent by pools with spotty boys in striped swimming trunks or back by a shack, below her father's garden where it was rumoured only the bravest of the girls went, because the mattress was kept on the shack floor for only one purpose; because any old town friend of Jen's would have, on being asked, described her as a real mover. And Jen never had any fears about hiding this fact – she liked sex, she liked it so much, she'd travel anywhere for it, with the person she chose to share the pleasure. So this was why, everyone guessed, from her neighbourhood, she had taken up with this elusive man named Richard, who lived to shoot and hunt, and stood near six feet four inches tall, and had bought a patch of scrub right in the middle of a bog somewhere south of Brazil called the pantanal, and apparently, so the neighbourhood heard, it was so much of a bog, there was rain and flood water on the porch six months out of every year.

That guy Richard – with that bushy beard of his – he must have something to keep Jen down there. How do we know? Well we haven't seen her for eight months, but we got a letter a month back, she saying she was deliriously happy and all that crap.

Richard had bought a little land in the pantanal, but he was never too bright with figures, and he soon learned he had not enough to make a farm work. And he had no more capital.

What should he do?

He schemed in his mind – and the one dream he had always relied on – to hunt – came back to him again and again. Why not advertise in the States? Real wild life hunting deep in the Mato? Hunt and kill what you like? An expert guide. A cook provided. The greatest adventure left to urban man – the wilds of Brazil. Well, to begin with Jen hated cooking; and secondly, without him realising it, hunting had been proibido in the pantanal for the last six years.

Richard blindly hoped on. He had his dream.

What Hemingway could do under Kilimanjaro, what Bill Holden could make of his Kenya wildlife sorties. My God – this pantanal made their places look like the Kent/Sussex borders.

One or two couples turned up. A wealthy missionary from the South American Protestant Mission with his wife; before they began their fieldwork, they fancied hunting onça with Richard.

A rather portly English company director – chairman of a small bank in Nicaragua – had decided to leave his family for a few months, and he stumbled across a tiny ad. of Richard's in an Idaho airport tourist guide.

Then, came Alston Reems and his Aunt Betty. And they were an odd sight indeed. Alston was nearly forty, he had never married, and his only surviving relative Aunt Betty just despaired of him. They came from a town in panhandling country a hundred miles north of Dallas. Aunt Betty had a small income and worked on Sundays with an Indian mission outside the town. Alston had long given up pump tending which he inherited from his father, on account of the fact the gasoline made his hair and his hands so dirty. Alston was a mild figure, he never played football, he never took girls out, he never drank much, in fact he had retained his boyhood passion for all soft drinks, he never fished with the boys, or played pool, or rode out on to the farms on a Sunday to watch the cowpokes' local races, in no uncertain way Alston all his life had been a mild thing. And what with his flat feet – large flat feet – well, Aunt Betty had now taken it upon herself to make a man of him, or die in the process. The one question she had never dared yet put to her nephew – the one sexual deviation she herself hardly dare speak of – was constantly, naturally, at the back of her mind.

The water in the pantanal was sinking nicely, and the stilts of Richard and Jen's casa de planta dried white in the sun. Richard showed Aunt Betty and Alston how to sleep in their redes hung out on the verandah, he showed them the latrine (a hole in boards), and the one prize a kerosene run refrigerator filled with a reputable brand of soft drink, and a few bottles of the sugar cane fermented pinga – that all Brazilian rotgut. Aunt Betty, of course, just to keep the family's name high, made the mistake of hitting the pinga. Jen's dislike for Alston was more than apparent. She hated him when he caught grippe, she loathed him when he had diarrhoea, and she laughed a lot when the mosquitoes and those tiny black borracho bugs dug into his flesh, and all the while Alston's hands just wouldn't stop sweating.

And Aunt Betty told Alston what a man Richard must be, and she kept telling him this, until one day, soon after they had set out on horseback across the pantanal (and you know how Alston takes to horses), when one night Betty discovered Jen and Richard making love together – then, strangely, she stopped telling her nephew what a man Richard was.

Sometimes they slept out under sheets, most often they hung their rêdes between trees, Richard lit a fire, and Jen tried to make something out of fried manioc and the odd bird or fish Richard would kill.

As for Alston, things got a little better. They were moving on to a higher plain, above the trees, and it was colder at night and the mosquitoes died off before midnight. He grew quieter, if anything, of them all, he was the one who spoke least. Jen liked to play with him, she insinuated so much. She talked to him a lot about her desires – and it was done in the way of a constant threat to Alston's manliness – as far as he could make out, her sole credentials for living were based on a man's strength, on the size and shape of him, on his potency and on his bravery; and poor Alston began to see Richard as a king of sexual prowess and as an eagle at a height he could never attain.

Richard started to hunt for serious.

Their rations were low now, and even Alston had none of that soft drink brand left. He even admitted that when hot, it did taste like some kind of soap fluid. Richard lay a base atop a stunted tree. He sat there with Alston from dark. Beside him he held his 30. magnum repeating rifle. Attached to the trigger was a wire which flicked on the powerful torchbeam he had tied to the top of the barrel. The plan was – no soon as wild hog or roedor could be heard, he would smell (so he claimed) the exact location of the animal, and he'd start firing. With the torchbeam full on, the animal would freeze, and three bullets would fix it. Well, Alston fell out of the tree, Richard opened fire on Aunt Betty who had brought them a little freshener as she relented and couldn't bear the thought of Alston suffering so much. And the first real adventure was a dud as far as Jen was concerned. She had looked forward to a particular thing she could do well. But a day later, she got her chance, Alston and Richard rode out for antelope. Richard brought one down in full flight, and if it took him six minutes to tie it to the back of his horse, it took him sixty minutes to find Alston who, on finding his horse bolting beneath him, just hung on grimly and let the wind take him. That was Alston for you. That evening, Jen made Alston cut and clean the whole animal. She showed him, and the more he did it the greener in the face he got, and Jen clearly had a ball with him.

Alston, one night, perhaps it was the night before Richard had promised him the big kill along the rio where the onça could be found, found Jen alone in the mato, her face covered in bruises. Richard had beaten her about the face over a petty matter. Alston rushed to get linament and he tried to bathe her face. After a while she became increasingly agitated at his womanising (she called it), and told him it was perfectly normal for them to fight like that, and that was all there was to it. Alston was angry. He tackled Richard about it, and little Alston held up his fist and told him if he saw him treat Jen like that again, so help him, why he'd lay one right on Richard's nose. Alston wagged his pudgy white fist. Aunt Betty hid herself in her rede, and Jen – watching at a distance – could not help smiling.

Richard was going to give Alston quite a lesson in onça hunting he decided. He had cut a thick long pole with a very sharp point to it. He and Alston left their guns behind with the women, and Richard showed Alston what he must do. Richard would imitate the sound of wild hog, and Alston must wait knee-deep in the water until the onça stepped out across a tree towards him. Then Alston must talk the onça towards him. He must talk gently, encouragingly, quietly, and eventually the onça would snarl forward until he was above Alston, and at that moment Alston must dig the pole into the mud beneath him, spread his legs wide, and talk the big cat to jump down on him. It was easy, said Richard, you'd never miss – once the cat jumps, you'll instinctively place the pole under its heart, it'll fall with you into the water, but don't worry, it'll be dead as it ever could be once its weight hits the pole.

Well, Alston waited, and Richard practised his wildhog voice, and with a full moon behind him, Alston saw the fragile shadow of the cat creep along the branch. The snarl, a slow curl of grating throat and tongue, chuckled in the dark noisy air of the mato close by the rio.

"Start talking... Alston," murmured Richard, from some way behind him.

"There you are ... just keep coming ... you keep on coming there you big cat..." and Alston's words trembled and trickled from his dry throat. And the cat leapt.

Alston gripped hold on the pole, and just as the front paws reached for his head, he instinctively placed the pole beneath the heart of the dark leaper, and a scream filled the rio with silence, as all murmurs ceased, and Alston fainted clean away. Richard stumbled through the shallows, as he reached down towards the body of the onça, and presumably Alston who lay prone under the water, the cat struck back at him. It was a last angry strike of breath and fear and agony. The paw bladed down into Richard's shoulder, his arm and his sinews through to his muscles and deep into the bone and shaved miles of unendurable pain through his body.

It was Alston who climbed out from beneath the dead weight of the animal. And it was Alston who dragged Richard out of the water. And it was Alston who tied the cat to the horse.

Betty volunteered to take Richard back, the closest town was Poconé, and there was a hospital there. She swiftly bound the deep treadmarks of the claws, bleeding as they were, and Richard sat on the horse with a pained, yet complaisant expression on his face, yes it seemed to say this is what hurting really is, and as you can see I do not mind, I can take it, but I cannot take the waiting and the inactivity. He waved a rough goodbye to Jen and threw her the steel compass he kept around his neck.

She would not touch Alston's wounds that night. They were not particularly bad, just a lot of scratch/bleeding around both his upper shoulders. In the morning, Alston did a strange thing – he began to explain how it was all his fault, that Richard had the cat speared in the water, but Alston was not quick enough to shoot it outright, once Richard had fallen back beneath the jumping weight.

"You don't have to tell me lies like that..." she replied. She knew what had happened. She told him that Richard was quite willing to see him killed. And slowly, as if taking part in a totally new experience, she stripped his cuts, cleaned and washed them, and felt a sense of amazement at her own tenderness.

On the way back, Alston found he could best bait for fish, and that and dried manioc served them well enough. Jen began to talk at last. She found Alston a good listener. And if he couldn't understand, he wanted to. All her youth, and now in her middle twenties, she had believed the greatest pleasure in life was to take the strongest boy in the class, or the best pool player in the town, and now she had married this hunter, Richard. Never once had she considered love and satisfaction to come out of tenderness.

"Why were you fighting like that?" he asked her. "When I interrupted and you looked at me so angrily as if to say – this is how we make love, don't you see?" Jen said that that was how they did make love. Richard hurt her, humiliated her, until she was exhausted, and then they loved.

Before they got within a day's horse ride of Poconé, Jen had made love with Alston. He only felt ashamed for being so puny and inadequate. She cried in his arms, and admitted she had never in her life before had such pleasure, of her own body out of her own orgasm, and she said to Alston she knew as little about sex as he did, if not less.

At the hospital, Jen sat beside Richard and realised how fully and completely she did not love or revere this man any more. She grew as stone. Aunt Betty made a number of flurried and hurried goodbyes. Jen made her own goodbye to Alston –

she kissed him and loved him, and told him that all his life he'd never need feel afraid. Whatever happened to him. And whatever, in her own right happened to her. Alston wanted to cry. She knew it. She told him she loved him, and that he mustn't – because as sure as eggs is eggs, Aunt Betty would notice, and frown.

In the crowded Norte Este ónibus back to Cuiabá, Aunt Betty sat beside her nephew. She didn't quite know what to think of Richard, she told Alston she believed Richard now, to be a bully and an atheist. Alston smiled dully.

"You know Alston," said his aunt, studying his tanned face, and noticing how the fat had slipped from his waistline, "I never before thought I'd have the courage to say – that at one time I really did believe you were going to turn into one of them homosexuals – now I think you got a chance in life, heck, but I don't know why!"

Alston lay back in the thick padded seat, with its tilt button at his finger, and he thought of gentle fingers, crying eyes, and a shudder engendered on another's thighs that begged for the heart but not the fist, that prayed in the perspiring skin of the night for the petal of love's touch and not the root. Whatever in his American past had kept from him the bruteness of competitive strength, had also hidden from Jen the magic wakening of tenderness.

"Well well well..." Alston murmured to himself.

And he uncrossed his legs from that overtly womanly posture he had always retained. In his slow smile, if you looked carefully, you could discern discovery and loss, all at once, and that was indeed just how Alston felt.

PADRE FRANÇOIS JENTEL: A REPORT

FRANÇOIS JENTEL WAS born in France on August 29th, 1922 and ordained at Juvisy on June 30th, 1946. In 1954 he was sent to Brazil by his superiors at the 'Petits Frères du Père du Foucault'. At first he worked for some years with the indians at Tapirape, a remote corner in the State of Mato Grosso. He then moved thirty kilometres to the tiny village of Santa Terezinha in 1964.

Santa Terezinha is a village of 1,000 inhabitants, many of whom have been driven by the droughts in the north-east to seek out a livelihood in the heavily forested regions of Santa Terezinha. With great difficulty they formed the forest and lived as small farmers on land unwanted by anyone else. Some of these people had worked the land for more than half a century and by so doing they considered they had acquired right of ownership i.e. squatters' rights. Padre Jentel helped the villagers to build roads and to flatten a field for a proper landing strip. He organised an infirmary, he opened a school, and he persuaded the farmers to set up a co-operative.

However, in the early sixties, spurred on by government fiscal incentives intended to stimulate the farming industry and increase Brazil's meat exports, land development companies began to take an interest in the Rio Araguaia area where Santa Terezinha is located. The land of the village and the surrounding area was bought from the State of Mato Grosso by a group of São Paulo bankers with high-level government connections under the name of CODEARA. This company has many strange share holders including, it is believed, senior Brazilian army officers and the American conglomerate ITT. CODEARA laid claim to 200,000 hectares of land in 1966 at Santa Terezinha, half a million, acres which they described as *uninhabited forest region*.

In 1967 Costa e Silva, the President of Brazil, signed a presidential decree in response to Padre Jentel's repeated request to have a certain portion of this land requisitioned by CODEARA expropriated for the use of his parishioners. In 1970 the Municipal Legislature of Luciara where the land is situated agreed that CODEARA should return the urban zone of Santa Terezinha to its inhabitants. But, when no further action was taken, Padre Jentel and his superior, Pedro Casaldaliga, Bishop of São Felix, charged that CODEARA had bribed the Mayor of Luciara, and that at a secret meeting the legal expropriation decree was rescinded.

Nevertheless, in 1970 CODEARA donated some 5,582 hectares to be shared between one hundred families. What at first looked like a generous gesture, soon came to be recognised for what it was. A blatant attempt to divide and destroy the unity of this co-operative. And in no way did this donation fulfil either the requirements of the presidential decree nor the expropriation order of the Luciara Municipality.

CODEARA brought in workers from the impoverished north-east to *form* the lands which they had acquired. But the conditions in the forest camp were appalling. Many workers fled the camp and appealed to the Padre and the villagers for help.

Illness was widespread, many were dying from malaria. The workers were frequently beaten and eight men were shot while trying to escape. Brasilia was not blind to all this, they did send down Federal Justice Department Officials to the camp to investigate late 1970, and though they willingly admitted they could not have a better case against CODEARA, to this day not one executive in the company has been prosecuted.

The Minister of Justice, Buzaid, made it clear to the Apostolic Nuncio in Brasilia that either Padre Jentel left the country or there would be trouble. This was a very sensitive period of relations between Brazil and France. Brazil was in the process of buying a large number of jet fighters from France and the French Ambassador in Brasilia took an active interest in the Padre's case. Both the Nuncio and the Ambassador made formal requests to the Padre to leave the country, but it was generally believed that the Ambassador felt considerable sympathy for Jentel. The Padre thanked them for their concern, but he replied he would stay on at Santa Terezinha in spite of the advances of CODEARA.

As a whole, it was wrong to accuse the Brazilian government of inactivity. At top level, in Brasilia, from the President downwards, there was a desire to be fair. But it was impossible to check the winking and bribery which went on beneath legislative control. Certain military chiefs wanted CODEARA's help in mounting anti-guerrilla operations in this area. And in 1972, army troops put down an active poor peoples' movement. There is evidence the troops were based and directed from lands acquired by similar land development corporations to CODEARA.

In January 1972, the Minister, Buzaid, met with Casaldaliga, Bishop of São Felix, and the Minister agreed to a month's truce to give the government time to study the problem and to find an equitable solution.

On the 10th of February 1972, while Padre Jentel was attending a retreat in Fortaleza, the manager of CODEARA, Jose Norberto Silveira sent 25 men to the Santa Terezinha mission with a tractor belonging to SUDAM, the government development agency which helped found CODEARA. The tractor, used as a bulldozer, destroyed the foundations of the dispensary the villagers had built, a well, a plantation of banana trees, and the CODEARA men smashed a camera which had been used to photograph the proceedings. A few days later, a corporal who attended evening classes at the mission and who supported the construction of the dispensary was brutally beaten by CODEARA workers and had to be taken to hospital. CODEARA justified the assault on the dispensary. It was directly in their path they said. For they were planning a new road. It was an arbitrary enough excuse, which had to be taken with a pinch of salt, for there already existed a road out of the village. This road had been purposefully made impassable by the CODEARA men the year before. The company had neither the approval of local authorities in Barra do Garças, nor of INCRA, the government agricultural body, to bulldoze the dispensary, let alone start building a new road.

The villagers did indeed have de facto squatters' rights. All along they were counselled by the Padre in non-violence. And article 502 of the Brazilian Civil Code specifies that – 'an owner whose property is being destroyed or robbed is entitled to act on his own to retain his property or demand that it be provided that he does so immediately'. So, the villagers stood by helplessly. Certain CODEARA men threatened the villagers, and they beat the representatives of the prelature to the ground.

On the 20th of February, the Bishop of São Felix ordered the Padre back to the village. The Bishop protested about CODEARA's actions to the legal authorities. The police were duly informed, and they advised CODEARA officially to keep their personnel away from the angry villagers. On the 21st of February the villagers began to reconstruct the dispensary.

Fearing a reaction to the attack, CODEARA virtually imprisoned their workers in the camp to keep them out of the way of Santa Terezinha. The two directors responsible for the aggression were withdrawn. Later, in conversation with friends, some of the workers said that the company had tricked them into taking part, and that they had expected 'more honest work'. The manager, Jose Norberto Silveira undertook to bring charges presenting CODEARA as the innocent victim of the *blows* from the prelature workers. This prosecution was unsuccessful.

On the afternoon of March 3rd, three planeloads of CODEARA men, and allied soldiers of fortune brought in from outside the state, descended on the mission house. Some of these men wore para-military uniforms. They carried between them two machine guns and various small arms. They aimed the guns at the workers rebuilding the dispensary and ordered all work to cease. After taking cover in nearby huts, the villagers brought out a number of old carbines and, fearing for their lives and deeply angered, they commenced firing at the CODEARA men.

The determination of the villagers panicked the men. They appeared to lose control of the situation. And no less than seven of them were peppered by shotgun fire. These intruders fled towards the CODEARA camp outside the village. The three CODEARA planes flew them back to São Felix immediately.

At the time of the shooting, Padre Jentel was a mile away in his own quarters. When he arrived at the scene, the intruders had disappeared back towards the camp. The following day a leading newspaper in Goiania published a headline story under the banner – 'PRIEST ARMED WITH MACHINE GUN WOUNDS SEVENTEEN PEOPLE.'

Padre Jentel promptly took an air taxi for Goiânia. He would personally inform the Church and the police authorities as to exactly what had happened. During his flight, the air taxi was pursued by a CODEARA aeroplane which constantly harassed the Padre's civil pilot. The man was forced to use all his skill to land safely at Goiânia.

Within the week, the military police arrived at Santa Terezinha. Almost eighty workers fled into the forest. There they remained for several months.

Before the Padre and the Bishop of São Felix completed their report on the incident a very curious thing happened. Copies of two strange telegrams were found in the CODEARA camp. They had been left behind by the men in their haste. The copies were signed by a ranking colonel in the army, who, it must be presumed, actually organised the assault. The two cables were directed to local police officials in the vicinity of the village. The first telegram suggested that indians had somehow been involved in the incident. And asked for an investigation. The second read—

> Obtain more information on the existence and distribution of arms. Give information on present police forces in Santa Terezinha. Identify and arrest the civilians of the organisation and arrest the civilian leaders of the organisation and take them to regional headquarters. Give information on necessary action to maintain order effectively in this area. How to establish permanent contact with the police prefecture. On the actions and situation of Captain Moreno. Give information on means of access to Barra do Garças and Santa Terezinha. Take preventative police action in Santa Terezinha.

Naturally, the Padre and the Bishop pointed out several questions raised by this telegram. They wondered just what arms other than those normally possessed by the villagers this colonel felt were being distributed? And they wondered just what *preventative police action* was required to justify the brandishing of two machine guns and an order to arrest a bunch of Santa Terezinha stone-masons? Furthermore they found it peculiar, to say the least, that the federal military government, who had followed the situation for five years in Santa Terezinha, should suddenly start suspecting a mysterious *organisation* in this area and consider arresting its supposed *leaders*. Further, they queried the logic of arresting civilians and not clerics from the prelature. Finally, they put the question – is it a crime to be a leader or to demand the most elementary rights?

But some angels in Brasilia were still listening to the appeals from the determined Padre. A month later, President Medici himself signed by decree law 70430 a declaration giving the settlers legal title to their land in Santa Terezinha. And, INCRA, the Brazilian association for agricultural development also agreed that a portion of the land claimed by the company CODEARA must be retained for the inhabitants of the area.

But for Padre Jentel this was only a beginning. Despite these official sanctions which appeared to validate all his efforts, the military police initiated a suit against the Padre in May, 1972. It took them one whole year to bring him to trial in a small room on the second floor of a military office in Campo Grande, State of Mato Grosso. During this time the Padre was held under house arrest. During this time one young couple, engaged to be wed, who worked at the prelature of Santa Terezinha, was arrested and tortured to extract a confession to the effect that it was the Padre who instigated the firing on the CODEARA men. There are witnesses in Campo Grande, today, who can testify to the burn marks on the girl's breasts and the lacerations on the young fiancé's genitals. During this time the entire weight of the Council of Bishops for all Brazil reiterated its support for the Padre.

The military trial itself was a travesty of justice. Two special prosecutors were sent from Rio de Janeiro. A brilliant carioca lawyer Heleno Fragoso well-known for his work defending political prisoners was employed by the Church to take up the Padre's case. A local lawyer from Campo Grande, Nelson Trad, also aided Fragoso. At the military trial were two presiding judges. A civil judge and a prosecuting judge. It takes little imagination to guess which of these two judges had the final say. The civil judge was a most remarkable man, Plinio Barbosa Martins; he lived in Campo Grande, and works there still today; but he is forbidden by law to take part in any kind of politically orientated career. In other words he can stand for no executive office in the body politic of present day Mato Grosso. Before the trial got under way the prosecuting judge made many efforts to replace Plinio, he was afraid that Plinio might dissent from the verdict demanded by the military representatives in the court room. He was right, as it happened.

The evidence presented at the trial ranged from the pernicious to the ridiculous. The abridged version of the twelve articles the Padre was charged with requires particular attention.

For the accusative articles were a strange mishmash of inciting not only villagers but indians to raise arms and cause danger to life and CODEARA limb, they included charges verging on Alice in Wonderland material—

no. 8. He held weekly meetings with peasants of Santa Terezinha at which he indoctrinated them to oppose the decisions of INCRA (National Institute of Colonisation and Agrarian Reform).
no. 9. He owned a rice harvesting machine, a co-operative store and a fleet of well equipped ships.
no. 10. He used only air taxis to leave Santa Terezinha.
no. 11. He aroused discontent amongst all the workers in the area.
no. 12. He owned agricultural machinery originating from the Soviet Union.

At the trial much was made of the evidence given by Commandante Euro Barbosa de Barros, head of the military police. His testimony did not address itself to the specific charges against the Padre, it was more of a diatribe against the entire metropolitan area of São Felix, and in particular on the person and motives of Dom Pedro Casaldaliga, the Bishop of São Felix.

Powerful interests supported the Commandante's attack. The same newspaper which carried the banner headline 'PRIEST ARMED WITH MACHINE GUN ...' etc. published a pastoral letter by the Bishop superimposed over a picture of wounded and maimed figures. It has to be admitted that the Bishop himself was not slow at returning the abuse. He accused all sorts of police and military officials with having financial connections in the company CODEARA. And there are plenty of people around who still say this is no mud-slinging-area a Bishop ought to be involved in.

In the afternoon of the 28th of May, outside the trial room, a curious scene occurred. One of the prosecuting attorneys could be seen leaving the court. This was before the final verdict had been declared.

The lawyer was tracked down in his room at the Hotel Campo Grande. There he was hastily packing his clothes to catch the next plane out to Rio. And still the final verdict had not been declared.

An enterprising journalist caught the lawyer up in the hotel elevator. Understandably, he was in no hurry to answer any questions. He was just in a hurry to get back to Rio. As much as he demurred and fobbed the questions away, he did at least murmur one intelligible phrase—

"The military are bringing a lot of pressure to bear."

In the court room, the prosecuting judge, for and on behalf of the military, found Padre François Jentel guilty on a majority of the charges.

The civil judge, Plinio Barbosa Martins, stood up and announced his verdict of 'not guilty'.

At this juncture of this curious state of affairs, it is worth recording the exact words of the civil judge, Plinio, if only to ascertain just how he arrived at such a reversal:

"I am in complete disagreement with the decision of the Permanent Council of the Justice of the Army. Although, up until now, I have always been in total agreement with their decisions. For I see absolutely nothing criminal in the conduct of Padre François Jacques Jentel. On the contrary, I admire his courage in abandoning a very developed country like France twenty years ago, to establish himself in the Mato Grosso in order to bring some civilisation and the gift of Christianity to the indians and Brazilians who live in these inhospitable areas. He has been exposed to numerous dangers, has suffered long bouts of illness, and all because of the love of human solidarity so often recommended and encouraged by various well-known encyclicals. People call the Church communist because she interests herself in those who have no social position. The real Christian cannot accept that the suffering of many is the price paid for the liberation of a few. The latter ought to accept that they must give up part of what they have, because by sacrificing a little themselves, they will help secure happiness of the economically destitute. Padre Jentel is a soldier of this manner of thinking. In his struggle on behalf of the dispossessed he obtained financial aid from Canada, intended for use in building a dispensary for the village of Santa Terezinha. A human agglomeration without roads to link it to other areas of the country. Then, the CODEARA society arrived. Rich and powerful. It decided to do what seemed good for the company. And felt that the social work of the Padre was eating into a few centimetres of a road drawn on a map which the company had prepared. The manager of the company, Jose Norberto Silveira, did not hesitate. In a deliberate way he destroyed the construction which was underway and the materials ready for use in building. He took judicial power upon himself. The peasants rose to defend the dispensary and their plots of land. Padre Jentel denies that he participated in this armed defence. And even if he had been present to defend by force the result of one of his works he would have been within the law. People who try to indicate the path to follow are of little interest to me. We ought to follow an independent route. And obey only our consciences. And my conscience cried out from within me that the condemnation of those who follow Padre Jentel put him far away from marxism. If he supported those sort of politics he would not believe in Catholicism. If he agreed with Marx, he wouldn't have established himself in the Amazonian forests, but would have gone to live in some large town to indoctrinate the masses and prepare a confrontation between the social classes. I see in the behaviour of Padre Jentel a Christian example to follow. May we have innumerable imitators in order that the face of the world become more and more a just one, and less one revealing social inequalities. Padre Jentel deserves a prize and not prison. His condemnation is shocking and profoundly ungrateful to sentence someone who has worked for nearly twenty years in the far-off interior of Brazil to try to integrate people into what is good and defensible. The injuries of which the suit speaks should be the object of discussions in courts of ordinary justice, at Barra do Garças. The law of National Security in all its severity deals with internal and external attacks upon the country. I honestly made an effort . . . I saw nothing in the acts of behaviour of Padre Jentel which constituted an instigation against the peace. On the contrary, I see in him a great deal of humility and sacrifice in a cause whose end is the respect of human beings. Later, the understanding of men will do him justice."

The prosecuting judge, by a unanimous decision of the Military Council, and by four military votes against one civil, sentenced Padre Jentel to ten years in prison. He was immediately taken back to the barracks of the 2nd Military Police Battalion in Campo Grande.

After the trial, the Bishop of São Felix would still not hold his peace. He accused the military lawyers from Rio of being servants of fear and self interest. Dr Flavio Benjamin D. de Andrade and Dr Olympio Jayme contrived to use 'patriotic and religious demagoguery' to achieve their ends.

Five days after the verdict, a detachment of about a hundred men, mainly military police, arrived at Santa Terezinha armed with machine guns. With them came officials from the Air Force and the Army. They were led by Commandante Euro Barbosa de Barros, chief of the Mato Grosso military police. Officers from the Federal police and the National Information Service were also present in this combined action. They carried with them orders from a General Domingues, (Commandante of the Brigada de Corumba). Throughout the visit the detachment remained in constant touch with the General's office by means of radio transmitters spread throughout the area.

A large number of workers were beaten. Numerous shotguns and working tools were confiscated. Houses were broken into. Interrogations were carried out with violence. The priests and nuns in the prelature were subjected to humiliation and ridicule. Those who could, ran away and hid out in the forest.

In his cell, the Padre was allowed pen and paper and books of his own choice. He wrote to a friend that it was not he but 'the Church which lives on, which moves forward, which suffers and which bears witness to the footsteps of Christ'.

The authorities allowed the Padre a regular visit from a priest. His sister from France came to see him. So too did his brother from Canada. Padre Jentel made it absolutely clear he intended to serve out his full sentence. But there was no doubt this was causing the authorities considerable embarrassment. The very last thing they wanted was a martyr to a cause.

Officials in Brasilia (many shocked at the severity of the sentence), the Nuncio, and the French Ambassador appealed to the Padre. In other words, if you will only sign a formal note of confession to the crimes charged, you will be released, and deported immediately.

But the Padre would have none of it. Even though his defence lawyer made a similar appeal. Even though, it was rumoured, other Bishops in the interior recommended the same advice. Padre Jentel was sticking.

He remained resilient and firm. He was not going to sign anything. Somebody else had to give way. But it was not going to be the Padre from Santa Terezinha.

He remained in the cell for 360 days, until on May 23rd, 1974, the following was reported in the press from Brasilia:

> Brazil's highest military court yesterday overturned a 1973 conviction of French priest François Jacques Jentel on anti-

government subversion charges. He was serving a ten-year term, charged with inciting to subvert the social order after a clash between his parishioners and a land developing company.

On May 25th, the New York Times reported:

> Rev Francis Jentel the French priest condemned to ten years in prison for encouraging Brazilian peasants to revolt against large landholders was freed last night, his lawyer declared today. The Brazilian Supreme Military Tribunal ordered his release after voting unanimously in favour of his appeal, according to a statement by the Brazilian National Bishops' Conference. The priest has been held for the last year in a military prison at Campo Grande in the central State of Mato Grosso about 600 miles west of São Paulo. His departure from Brazil was the condition of his release according to Church sources. The Bishops' statement said that the tribunal had ruled out subversion in the case, declared the military court incompetent, and turned the matter over to civil justice.

This report must not be seen as an across the board condemnation of the Brazilian authorities. It is wrong and too simplistic a resolution. There is much to indicate that those in the highest level of government did indeed try to find a fair solution to this case. And what created all the damage happened somewhere down the line of delegation. Where the hand of corruption can more readily stray. If this point is not understood, then nor is the sheer geographical size of Brazil understood. Where communication is often impossible, where States are like little nations and where village communities in the forest become as isolated as certain Pacific islands.

Two Brazilian Presidents personally intervened. In 1967 President Costa e Silva signed a decree expropriating land back from the CODEARA company. In 1972, President Medici signed a further decree law. INCRA for national agricultural development recommended inalienable rights for the villagers. The Minister Buzaid met on conciliatory terms with the Padre and the Bishop. Even CODEARA can say they offered 5,000 hectares back to the villagers. The French Ambassador was deeply embarrassed by the Brazilian government over the subject of Padre

Jentel. The lawyer from Campo Grande, civil judge Plinio Barbosa Martins, put his neck on a chopping block to justify the Padre's case. Even a lone corporal, isolated single striper in the village of Santa Terezinha, collected a severe beating for standing up for what he knew to be right.

If the truth of the matter can be found anywhere, it is somewhere between, murky area of bribe and wink, a few colonels and minor state executives, and the directors of the CODEARA company itself, and the undeniable bravery and stubbornness of the Padre from Santa Terezinha.

Padre François Jentel is living in France.

AT LAST

YOU DON'T ALWAYS strike it lucky out here. Then again when you do . . .

I wasn't, in effect, inside the dustbin, but jolly near to it; when I found yesterday's copy of Estado do São Paulo or, what was left of it between the torn furniture advertisements, foreign noticia nonsense and the entire *wanted* column, mixed with deep coffee stains across the photograph of a sulky swarth (if you can put it like that) the champion tennis player of Mato Grosso State who had gone down rather badly at Wimbledon this year – 0-6, 0-6, 0-6: later in a shady spot, I found the most peculiar and unexpected announcement in the *wanted* column I suppose I was ever likely to come upon.

A reward will be given, it said in three languages, Portuguese, French, and English, of 50,000 cruzeiros to anyone who can provide information to the whereabouts of one – Anthony Last Esq., late of Hetton Abbey, England, and last heard of in the southern Amazonas, 1933.

Furthermore, it went on – if anyone can help at all in this enquiry, they must present themselves in suite 606, São Paulo Hilton, the morning of the twenty-third.

I studied the date on the newspaper. It was already the ninth of the month. It would take me at least ten days to reach São Paulo, the way I travel.

I had better put my skates on. This was a wake I certainly had no intention of missing.

Think of it. A genuine mystery. The romantic forgotten stirrings of forest tales. That 50,000 cruzeiros reward. And from the information I possessed – why, it was already as good as mine!

I was talking to myself as I climbed out of the back of the

banana lorry, in a suburb of the great city – I could do no end of good to myself with 50,000 contos, as they used to call the green stuff, in the old days, out here.

But I still had quite a way to go. It wasn't that easy, either. I kept to the main streets in the evenings, but during the day I was careful to stay in the little travessas. And if I saw the occasional police, I assumed a certain rigid formality, a calculated mien.

The rodoviárias were my safest bet. Bus stations were crowded with delinquent figures. Who would mistake me for anything else? But, there was always an unfinished paper cup cafezinha, or that delicious quarter pint of milkshake some people who don't know the tricks leave behind in the shaker below the counter, that was always up for grabs, as you might say.

I don't really know what I did with myself in the intervening days. I had arrived in São Paulo two days early, and there never was anything wrong with promptness, people think better of you for it, and indeed it's corollary – politeness; I managed, I used the time up, there were other people's little foibles to study.

But I was gripped by the mystery of it all. What an extraordinary stroke of luck I should find that announcement in a crumpled paper concealing the remains of what I'd guess to have once been quite a cheerful churrascaria.

I could hardly control my curiosity. It bubbled in me. Just who were the occupants of suite 606? Why had they come to Brazil on such an absurd mission?

The day arrived. You would think any Brazil nut fool could direct you to the famous Hilton, the new and glorious modern Hilton, but as it happened I had a little bit of trouble finding it. People weren't in that much of a hurry to direct me. And I had to move cautiously. A person in my condition. A person in my situation.

I could hear the heavy thunder of the traffic on the huge avenida before I was two blocks nearer. It produced in me a sense of fright, yes it was, face it, and I knew such roaring metropolises were not for me. Speed kills were the new words, and, noise deadens, yes those were the modern catchphrases. And I'd heard them.

I stood in the sudden sunlight on the wide pavement, heretofore I had been careful about that, keeping to the dark side of the streets, naturally, and I blinked in the garishness of it all. The white haze from the azure concrete. The dreadful black exhausts from the ónibus. I could see the Hilton Hotel. Epic of construction. Mad gambit in an inhospitable place. I do admit, without any hesitation, that – when I saw the doorman, I took the most instant dislike to him. He had that certain temerity only the vulgar can show without as much as a word. It was all in his eyes. Eyes that, if you will, commence at your shoes, the polish of them, travel to the very trim of the hair on your collar, and like a bull-terrier in lockjaw battle will not leave sight of your heels, and their quality of finish, until you have reached the far turning of the lobby. As it so happened, on this occasion, I was not wearing any shoes at all; and I'm afraid it was confrontation all the way.

He stood four square in front of me as I pushed the glass door. He was shaking his head, his finger waggling in a lateral motion, the polish on his black boots reflected the sunlight outside.

"Out!"

"I'm afraid you don't understand..."

"Out!"

"I'm a terribly busy person and—"

"Out!"

"I think you and I ought to get something straight between us, my man—"

"Out!" There was a certain repetitive quality about him.

"Call the Manager, immediately!" I said in a loud voice.

Passers-by, Paulistas in black silk suits and Americans with heavily painted wives and one or two darting little Chinese gentlemen made hurried steps between my opponent and myself. As if they just couldn't bear to look at us. He and I were pariahs on a desert shore, locked and alone, immutable figures; giants from an old and all but extinct race.

One American lady clutched her nose as she passed between us. Hastily averting her eyes. Poor dear, I'm not surprised, she must have caught a whiff of the doorman's foul breath, I imagine.

I think – by asking for the Manager – I had managed to slow him down somewhat. The very mention of higher authority promptly tickled doubt and a fraction of fear in his servile shell of grey matter.

I knew I had made my point. He hovered. His weight shifted from one great haddock of a foot to the other. Perhaps he felt slippery ground under him. He didn't want to be seen talking too long to the likes of me. Best get it over and done with he was thinking.

"I don't think you want to come in here," he said, trying on the surly benevolence only the most vulgar imagine pulls any weight at all with me.

"Oh indeed I most certainly do!" said I.

"Let us start with your shoes shall we?" and he underlined the '*sir*'.

"I happened to be in a hurry this morning and—"

"You forgot them, sir?"

"Quite..."

At least we had progressed to *sir*. He might have been confused by the accent, and I am not surprised, but he knew he was addressing a superior mortal did this overdressed Brazil nut, and I intended to ram it home.

"I have an appointment here, my man "

"Name?"

"There isn't one."

"Room?"

"Suite 606," with emphasis on the sweet suite.

"If you'd like to go across to Reception they will phone up for you," where had the *sir* gone?

"I'm perfectly capable of finding the sixth floor myself," using my initiative, "and my friends up there are expecting me."

It wasn't going to wash. He took a step and waved across another servant. Now he turned round and was trying to catch the eye of a respectably suited figure in the corner clearly in the junior managerial league, and I made a run for it. You can't call it anything less than that. I made a bloody good shuffle and skip and my God was that your toe madam towards the lift. And I made it. The lift hop barely glanced at me. My voice was a clear command of confidence.

"Six, please!"

At the floor, I was out of that lift door like a leveret from a lurcher.

The hop had no chance of seeing me.

My goodness me ... the strain of all this gallivanting. Paper chase gone cuckoo on Hilton mozaic corridors lined with aquatints of bandeirentes and Jesuits converting indios poor little brown bleeders God wot they need cant like I need a set of identity papers!

I found the door. Double grand doors with giant handles

styled in *figa* bronze shapes, recessed archway and louvred upper panels (in other words just a touch of Spanish/Portuguese colonial). I straightened what was left of my collar. I waited quite erect. Stroking my chin I thought well, at least, there is something quite nautical about a beard this size.

A moment after I knocked the doors were flung open and after one brief and uncomfortable glance at me during which time the hop's eyes became paralysed gobstoppers, he gestured for me to go forward. There came from the rooms in front a fair buzz of many languages. Like an air-conditioned mini-babel floating on a carpet of ankle-deep comfort (and were my feet grateful!), and when I entered the right room, I found I was standing in a palace-sized reception area which overlooked one floor below us the front rooftop swimming pool. I had arrived.

Naturally, it took the several people in the room some time to get accustomed to my presence. But I was far from being the person who stood out the most. There were a couple of real roughneck seringueiros there. Couple more had that closed lidded look of forest people, river men you can recognise anywhere, and I was not ill-at-ease.

I was introduced to an upright Englishman, a Mr Ebenezer; white hands freckled with ginger, soaked under-arms beneath a shirt that clearly was not made of pure cotton, and all the more surprising when you consider the air-conditioning horror vents beside me blasting full tilt. I will refer to him, in future, as the interrogator.

The second Englishman was considerably younger, flush fat body in a cream silk suit, quite a paunch, bull neck and public-school exuberance about him, by flush I mean he gave you the immediate impression of privilege and class and education the kind of thing which drives the bolshevik to distraction. He was called Neil.

I stood by the long table where the drinks were so hospitably laid out. I said thank you very much but I'll stick with batidas. Gin fizzes never go down well in Brazil, it must be those half lemon half lime fruits they slice up – they give a rough edge to the gin.

Do sit down, please, the interrogator admonished us as if we really didn't know our places or our good luck to be here in the first place. In my turn, the drink hop was over anxious to embarrass me. He insisted on placing a sheet of paper between my seat and the soft armchair. I couldn't possibly have appeared that uncouth. It's just the lick service Brazils pay to Messrs Hilton. They take such pride in skyscraper buildings and modern aerodrome waiting-room fittings.

"Gentlemen ..." I looked around at the six of us in the bright room filled with a glass wall window which overlooked the swimming pool, as the interrogator started to speak, "I must say to you ... in all frankness ... we didn't expect anyone to come here, this morning. Whatever comes of this meeting please do allow us to meet whatever travel expenses you might have incurred."

Rather!

"Now to get down to details ..." he was saying, "My junior partner, here, and I represent Wilcox, Ebenezer and Carter. We are London lawyers and we act for the residual estate of Mr Richard Last, late of Hetton Abbey. Now I know all this may sound strange to you – you must bear with me – but Mr Richard Last's will very much concerns his cousin Anthony Last. And it is of paramount importance we make this final effort to assure ourselves that Anthony Last is, as it were, *and sadly*," he hastily interjected, "but quite definitely dead. In order we might file probate and waste no more time with eccentric wills."

I don't quite know what he was referring to; but it sounded to me like Richard Last had this minute snuffed it, and left behind him a mad will deeding all his property to the missing, hopefully feared dead, cousin Anthony. Turn up for the bereaved etcetera, what? No cash for poor wifey? Can't sell the loved heap of bricks to an arms manufacturer?

The interrogator filled us in with odds and ends. I don't know how the others understood. The Swede in the corner spoke good English. So did the Frenchman. But as for those two barqueiros with the lidded eyes, God wot they lit their minds with! The young Brazilian with curly hair and well pressed baggy US Army-type trousers was listening very carefully. Perhaps he could keep up with us.

All in all, what it amounted to was this – all sorts of relatives were in line for the dead man's money. The lawyers weren't prepared to give a definite word on the missing Anthony Last until they had completed their enquiries in Brazil. Then they would feel free to release the money and bonds and property to the rightful heirs.

After all, this Anthony Last was some kind of mad man who disappeared years ago in Brazil; and although the cousin took over the estate and bonds etcetera, the cousin always maintained a shadow of doubt over the true fate of Anthony Last. There was just a chance he could still be alive somewhere. Made his mark in Brazil. Married here. Started a new life. Prospered ...

The flush younger man Neil was speaking—

"... Naturally, we are talking about a man who disappeared more than forty years ago. My partner, Mr Ebenezer and I, we don't expect miracles, but any help, no matter how small, might put at rest the tormented minds of our clients in London."

"May I be so bold as to ask ..." I began.

"Yes, by all means."

I think the accent must have foxed them. It was neither English, American, nor Brazilian valley of Araçatuba British colony style, more a thick Dutch or Belgian feel about it; born of years with mainland European emigrants in the southern interior of Brazil.

Ah ... perhaps they mistook me for a New Zealander, outpost emigrant from the shared language Empire; with still, a dash of clear tongue (none of your Australian belch and outback digger mouthrun).

"I wonder ..." I hesitated, "could you explain a little more about Anthony Last. Of course, that is why we're here. And no doubt each one of us might be able to help, but – what about his own folks? Have they tried to contact him? Why is it left to you gentlemen, the lawyers?"

"That," said the interrogator, "is not easy to answer. There was a wife, once. After an – albeit – near unsuitable length of time, she married another. She became Lady Grant-Menzies. But alas ... alas ..."

The interrogator paused.

"Oh dear ..." I murmured.

"The Lady in question disappeared off a ship's bridge in a hurricane outside Cape Wrath."

"Tragic ..." I demurred.

"There was a son – but he died in an accident. Very young at the time."

"Nothing but tragedy after tragedy ..." I demurred again.

I kept a very long face on me, but I suspected, from the quick sidelong glance I received from the interrogator, he believed I was, in some way, sending him up. I adopted the most urbane composure I could muster.

It was time to get down to business. The younger partner

produced a very nifty electric tape-recording gadget which he placed on the table beside him. He had a microphone on a long flex, and he placed it on the floor, upright, so that it lay between us.

Oh ... and my dears ... the stories were endless. Each of us had clearly come here with a tale to tell; and the more convincing it could be made the closer one got to that lovely 50,000 cruzeiros.

The first was the Swede. Gustave he was. In an easy but halting English he described his early years in Brazil. He panned for diamonds up in Minas Gerais. He and his friends heard of a strange britisher who had made a great collection of precious river stones. But the man never sold his finds. He kept them in a cave up in the serra, and nobody could find the secret hoard. It was baffling for true garimpeiros. If you found a good stone you laid your claim and cashed your gem in quick as you could reach town. Why did this britisher hoard the gems? Gustave tracked the englander for months. There was trouble in the air. Nearby other diamond panners had been shot at. Gustave forced his way up to a difficult point in the serra. And there he found the britisher. The man wouldn't allow him any closer. He fired round after round at Gustave. Until—

"Well, until ..." in the Swede's own words, "I knew the man had run out of bullets. I fired one or two warning shots in the air. Then I saw him on a high ridge – without his gun. He turned towards me – very sinister look in his eyes a mad man's look and when I began to fire off these warning shots he stumbled and fell over the other side. He screamed. It sounded a hopeless fall – to his death, you know. And I made my way up to the cave near the high ledge," the Swede paused, as if to take breath.

"What did you find in the cave, sir?" asked the interrogator.

"Now that was the strange thing – yes, I found his rifle, an old single-barrelled breech loader, real old piece you see. He had run out of shells. And you know – the barrel of the shot-gun was so warped – a miracle he could hit anything with it."

"But the diamonds?"

"I found the tin box in the earth – yes, it was full. But when I opened it – I looked, and I am an expert on these matters, all the stones were useless glass. Oh yes, they were like diamonds but it seemed to me so tragic – so sad, you know?"

"What did?"

"A man – crazed maybe – spends all his life all those years

searching for diamonds – he might even have found true diamonds and thrown them back – because he clearly had a fixation about these glass things."

"In other words he had wasted his whole life?"

"I would think so."

"But what evidence is there that he died? And was this Anthony Last the man we are seeking?"

"How could a man survive a fall like that?" the Swede asked. There was a murmur of consent.

Well, that may be so, but it strongly depends on what is underneath the descent. Suppose, for instance, there was a swift and deep river beneath the ledge? A river the Swede could never have seen.

"You ask me what evidence I have," the Swede said, as he reached into his pocket, "I think I lost the old rifle long time back now. But I always kept the lid of the tin box. Here ... you see ..."

He placed a rusted blue-painted tin lid with torn edges on the table. The young lawyer, Neil, held it up for all of us to see. On the inside of the lid were the initials A. L. daubed in white paint, now flaking a little, but clear enough.

"I wonder ... you see ..." said Gustave, the Swede, "could this be the englander you advertise for?"

At this juncture we took a rest. Addresses were exchanged between Gustave and the lawyers. And the tape-recording machine was switched off. I had recourse to make for the drink hop behind the bar table – my tongue was rather dry.

The next speaker was the young whipper-snapper the Brazil, a mere boy, he said his name was Bosco. And his story he assured us was, at least, third-hand.

His father, now dead, learnt to speak fluent English from a britisher who succumbed to a very peculiar fate. The father lived up in Acre, east of Feijo, where there were, in those days, some very unpleasant leper colonies. After some months of language tuition, the britisher fell in love with a very beautiful daughter of a leper family. He insisted on marrying her and he went to live with the family, because the law forbade him to take her out amidst normal healthy beings. Bosco's father told his son the curious end the britisher came to—

"... My father later heard that this britisher caught a very dreadful type of leprosy. The worst you can come by. And at first, only his fingers and some of his toes fell away, but he still loved this girl so much nothing would make him seek medical assistance. Unless she came with him. And she was terrified of the outside world. Rumour had it, according to my father, this britisher's love became an insane thing. It ate into his brain. He believed the leprosy was about to lop away his most important finger – his penis. And the rumour had it he almost killed himself making love to the beautiful girl every hour of every day in a frenzy – just in case the worst fell on his favourite finger."

"What happened then?"

"My father told me the girl killed herself when she found she was pregnant. She did not want to produce a leper child for this man who loved her so."

"And the man?"

"Rumour had it – he wandered deep into the forest, never to return, sick and exhausted, and totally distraught."

"What name had the man?"

"My father always told me it was Anthony ... Anthony the Englishman. That was all I knew. I came here when I read the advertisement because – well, I have no proof except that, my father lived up in Acre in 1934 and 1935."

"May I possibly come in here ..." I was afraid to push myself forward, but I thought perhaps I could be of assistance by throwing in the odd question, and nobody seemed to mind, "Could I ask you this – what proof had your father that the man's digits were eaten away by this hideous disease?"

"None at all, none," Bosco replied to me, "because nobody fit and well ever went near the leper homes."

I thanked him.

Although the others looked at me curiously, I did consider that I could not be at fault for opening up the enquiries.

The heavily lidded brasileiro introduced himself as Ireis. I could not have precisely guessed his age, but even in his mid sixties he was merely a whipper-snapper; everybody in the room treated me with the necessary respect the aged can command, and I did nothing to hinder their ministrations.

Young Ireis had an artful tale. He placed his nose close to the recording microphone device, and with a stumbling English and no little hint of Spanish he told us—

"I know nothing senhores, but what I hear ... and it was long time gone now heard it ... if excuse."

There was no stopping him for sheer lack of invention. He knew a trick or two.

Sometime in his forties he was apparently living down by the Chaco, the border wasteland between Paraguay and Brazil. He kept a number of small river boats. Light haulage craft I imagine aimed for Corumbá beef drives and trips below the falls where the Madeira River breaks up.

Ireis was clearly a bit of an adventurer. Liked to pack a revolver in his trouser belt. Was always willing to shave legality for a quick profit. Just after the war ended he heard of the infamous Nazi Martin Bormann. There was a prize on his head. The new Israeli authorities were prepared to cough up their last pretzel in exchange for Bormann, alive or dead.

Ireis, living close on the Paraguay border, learnt that Bormann, or somebody very much like the fellow – you know what I mean, twenty bodyguards and curtained limousines – had slipped across the border with a little bit of bribery and headed up by road towards the Bolivian/Brazil border at Guajará Mirim. Now Mirim was nothing. Just a fluvial port and you crossed the river into Bolivia no questions asked.

But when Ireis reached Guajará Mirim, it was too late. Yes, indeed, a very strange convoy of bodyguards and limousines had tried to cross the river to Bolivia. Tried? Ireis asked the customs officer.

After a couple of beers, the officer unloaded the tale of Bormann at Guajará Mirim. Apparently a peculiar if not downright eccentric Englishman was acting as courier and advance-man for Bormann, (if indeed it was the notorious Bormann because no passports were stamped at the river customs house), (nothing gets stamped anywhere out here if you pay enough), and the customs officer took quite a liking to the Englishman. They had plenty of time together, fixing up the raft to take the cars, organising the bribery, and the Englishman always called the Germans his 'bandeirentes friends', for they definitely were Germans, thickset ghastly shapes with dark glasses and crumpled suits heavily lined with small bore arms.

The customs officer learnt that the Englishman had lived most of the war years in Paraguay. He had tried to persuade the then government to build a flying squadron to defend Japan and Germany in their race for world domination. The English fellow – curiouser and curiouser – had a vague idea that the Fourth Reich could be reborn in Latin America. Anyway, he couldn't quite persuade Paraguay to descend on beleaguered Europe with all sixteen of its De Havilland freight engines, and the Englishman became the great buddybuddy of all new German immigrants. Clearly, he became a kind of focal point for the retreating czars of the old reich.

Alas and alack ... the britisher made quite a boob for his heroic new employers in little Guajará Mirim. He had volunteered to take all the gleaming limousines across by raft, and this was his sole responsibility.

He waited for the first raft to ferry the Germans and their bodyguards. They stood on the opposite bank safe on Bolivian territory and watched him organise the craft load of gleaming limousines. And, yes, you guessed it ... the worst happened. Halfway across the river, a sudden surge in the river flow, and the entire raft sank into the brown mud watery depths of the Rio Guaporé.

The ungrateful Germans and their bodyguards wasted no time. They drew out their guns and fair peppered the bubbling swell where the britisher was last seen attempting a pretty inefficient dogpaddle towards, of all places, the Bolivian side where his Nazi masters waited, guns flaring.

No more was heard of the britisher, luckless ally of the master race, he disappeared under the river swell, the hail of bullets all around him, dogpaddle unavailing.

The customs officer told Ireis a boy found a crumpled damp passport a few weeks later by the edge of the river. It was the dry season now, and the river lowered itself. The officer said to Ireis he could buy it from him if he liked. And this Ireis did. It was a kind of memento from his Nazi 'hunting' days. For Ireis admitted to us in the hotel room, he never looked for the wicked Martin Bormann again.

Ireis stood up and fumbled in his pocket—

"You want see it? ... I got it! ... Look this, ne?"

He held up what appeared to be, on first sight, a blue-rinse lettuce omelette with scalloped edges. He laid the ancient and river worn passport on the table. We each studied it. When it was my turn, I tried to leaf the pages through, to the most important section – the Royal Seal and the owner's picture – but I'm afraid the river and time and numerous insects had long done away with that page.

But, on the front cover, chewed as it was, set into the cut-out panel you could just make out the blurred name of A. Last.

Ireis was profoundly pleased with his exhibit. He could see those lovely 50,000 contos dancing before his eyes. I glanced across at the interrogator. I was surprised at his silence. Surely he wasn't going to allow this man to get away with such a dubious saga as this? I made up my mind to represent sanity and common sense. I asked Ireis—

"What evidence is there that this passport – admittedly Mr Last's – belonged to the britisher who sank with the raft?"

"Desculpe . . . ?" Ireis looked profoundly blank.

"Quite . . ." murmured the interrogator.

"Furthermore, I'd ask" clearly I was in ramping good shape, blood of the law, what? ". . . what evidence is there to prove the veracity of the customs officer?"

"Quite so . . ." the interrogator studied me mournfully. Perhaps the heat, even with the air-conditioning fans, was getting at his British clear-headedness. Perspiration matted the shirt to his chest.

Ireis sat back, a trifle confused, although the interrogator was waffling on about grateful for coming and that kind of thing, I felt I had struck a blow of truth.

But I must say – seeing that passport on the table was a bit of a shock to the old system.

And a small setback to my chances of getting a hold on those 50,000 greens.

After a really superb early luncheon of churrascos mixed and no end of cheeses and fruit and cafezinho we settled down to business.

This did not stop the drinks hop making a great fuss about my health and wellbeing. He led me to the suite bathroom, all tiles and mirrors and soft towels, and he helped me wash my feet, mindful of the sores, and feeling so encouraged I gave the scabs and the dirt engrained into my cheeks a quick rinse in the hand basin. In truth, after these years, living as I have been, a bar of rich soap and a soft towel can do very little for the habits of a lifestyle like mine.

João– the second seedy brasileiro – made it very apparent from the start that most of his living came from one form of proselytising with the Roman Church or another. Some sort of rambling account of his childhood in a monastery, his father who worked the gardens, and his dim memory of an English eccentric, a common tramp called Anthony, who appealed to the brothers of this particular Roman house of God to take him in and convert him to the Popish Empire they represent. João's tale included this poor tramp having a mental seizure in the pulpit of the monastery's place of worship and reciting at great speed to the gathered brethren a chapter out of Charles Dickens. He then, so the story went, tore all his clothes off and raced screaming into the forest, hair on end like electrified spikes, and was never heard of again.

I suppose João was in his mid fifties, thereabout; and we were given the impression that he could not have been more than a lad at the time of this strange event. I looked at the interrogator. If he was not prepared to tear this hapless account to shreds, I most certainly was.

"My mother worked for the brothers in the monastery," João continued, "and she cleared out the britisher's cell after he had vanished. She found one book which must have belonged to the mad man. She brought it home. And I have kept it."

João fished into a canvas bag which lay at his feet. He pulled out a soiled ex-public-library franked novel published by a well respected London firm. He placed the exhibit on the table and opened it to the first page. We could clearly make out the title – *Nicholas Nickleby* by Charles Dickens; and neatly penned in a curious antique lettering on the inside panel of the cover was the name *James Todd*.

"This is all very well ..." began the interrogator, "but what has this got to do with Anthony Last? What has Dickens to do with it?"

"No no no you don't understand..." João replied, "my mother said – the britisher told her his name was Anthony Last and this man called Todd – the Todd written in the book was the britisher's great friend. They spent years in the forest learning books by this writer Dickens learning them off by heart. My mother swore that!"

The stricken silence was quite amusing. The interrogator boggled at João; the younger man, Neil, clasped his hands to his eyes and shook his head.

"May I ask ..." the interrogator had difficulty in finishing the sentence, "why these two men sat in the jungle reading Charles Dickens to each other?"

"My mother said... it was very good medicine for the britisher. He had become crazy. He could not think properly. And this man Todd rescued his sanity with the Dickens books. It was like a treatment ..."

I smiled under my beard. The only two front teeth I had left grazed my upper lip.

"May I ... ?" I asked politely. And I cleared my throat. Nobody seemed to object.

"Now look here ..." I commenced, sternly staring at the somewhat descredited João; my Portuguese fairly spitting teeth (that is if I had any to give away), "who told you this man was called Anthony Last?"

"Mother did ..." the hapless João.

"What evidence had she?"

"None ..." his head lowered.

"Whose tale was it – about two britishers – or one britisher this man who went mad in the monastery – sitting in the forest reciting Dickens?"

"Mother did ..." poor confused João.

"I put it to you ..." I turned to the English lawyers, "no more absurd fantasy could be developed than that? What are we talking about? A madman who reads Dickens in the woods for years, or a gentleman of high birth – I'm presuming of course – who lost his way and perhaps died nobly on some distant shore? As many Englishmen are known to have done!"

"I must say ..." the interrogator reddened at the cheeks, "it is a far-fetched tale, this one."

I was quick to agree. I heaped scorn on such preposterous anecdotes. Were we going to sit through such arrant chatter? Why, when you consider how much more I had to contribute, if this was to be the level of intercourse here, I was wasting my time. And time, in this new world of speed and instant communication, is very expensive. I sincerely hoped they appreciated my point.

The tape-recording machine was whirring once more. The younger man, Neil fiddled with the microphone speaker on the thick carpet in which my toes wiggled so deliciously. There was a fifth man, one Georges, speaking now: burly khaki figure in pressed razor edge pants and thick waterproof brown boots; had lazy eyes and a fat unsmoked cigar stub between his teeth. Certain assuredness about him, he must be a small fazendeiro, enough land and river to keep him in whores above shampoo lojas in downtown Campo Grande or whatever ...

There was a ludicrous beginning to his career. He spoke a perfect sweetly singing Guiana English where he was born. He made a small fortune collecting Amazona bugs for a dealer in Leticia on the tri-border-line of Peru, Columbia and Brazil. This dealer smuggled everything Georges found for him out of the country. Believe it or not, and I did prefer to believe it, Japanese and American bug farms were prepared to pay the earth for the rare bicho ticks Georges could hunt out.

"But I had to give it up ..." said Georges woefully.

"Why was that?" the Neil fellow looked up.

"I was dying ... those bugs were killing me ... they were in my blood in my stomach in my brain ... too much for me the bugs ... I told the dealer in Leticia he could get a good price for me if he smuggled me out in a crate – I had bugs like some people have pores!"

The upshot to his activities in the forest of bugs was a curious half legal affair. Georges heard of a white man, a foreigner, who lived deep in the State of Mato Grosso close on the Bolivian border. Rumour had it, this man, said to be a britisher, had a kind of slave farm. He had stumbled through the forest, and after weeks of privation, he met up with a colony of black Africans, the heirs of the seventeenth-century colonial traders, who had never seen a white man before. These Africans, though they spoke an archaic colonial Portuguese, had all the appearances and servility and humility of true colony slaves. In other words, though Brazil banished slavery in the 1880s, this peculiar lost colony huddled together for centuries, through birth and death and contagion, with only the knowledge that they were slaves to masters who must eventually return to them. The britisher they discovered stumbling through the forest was not slow to see a good thing. He promptly recovered his health, and claimed ownership of this black slave estância. The slaves loved it. They had been waiting for some two hundred years for their masters to return – here he was in the flesh.

Georges' account was explicit with disgusting sexual connotations, suggestions of outrageous behaviour no normal English gentleman would have known about. Such lusting with the slaves was a sad reflection on Georges' own imagination, no wonder he was so keen, those years ago, to find this slave estância for himself.

Georges set out into the Ricardo Franco hills which border Bolivia. It was a kind of lost world the novelists love to write about. The nearer he got to the place, the more rumours he heard. The britisher was training these slaves into serfdom. He had contacted rich landowners on the Bolivian side who were willing to pay high prices for parcels of slaves, and even the young children were indoctrinated with their dreadful prospects, as if life offered no other choices to such beings, and slavery was their true role in life.

But Georges got to the estância too late. And the entire colony of Africans had disappeared into the forest.

"Why was this?" asked the interrogator.

It appeared that our britisher had made one frightful mistake. He had become addicted to a game of cards – 'Animal Snap' it was called – and when his last pack ran out he sent a supposedly trusty black youth downriver to a village to buy another pack. The black trusty was away a long while. When he returned he was a different black altogether.

"How different?" I humbly interjected.

To begin with the villagers explained to the trusty we were now all living in the twentieth century, slavery was abolished, slavers could be executed, World War One, the Great Slump, David Windsor married a divorcee, Jesse Owens was the world's greatest athlete, The USA was a great republic of many States ... in other words, all those wonderful miracles of Marconi and Edison and Madame Curie and Charles Lindbergh and Henry Ford, Trotsky and Lenin, Disney and the sinking of the Titanic – that an erstwhile hardgrinding antediluvian black African slave couldn't survive without for one more minute.

"What happened to the British slaver and his colony?"

There was, it transpired, a revolting revolt. The slaves learned they had been deceived for nigh two hundred years, and they took it out on the britisher, their supposed boss whip man.

This britisher was boiled in oil. His bones were used for soup stock. Children played marbles with his eyeballs. His skin made suitable water sacks. Just the run of the mill African tribal vendetta stuff. Nothing out of the ordinary.

And our friend Georges found the estância in a lost valley, hidden from all the world, but alas ... in ruins.

"I am beginning to wonder ..." the interrogator murmured softly, "just what has all this to do with our quest?"

"Ah, sir, now I come to my point," said Georges, "for the moment I reached the ruined estância I knew I'd find no one alive there. But in the dereliction of the main casa – obviously the head man's home – I found a carefully worded name etched out in the wood on top of a little wicket gate that was, presumably, the garden compound for the britisher's hut. For I may say, there was little else left in the whole estância."

"What did it say on the gate?" pursued the interrogator.

"It said simply – *Hetton Abbey*," replied Georges.

The interrogator's eyes widened. The young Neil fellow sat up. I could not disguise a sense of genuine fear in my own boots (had I a pair to quiver in).

"You say – *Hetton Abbey*?" from Neil.

"Just so, sir."

"Good lord . . ." the interrogator sucked at his teeth.

"A terrible end," I added, ever mindful not to disturb the funereal air-conditioned calm with my barely concealed all engulfing hilarity.

Georges had made a pretty good case for himself, I thought; and without my own presence in the room, that 50,000 conto cheque was in his bag. I say bag with some deference, because one moment later friend Georges was unzipping a strong brown leather grip in front of us and heaving at something nasty and awkward which lay inside.

"Now, sirs ... see this!" he spoke out triumphantly. And he clasped between his thick fingers a yellow or off-white or even gingerish coloured human skull equipped with the most splendid set of natural molars.

This, Georges triumphed at us, was the skull he pulled out from the giant earthenware cooking pot which stood in the centre of the estância. This was the final clue—

"I take leave to introduce you to ..." Georges barked, "Mr Anthony Last, the late!"

The skull stood on the table before us. A smiling apotheosis of homage to the art of dentistry. I think, like a cold drip of a tap in mid winter icicle sharp when you least expect it, something prickled and crept and tickled down my spine until I could tolerate it no longer: it was a nerve ticking away like a clock's second-hand, and I squirmed in my chair.

I had to smooth the shock of it all to my system.

"What evidence is there – this skull belongs to this gentleman Mr Last?"

"But sir ..." Georges was fighting for his money now, he could smell that 50,000 prize all right, "the name of the house *Hetton Abbey* ... all the local rumours in the forest that it was an Englishman. Look – look at the skull – is it not a fine head?"

"Well . . . yes, it is that," the interrogator stirred.

"It is a fine English head, no?"

"You could say that . . . I suppose."

"This is your lost Anthony Last!" Georges proclaimed.

But I was far from finished.

"Let us start ..." I said, "with the teeth. Have you a chart of the late Mr Last's teeth?"

"I do believe we have ..." the interrogator made knives at me with his eyes, as if to say I don't need any Sherlock Holmes prompting thank you. He abruptly turned on Neil.

It took Neil but a moment to produce from out of a deep and broad Gladstone bag the correct file. Yes, there it was. The London dentist's report on Anthony Last's teeth. The interrogator flipped through the pages. He barely glanced up at the smiling skull.

"Well ... ?" I asked with a sharp ring to my tone.

"I'm afraid ..." the interrogator slapped the file to, "according to this report – Last's teeth have nothing in common with the skull here. In fact, Mr Anthony Last's teeth were in a very sorry state when he left England. Hardly any of his front ones could be called his own."

Georges looked a little downcast at that. The interrogator had a mournful expression, for it seemed, I was intent upon destroying every conclusion the interrogator greedily anticipated. He began to positively hate me. I was the wrecker of his plans. He was thinking – I must be the one who believes he has the answer to the mystery. I was the one (if you knew how mild and uncompetitive I really am) the interrogator blamed for raising the ante of tension in the hotel room. And he would destroy my tale just as I had undermined the others. It was in his every movement.

All he wanted was – to wrap up the proceedings, thank us all disarmingly for wasting his valuable time, pay his bills and depart back to London. He had made this one vain effort, in what he was convinced was a hopeless quest. The whim of a dead cousin of this Anthony Last. The whim of a will the interrogator had to put through abnormal legal twists in order that certain money hungry heirs might benefit.

The cafezinho flowed. The afternoon wore on. Various wives in those novel next-to-nothing bikini strips finished their oiling rituals down below by the swimming pool. The interrogator was wilting. He longed, I knew, for dear old England. Fortnum's teas. Luncheons at Bratt's Club. Those *weekend rooms* on the upper floors of the Cavendish Hotel in Jermyn Street, and dog Kippy's basket by the front hall door (or Kippy's heirs). Those delicious Saturday nights down the grand stairway in the Café

Royal (would we catch a glimpse of dear Noel there?). My mouth watered with nostalgia.

And could it be still like that? Those wonderful places which became such a habit of living, and of loving. Things you cannot imagine the old country without. That feeling of sameness, continuity, the world outside changing, but at home gleaming spires of permanence; the intactness of our days. Or, shall I say – those days; or – his days, the interrogator's.

They were looking at me now. Clearly it was my turn. And I had better make it good, they were saying to themselves. This cocky old devil, wrinkled malingering twerp ... what can he know?

I wanted to make sure of my ground. There was no reality without a past. And I could not grasp every facet of the situation without help. I had to turn to the interrogator; enquire a little more ...

"Before I explain what I am doing here," I was charming if tentative, slow but quite assured, "... could you give us any clue to this man Anthony Last? Obviously each one of us has got a picture of him, but – whatever the outcome of this meeting, it would be nice to know a little more about him?"

I appealed to the others in the room, and they gave me a murmuring of general assent. The interrogator was on the spot, once more. He coughed discreetly and let the perspiration joggle under his nostrils—

"Well ... there – I – you see I was never Anthony Last's lawyer. And much that I heard is hearsay."

"He had a wife?" I asked.

"Yes. Lady Brenda—"

"What happened to her?"

"She married the best friend of Last's – Jock Grant-Menzies."

"After a suitable time? After this eh – Anthony Last was declared gone for ever?"

"Not exactly a 'suitable time'," the interrogator sniffed as if he had just discovered an unpleasant smell beneath his nose, "but yes – they did marry."

"And—?"

"She disappeared from a boat during a storm ... quite suddenly."

The poor dear.

"Did they have children – the Anthony Lasts?"

"A boy – died young, fatal accident."

"Sad sad sad ..." I stressed.

"Yes, sad ..." the interrogator fiddled with his knuckles he longed for it to end. What was the point of my silly questions? Let us get down to you and your nasty Brazil tale, he was thinking, as he stared balefully at me. But I was like a hound on that second run through the woods, fox had routed hare as a kind of smokescreen, but my nose was pretty keen ...

"Did Anthony Last have friends?"

"All dead and gone I'm afraid ... there was a certain Princess Abdul Akbar, a mistress at one time I heard. There were friends of Lady Brenda – Marjorie her sister and a Polly Cockpurse. And there was rumoured to be a dark figure in the Last closet."

"And who might that be?"

"Wretched fellow by the name of Beaver – it was said he caused the split in the marriage. Took all the blame for it and died a hero in the Second World War," said the interrogator.

"Now there is nothing left of Anthony Last's background?"

"The house – Hetton Abbey."

"Ah, yes."

"But I ..." the interrogator hesitated, "I do not know if you have been to England recently, things have changed dramatically. The heirs of Richard Last want the estate sold off quickly. A large bungalow development corporation has put in a sizeable offer."

"A bungalow corporation?"

"Yes."

"A sizeable offer?"

"Indeed ..."

"A lot of money must be involved?" I couldn't resist.

The interrogator was quick to side step—

"If the land is not sold off – after all most of the great house roof is already in ruins – the ceilings are crumbling – there is strong talk of a new Labour government turning the whole place into a New Town project like Basildon—" that place didn't strike a bell with me, I'm afraid, "and if not that – then it could be – all the estate could come under compulsory purchase orders and there are plans threatened of a major new jumbo jet airport."

"We are talking about Hetton Abbey?" I insisted.

"Quite ..."

"England doesn't appear to be the same old place," I murmured. The interrogator shifted in his seat and smiled condescendingly as if I had just uttered the most crashing cliché.

I was about to begin. Though what I had to say could hardly be called a peroration. And all my questions and sharply wielded barbs at my opponents were meant for the good. Why the interrogator himself didn't take up many of my points was beyond me.

Here gathered were six strange Brazilian characters, (albeit in search of a lost soul?) and these two lawyers from England; what was it in aid of?

Here was a man who, from all accounts, only wanted to escape from changes and habits of a lifestyle which were breaking before his very eyes – his wife led astray by an idiot, a great chum marries her instead in undue haste, cousins steal the estate and loved only son has an appalling accident; too far back in the past now, nothing but dust and crumbling memories, echoes of common chatter in ceilinged palace-sized rooms all mown in a remorseless season of near a quarter of a century; all kindred souls exeunt left and right, this poor devil who chose the shadow of the green forest out here now even less than a legend in an air-conditioned hotel room of strangers in São Paulo. A victim of petty tyrants, those heirs of cousins demanding final confirmation, yes – Anthony Last *is* gone, yes – there is enough proof now to bend the Attorney General's knee with.

What is it we most seek when we can no longer control our lives in the known daily world? That secret kingdom, a warmth, a death before death enters, womb of mercy no man faced with too many over-riding odds can do without; for the dead, if they have had nothing but their illusions to take with them, have at least gone down with the appertainances of mercy, this mercy, not necessarily made manifest, but at least made into an inkling shadow hint of a greater charity. At last ... at last ... a tribute no human frailty need jeopardise: there was light in the unpeopled void where no nasty feminine emotion could hurt, or where rats' blood relatives might multiply.

The interrogator was asking me when I'd like to commence. He was studying his watch at the same time. Something or another about an embassy engagement, a trade drink I think he called it, of course, of course ...

"Ah indeed ..." as I stood up, dirt falling from my clothes on to the hospitable carpet, "I am not going to waste much more of your time. I have listened carefully to all the anecdotes and I hope I have contributed somewhat to tidying up their edges. Now ..." and I was looking about me, feeling a little dizzy, there was so little to focus upon, just their eyes, worried and beady, money drinking lazy lids, imagining thousands of contos in reward, here I must go, as they say, in deep – "Now ... it is my turn. And I do not intend to beat about the bush. Gentlemen, there is no tale to unfold. Nothing to prevaricate about. I cannot tell a lie. You see – I am Anthony Last, the very same! He is me or I am him, what you will, but – I am here! I am Anthony Last ... !" And I paused. The silence in the noisy room filled with air-conditioning hum. The wall of antagonism I had created all around me. Their cold eyes demanding retribution.

I tried to laugh in my throat—

"The very man you are seeking! I am Anthony Last!"

They were carrying me out. I was halfway down the corridor towards the lift before I could bite their inhospitable hands away from my mouth. My legs were contorted. No matter how much I screamed the froth kept coming back into my throat. I choked on it. They had me tied in what was fashionably named a 'strait jacket'. For those in straits, ha ha. And the rest of the hotel staff rushed towards me. They were pounding along the comfortable pile carpets. And I screamed, dear heaven oh dear. My voice high and monstrous clear in the air-conditioned cool. All my body weight heaved. Jock, I was telling that, that devil's undue haste. Brenda poor darling off the ship's deck cruel water end those ruined hair Permanents all that salon money wasted. Driven no doubt to suicide. Couldn't tolerate Jock Grant-Menzies anyway! Why not admit it! My feet hammered at their black lidded eyes. And the Princess – that mistress no self-respecting bank manager deserved. Where was Polly? Where was Marjorie – no true ally but to her self! Good God, Beaver! It's you! I ought to have kicked you down the portal steps of Bratt's Club! Mr Todd I am coming! Soon I would have to confront that doorman oaf downstairs in the hotel vestibule now that they are squeezing me into the lift. His arrogance as he bundles me into the back of an ambulance. My cries unavailing. Their disbelief. Asylum eyes shaking their heads at me. I'll play you Animal Snap and toss you in all Hetton Abbey bungalow sites on the third shuffle! My shrieks out loud. The entire hotel clientele in bikinis outraged at the commotion. Their doors slamming in haste: 'Honey, some maniac gone ape loose on the sixth floor.' Give me that money. Read me the fine print, what it say – young John will inherit when a grown man the entire diamond minefields of Hetton Abbey with a private army of black slaves whose habits have never changed? Rather!

UNIMPEACHABLE DAY

COMING OUT OF the interior. The light changes. River friends shout goodbye. You not come back. You too soft. What is there here to come back for anyway. Tell your rich branco friends Aristonico fart in their eye but he share his chá de mato with them come see him. He put his hand in their conto pockets.

First shock you get. Realise that Americano Express really do work. Sick as a dog for a week, what is wrong? Shakes. High temp. Can't walk up stairs. Sudden profuse sweating. Stomach worm you got. Something in the blood and piss arse old-fashioned grippe. You fucking fault, man; you insist no salt tablets no boiling no straining, so that's what you get for thinking you can drink river water like Coffee could out in the nowheres Coffee got pinga intestines don't you know!

First shock that Americano Express card really does work. The Varig air-conditioning cool ice prickles frost glass touch about it. Sitting right up front of me bunch of *all american* tipo pop group, girls with long hair, Levi's, guitars, guys fat overfed money youth adopting alien customs Paulista kids with badges, cheque books and hip swivel yankee cuban-heeled arrogance. Talk of good grass in Bahia. And a nova carimba sound from the north-east.

Somewhere below in the green forest canyons and red sand earth sertão, this far north they mix together, by river long way in and far from the enemy the new highway, must be my Emilio pigshit porceiro poor white trash counting his manioc tubers for the dry season, will they last him out? He can eat cana if not. He that poor all right but if he gets a good day an over-generous fazendeiro's gladhand day, he could earn enough to lie in the gutter all the dry season and keep a hold on that pinga tap with his money. He like that. He forget the future then. He fine.

Sitting on the Leblon beach a week in Rio rest up marblehalled international first-class hotel; too weak to walk further – sit on beach all day eating hamburgers. Need a doctor.

British Caledonian. You been on a holiday have you? If you ask that hostess nicely she's got last Sunday's newspapers.

A President impeached in the USA. French frenzy about. German blandness over. Ex cabinet minister stashes bullion in Cayman islands.

Friends were so kind. That – I don't know we've done nothing since I last saw you look. Dinner in candlelight. Wine bottles like skittles. Do indians actually smell? More children? How *many* more can you *have*! End of summer and Tom is laughing on the lawn beside me. He keep pouring that Buck's Fizz he like to swim in, more fresh orange and champagne please! For fuck's sake why don't you and your sort leave those bleeding little bastard indians alone in the forest why don't we all leave them be and god in heaven forget about them! That's all! The perfect English landscape is filled with pylons.

Perfect summer days like promises. And childhood made of promises. And blue skies the same. I remember it was a promise to hurtle round the house in a Chinese silk dragon suit beheading grandfather's caterpillars. They did indeed belong to grandfather in those days, too.

And I was promised my first cousin Jean the toad she was. Thanks! I sniffed. Some holiday this will be. (Uncle Eddie's wood chalet was cheap on the beach at Frinton-on-Sea.) At night toad cousin would scream to die at my black ghost tale tongue, red sand lips and salt nostrils lit with matches and candle. Windy tales, all right . . .

Tried to write and began to cry when the words would not rhyme. Foot petulant stamp. Wild running finger scythes through hollyhocks. Time was promised to you.

My mother loved a man twenty years, wrote him two letters a week for twenty years, and he never came back to her. She broke. And I remember the pieces like shattered window screen glass tears at the bottom of her handbag. She didn't believe in drugs. She was silent, for ever, a still silent scream of withdrawal. Time was promised. Days were.

Michael, do you remember that day on the beach at Frinton when the tide was so cold you refused to paddle until you had emptied a boiling kettle of water into the sea?

I heard it said Uncle Eddie smoked fifty Woodbines from dawn to dusk. Gracious! The spendthrift of it!

Frinton promise ... night scuds raffish with slats of wood prised eyelids; ask Aunt Marj come outside see her deckchair gaudy cloth do a belly dance, it gust so.

That path is still the same those pontoons
by the lock are, as are trees still planted
in first earth. Light as fright shutter quick
cabbage white race the eye; sun too soft
on mist too grave to let light touch, but –
morning make blue day yawn a promise.

When first I came I only wanted
just the one memory and no more;
just the one without the purple words
just the heart and the head once knowing.
It is that I cannot be the same,
not that path or first light or grave earth.

A thief robbed a bank and shot a guard
in Brazil. A student was tortured
to confess. When they caught the real thief
they put a magnum bullet in his head.
Then they showed the student to the judge
who gave him two years for perjury.

You do know ... when you put the croquet
on the lawn I will play, should you see
the child cut his finger I will say
yes it bleeds, if you fill the meringues
with strawberries ... that I will eat them.
For what my grandmother made me so

accustomed to I'll surely die from.
What I know must be outside of here.
Sorely fragile as irrelevance
it's outside the skin of the outside,
of childish fat cries and purple lips
drenched in new fruit, outside of all that.

And in my knowing it is ice to flame.
Beside what that path is to the trees
and those pontoons are to the lock and –
day make breath – what moisture in the mist
is to flutter of cabbage white wings,
I am less than cinders to diamonds.

Outside, blood cries instead of fat mouths,
genitals vault from electric probes.
Outside, perfectly trumpeted truths
tell lies, dice and Gods praise rabid men.
Outside tall grasses where the meringue
on the mallet strokes the yellow ball.

Effortless with pity that green laugh
across the hedge is embroidered with
horror. Recognitions will bury
that old path. Stratospheres from charm beg
the *outside*, not of our handmaking,
a good day made unimpeachable.

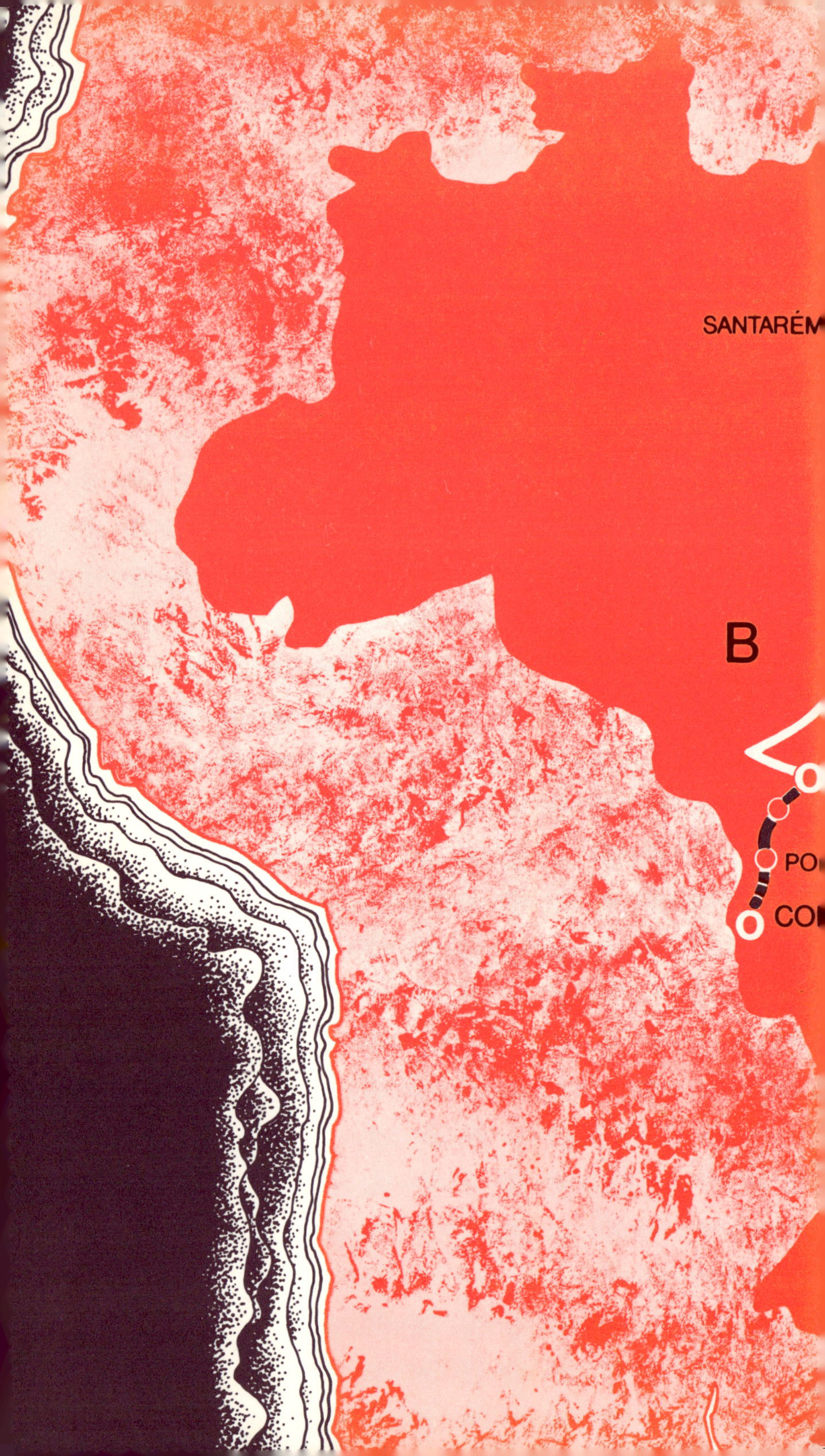
SANTARÉM
B